DARE ME

a dare me novel

REBECCA SHEA

xo, Rebecca Shea

Dare Me
Copyright ©2016 Rebecca Shea Author, LLC
All rights reserved.
ISBN-13: 978–1523784707
ISBN-10: 1523784709

Except as permitted under the U.S. Copyright Act of 1976, no part of this publication may be reproduced, distributed or transmitted in any form or by any means (electronic, mechanical, photocopying, recording or otherwise), or stored in a database or retrieval system, without the prior written permission of the author.

This ebook is licensed for your personal enjoyment only. This ebook may not be re-sold or given away to other people. If you would like to share this book with another person, please purchase an additional copy for each person. If you are reading this book and did not purchase it, or it was not purchased for your use only, then please return it and purchase your own copy. The scanning, uploading, and distribution of this book via the Internet or any other means without the written permission of the author is illegal and punishable by law. Thank you for respecting the hard work of this author.

This book is a work of fiction. Any resemblance to any person, living or dead, any place, events or occurrences, is purely coincidental. The characters and storylines are products of the author's imagination or are used fictitiously.

Cover design by:
Regina Wamba, Mae I Design

Edited by:
Megan Hand, Story Girl Editing and Beth Lynne, Hercules Editing

Interior Design and Formatting by:
Christine Borgford, Perfectly Publishable

AUTHOR'S NOTE:

Always accept the dare.

PROLOGUE

"RIGHT THERE. SEE it?" My father points to the perfectly aligned stars in the dark sky. "The Big Dipper," he says quietly as not to disrupt the lightning bugs dancing around us in the humid evening air.

We lie on our backs, taking it all in. The endless sky you can see for miles, the crisp summer air tingling at my nose, and the quiet. You can hear everything here on the farm.

I'm beginning to get used to the silence. We moved back to Deer Creek, North Dakota, after my father lost every penny we had in an investment scheme. Everything he'd worked so hard to provide for our family was gone overnight—vanished into thin air at the hands of a so-called friend and mentor. Mom and Dad sold everything to pay off the debts he owed. We went from living a comfortable life, in an upper middle-class neighborhood of Chicago, back to my grandfather's farm. This was where my mom grew up, and my uncle recently took over after my grandfather passed unexpectedly two months ago.

To say life has been full of changes lately would be an understatement. I pretend not to notice because I'm only thirteen. I'm supposed to believe that my family wanted to move back here, to northeastern North Dakota, for a simpler way of life. Except I'm wise beyond my years and learned to smell bullshit from a mile away a long time ago.

Murphy, the lab mix puppy that my dad gave me today for my birthday, sniffs the ground between Dad and me, and then settles into the cool grass at my feet. "Dad," I whisper as I lace my fingers behind my head and focus on the Big Dipper he just pointed out.

"Yeah, kiddo?"

"Thanks for Murphy. He's honestly the best gift I've ever gotten. You know I've been asking for a puppy for years." I turn my head to the side to watch him as he stares at the sky. His Adam's apple bobs ever so gently under the tan skin of his neck, and he inhales sharply before turning to look at me.

"I love you, Saige. I hope you remember that." His voice breaks. He quickly clears his throat, burying a wave of emotion. "I wish I could've given you more." He reaches out and squeezes my hand. His touch is firm yet gentle, and my normally hormonal self would shrug off his touch, but tonight, I let him hold my hand.

"I love you too, Dad."

He sits up, leaning over to press a firm kiss to my forehead. Reaching down, he rubs the soft yellow fur on top of Murphy's head before he pushes himself up from the ground. "Don't stay out here too late," he tells me, brushing the freshly cut grass from the back of his jeans.

"I won't. Night, Dad."

Dad shuffles his feet across the large grass yard toward the gravel drive and over to the barn that sits downhill from the house. The old barn door squeaks as he opens it and closes it behind him. When I can't see him anymore, I settle back in to looking at the sky and searching for the Big Dipper again. It's the one constellation he showed me that I could find time and again.

The metal screen door from the house hisses as it opens, and Uncle Brent bounds down the front porch steps toward me. "Whatcha doing, Piglet?" he says with a laugh.

"Don't call me that." I roll my eyes as he stands over me, blocking my view of the stars.

"Sorry, but you'll always be a little piglet to me." He chuckles. Brent is only six years older and more like a brother than an uncle to me. When I was born, he said I squealed like a baby piglet when I cried, and that's where the nickname came from.

"I don't like it," I admit.

"I'm sorry," he says half-heartedly before bending over and scooping Murphy off the ground. "Well, would you look how cute this little mutt is," he says, rubbing Murphy's muzzle.

"Dad got him for me." I look at the fluffy puppy and I already love him.

"What's his name?"

"Murphy."

He smiles. "I like it; it fits him. He's going to make a great farm dog, Saige."

"He's not going to be a farm dog. We won't be here for long," I snap, sitting up quickly.

Brent side-eyes me but doesn't say anything. He knows what a touchy subject moving back to the farm has been for all of us.

"As soon as Mom finishes school, we're moving back to the city," I tell him as if I know what our plans are. I don't, but I like to believe this is only temporary.

"Well, y'all are welcome to stay here as long as you need—I mean, want to," he corrects himself. I know he feels sorry for us and he's lousy at hiding it.

"Are you going to keep the farm?" I ask, because my mom has been pressuring him to sell it. She says that nineteen is too young to run a farm, that he's got an entire life ahead of him away from this place. But I know this farm is all Brent really cares about.

"I think I am," he admits with a smile. "It's all I know, Piglet. I was raised on this farm, and it was Pop's pride and joy," he says. "I'm not ready to sell it, not sure if I ever will." He sets Murphy down and stands with his hands on his hips. "Plus, I kinda like y'all being here with me." He smiles at me and digs the toe of his tennis shoe playfully into my hip. I swat at his leg, and he jumps back with a boisterous laugh.

Suddenly, a large boom rings out and my body goes stiff, goose bumps instantly rising on my arms. "What was that?" I ask, my voice shaking with fear. The horses in the barn begin screaming, and it sounds like all-out chaos.

Murphy lunges to his feet and begins to bark in the direction of the barn.

"Saige, stay here," Brent says as he takes off running toward the barn.

I've always been terrible at following directions, and I take off in a full sprint after Brent. My lungs burn as I gasp for breath while my feet try to keep up with him. He's taller and faster than me, and I finally catch up as he's throwing the barn door open. As I push past him, I'm the first to see.

The gun, the blood, my father with half of his head missing.

My stomach drops and I can feel the bile twist in my stomach. "Dad. Dad," I try to scream at him, but I'm barely able to breathe.

His limp body is lying in a pool of blood on the old wood floor next to a rifle. This can't be happening. This can't be real.

"Nooooo," I finally cry out. Vomit rises from my stomach as my legs go weak, and I fall to my knees.

The blood in my ears pounds so loudly, I can barely hear Brent screaming for help. Then I feel him pulling on my arms as my knees scrape against the wood floor. He's dragging my limp body out of the barn, and I watch a stream of blood roll under a hay bale and inside one of the horse stalls before I finally close my eyes and give in.

ONE

Saige

"SAIGE!" EVELYN, MY roommate, yells at me as I gasp for air. "Breathe. Just breathe," she says, stumbling into my dark room. My lamp on the bedside table flicks on just as she sinks down next to me on my bed. She reaches for me and begins rubbing my arm. "That's two nights in a row," she whispers and frowns. I drop my head back against my headboard and try to get my breathing under control. "You need to talk to someone, Saige. You can't keep having these nightmares. You need to sleep."

I nod my head and stare at the ceiling. "I'm sorry," I muster between breaths. *Breathe. Breathe,* I tell myself as my pulse begins to slow down. I moved to Chicago and in with Evelyn a month ago. The nightmares started back up about that time. As I began to live my dream—his dream—the past came crashing back into my life like a freight train with no brakes.

Every street here in Chicago, every chilly evening, and every sunny morning overlooking Lake Michigan reminds me of my father and the life we used to have here.

"Same nightmare?" Evelyn asks, her blue eyes wide with concern.

"Same one."

She stands up to leave now that I've begun to settle down but pauses.

"Saige—"

"I know," I groan. "I promise I will. There's just been a lot of change lately. I need a little more time to settle into a routine. They always get worse this time of year."

She knowingly nods. Every year, in the weeks leading up to my birthday, I tend to regress with my nightmares. She sighs and backs up toward the door. "Two more weeks, and if this doesn't get better, I'm making the appointment for you."

"Deal."

She flips her long jet-black hair over her shoulder as she turns on her heel. "Dream of that sexy boss you told me about. What's his name ... Holt?" She winks at me. "Think about happy things, Saige. Hot men, rainbows, or fucking unicorns," she quips.

I exhale loudly and narrow my eyes at her, then shoo her out of the room. Tugging the sheet up over my legs, I lean back against the headboard and rub my temples. "Holt," I mumble and smirk. "Think of Holt."

I STAND AT the small sink in the attached bathroom, dabbing concealer on the dark circles beneath my eyes and brush red lipstick across my lips, smacking them twice to distribute it evenly. *This is as good as it's going to get today.* I take a sip of coffee from the mug Evelyn shoved into my hand as I was getting out of the shower this morning and groan at how good it tastes sliding down my throat and settling into my belly. Over the giant mug, I notice in the mirror how my green eyes pop against my fair complexion. I tuck my nearly black hair behind one of my ears and like the way it falls in long loose waves down my back. *One positive*

for today—a good hair day.

Shimmying into a tight black pencil skirt and an olive green silk sleeveless blouse, I take one last look in the full-length mirror. I finish off my outfit with pair of nude heels and grab my purse off the counter, shoving my cell phone into it.

"I'm outta here, Ev! Don't wait up for me," I shout as I shuffle out the apartment door and down the hallway of our old brick apartment building. A quick train ride later and I'm pushing through the revolving doors to Jackson-Hamilton Aviation.

"Morning, Larry!" I wave and hustle past the security desk where Larry sits.

"Mornin', sweetheart," he yells back, never once taking his eyes off the newspaper he's reading.

My heels click loudly on the granite floor of the open-air atrium as I hustle over to the elevator bank. I frantically press the call button for the elevator and glance at my watch. I'm already five minutes late. I hate being late. Punctual is my middle name. If I'm not five minutes early, I'm late. That's how I roll.

Groaning, I tap the toe of my shoe impatiently. When an elevator finally arrives, I scurry in just as a voice from behind me hollers out, "Hold that elevator, please." I grumble but hold the doors as Holt Hamilton glides in, a cell phone pressed to his ear. With a curt nod, he steps aside and the elevator doors close while my heart pounds wildly in my chest.

Holt Hamilton. The sexiest man I've ever seen and the Vice President of Jackson-Hamilton Aviation—basically my boss. Standing at least six-foot-three, he could be Henry Cavill's twin brother. With striking blue eyes and dark hair that's styled back off of his face, he's the perfect combination of businessman meets runway model. His cut jawline is accentuated by one very perfect dimple on his left cheek.

His athletic frame is highlighted by his custom-tailored suit that hugs each and every curve of his shoulders, arms, and waist, showing every muscle the man owns as he leans against the side of the elevator. Today he's wearing a charcoal suit with a blue shirt and striped tie. The blue shirt makes his blue eyes stand out against his tan skin. I catch myself staring and quickly turn to face the doors of the elevator.

"Morning, Ms. Phillips," he says with a tight smile. He shoves his cell phone into the pocket of his suit jacket.

Again, my heart is racing. "Mr. Hamilton." I nod and keep my eyes on the digital display showing the floor numbers. *Fifty-seven, fifty-eight*, I silently count as we continue to rise. Only thirty more. I take a deep breath, trying to calm myself.

"How are you settling in?" he asks, his voice deep and commanding. I half-turn to speak to him and catch his smirk, but he quickly composes himself and adjusts his tie.

"It's going well. I submitted the final orders for both planes that were overdue. Mr. Jackson emphasized those were priority." I raise my chin confidently, but my heart continues to race with nervousness.

"You closed both orders?" he asks, surprised. "As in, you got both clients to agree to every last detail?" He looks skeptical. These particular clients were a nightmare. I knew when I accepted the job that I'd have demanding clients, but those two were the cream of the crop.

"I did." Another confident nod.

"Huh," he mumbles, giving his head a little shake. "So how'd you do it? Rachel had been working for months with those clients, and they wouldn't agree to anything she recommended. She tossed their client portfolios on my desk the day she resigned and swore we'd never close the deal on those planes."

I try to contain my smirk. "I get to know my clients, Mr. Hamilton. I make an effort to really understand their likes and dislikes—their personal preferences. What excites them. What motivates them. Not just shove today's best-selling aeronautical features down their throats. I work with them and, in the end, they trust me and my recommendations—we're a team."

"It's that easy?" He cocks an eyebrow in amusement.

I cock an eyebrow. "It's that easy. Payments are finalized and in the Jackson-Hamilton account, Mr. Hamilton. Planes are scheduled to be delivered to both clients in the next ninety days." I rub my sweaty palms down the sides of my pencil skirt.

He stares at me silently, just chewing on the inside of his cheek when the elevator finally slows to a stop. The doors open and Holt reaches out and places his arm against the open door so as to not let them close on us, but in doing so, places himself shoulder to shoulder with me. Too close. So close I can smell his body wash and his minty breath.

I quickly step out of the elevator and into the lobby of Jackson-Hamilton Aviation and begin to walk down the hall toward my cubicle, the opposite direction of Holt Hamilton.

"Nice work, Phillips," he says from behind me.

I smile and race to my desk, internally high-fiving myself.

"What's put that shit-eating grin on your face?" Zay asks.

Isaiah, or Zay, as I've been told to call him, is our private sales coordinator. He works alongside our customers to determine what type of plane they need. Once they agree on the bones of the structure, he tosses them over to me, where I work with the client to customize and build their dream plane. Kind of like *Pimp Your Plane*, only it's not reality television; it's my job.

I'm the interior designer. I get to work with clients on the "fun part" . . . although, to be honest, it's a difficult job. Our customers are premier, the elite—celebrities, Fortune 500 companies, and CEOs. Even royalty. I work with people all over the world. They want the best for the least amount of money, and it's my job to make them happy while making Jackson-Hamilton Aviation some serious money in the process. No sale is complete until I submit all the final details back to Zay and payment has been received, then the planes are customized.

I shrug and slide my sleek laptop into the docking station, powering it on. Zay sits on my desk, bumping his shoulder into mine. "Talk to me, Phillips. That look on your face. What put it there?" Zay has the best smiles. His perfectly straight, bright white teeth stand out against his dark olive skin.

"Nothing." I try to hide my smile, but I'm failing. "I'm just in a good mood. It's Friday, We received payment on the Zamora and Dubai planes."

He smacks his lips before he speaks. "Well, good. Then you'll be joining us for an impromptu happy hour after work tonight."

I turn in my chair and smirk at him. "I'm not sure I'm ready for another happy hour with this group." I twirl my hand around the small workspace that holds all of our cubicles.

I actually work with the nicest people I've ever met. We're an eclectic bunch, with Zay bringing the spice. He's half-Mexican and half-Caucasian and the epitome of the term "Latin lover." Then there's Emery, your classic hippie; mid-thirties with essential oils lining her desk, a cup full of some herbal concoction, and a foul mouth to boot. She's honest and sincere and the matriarch of our little group.

Of course there's the token gay man, and that's Rowan. He's sarcastic and witty, and if he weren't twenty years older than me and gay, I'd find a way to make him love me. He's kind and nurturing and has the sense of humor and quick wit of Jimmy Fallon. Rounding out our little group is a spitfire named Kinsley. At twenty-five, she's only two years older than me and the closest in age. Everything she says or does is borderline inappropriate, and we love her for it. Our group is fun and sassy and Human Resources' worst nightmare.

"This group. You say it like we're a bunch of lepers." He laughs and leans back against my desk, crossing one of his legs over the other.

"Morning, sunshine." Rowan air kisses my cheek and sets a piping hot cup of coffee from the local coffeehouse on my desk. He's our early bird, and if I'm not here promptly at eight o'clock, he'll walk to the coffee shop down the street and bring me back my coffee. God forbid he waits five minutes for me to get here. He's a creature of habit, and I love him all the more for it.

"Non-fat caramel mocha," he says, nodding at the cup he just set in front of me. "What are you two up to?" He glances between Zay and me. "Looks like I interrupted something."

"Zay says we're doing happy hour tonight—"

Rowan claps excitedly. "Damn right we are. I need about six stiff drinks and—"

"That's not the only stiff thing you need," Zay jabs at him.

Rowan looks forlorn. "If you only knew, child . . . if you only knew." He recently broke up with his partner of sixteen years, and he's anxious to put himself out on the market. He shakes his head and takes a seat in the only extra chair I have in my cubicle.

"What are you whores doing?" Kinsley asks as she walks by, throwing her purse and laptop bag onto the floor of her cube. She sits directly across from me and always keeps me entertained. She kicks off her flip-flops and steps into a pair of four-inch heels that look as though a hooker on Cicero Avenue should be wearing them. She strides across the hall and leans against the opening of my cube. "Did you get me a coffee?" She asks Rowan, batting her eyes and pouting her lips.

"Do I ever get you a coffee?" He rolls his eyes.

"Asshole," she mumbles under her breath and rolls her eyes. It's all in jest. Rowan and Kinsley could insult each other all day, but it's always for fun and shock value.

"Didn't get laid last night, sweet cheeks?" Rowan laughs.

"Nope. That's the plan for tonight." She smirks. "I'm taking someone home, and if the pickings are slim, it's going to be one of you two." She looks between Zay and Rowan. With Rowan being gay, that leaves Zay as her target and she gives him a flirty smile.

"And I'm out of here." Zay pushes himself up from my desk and walks away, mumbling something under his breath about crossing boundaries. We all laugh and Kinsley slides into the spot Zay just vacated.

"So tonight," she says, pulling my coffee from my hand and taking a sip. "You're in, right, Saige?"

I roll my eyes and smile. "Do I have a choice?" They never let me say no to happy hour.

"Nope." She giggles and taps my nose, handing me my coffee back.

"Do I at least have time to go home and change?" I feign annoyance.

"No. We're outta here at four. It's just down the street. There are always good-looking suits in there. Suits and cheap drinks, girlfriend. That skirt you're wearing is exactly what you need. You look hot, Saige." She gives me a little wink.

By "suits," she means businessmen in their suits. "I'm not looking for a man or free drinks, Kins. I'll come for a quick drink. That's it."

"Drinks," she corrects me. "We're staying for drinks. Plural."

I roll my eyes at her and log in to my computer.

"I'll look out for you, kiddo." Rowan pats the top of my head. "Until then, I've got work to do." He starts walking away but turns around quickly. "Oh hey, great job on the Zamora and Dubai planes. Tonight over drinks, you're going to have to tell us how you got those bastards to agree to anything because I was convinced we were losing those sales."

I nod at Rowan and bite down on my lip as I fight back the smile forcing its way across my face. I've always prided myself on doing good work, but closing these two deals hopefully solidified the fact that I'm serious about my job at Jackson-Hamilton.

TWO

Saige

ZAY OPENS THE large wooden door to Bar 51, and we enter the dark bar. The place is packed wall-to-wall with bodies. I can barely hear myself think over the roars of laughter and loud conversation that fills the air.

"Holy shit," I mumble as Zay grabs my wrist, and we wind through the human sea. Tall pub tables are surrounded with people that chatter away and laugh, enjoying Friday night's happy hour festivities.

"Over there," Zay announces. I glance to where he's pointing and find Kinsley waving her hands in the air to get our attention.

"'Bout time you assholes got here," she chides and pulls her purse off a chair she was saving for me.

I slide into the tall chair and look around the packed bar. Leaning in, I holler across the table, "This place is insane."

"I know," Kinsley responds, flipping her long blonde hair over her shoulder. "They opened about six months ago. It's the 'it' place to be on a Friday night. Drink specials until close." She lifts a martini glass full of pink liquid and takes a sip.

"What're you drinking?" I ask. Whatever it is looks delicious with a raspberry floating on top and a twist of lemon peel perched on the rim.

"Sex on the beach. It's good. Want to try it?" She shoves the glass in my face, and I take a little sip.

"It's really sweet . . . and strong." I lick my lips and give my head a little shake.

"What do you want to drink, Saige?" Rowan asks. "I'll get this round."

"Umm, let's try a vodka-cranberry. And a large ice water, please."

"Pussy," Kinsley mumbles, then starts laughing. "Just kidding. Ease into it, kid." She calls me "kid" as if I'm ten years younger than she is, and I can't help but laugh at her. "I'll have another one of these." She lifts her glass to Rowan, and he nods.

"Since our waitress hasn't been by, I'm just going to get them from the bar," he says before disappearing into the dimly lit space.

This is my first time actually going out since I've moved to Chicago. I've been here six weeks, and I've been somewhat of a homebody, only wandering out to explore the city for a few hours during the day on the weekends.

The city seems larger than I remember, but I only ever explored with my mom a handful of times before we moved back to North Dakota. Millennium Park and Navy Pier, although touristy, were my favorites as a child and they still are. But I have yet to experience the nightlife Chicago has to offer.

Evelyn, my roommate, is a nurse, and she works the night shift at Rush University Medical Center. With her being the only other person I know in Chicago, my evenings have been limited to watching marathons of *Property Brothers* and *House Hunters* instead of wearing slutty dresses and traipsing through every chic club.

"Where's Emery?" I ask, noticing her sweater and purse

on another chair, but no sign of our sweet hippie friend anywhere nearby.

"No idea," Kinsley says, sipping her drink. "She dropped her shit and disappeared."

Zay snags an open chair from another table and squeezes it into the small space between Kinsley and me just as Rowan returns, juggling four drinks in his hands.

"This place is a madhouse!" he says, sliding the drinks on the table. "Our waitress is coming with your water," he hands me my vodka-cranberry, "and to order us another round. I'm planning ahead." He winks.

"I like how you think," Zay says, grabbing his bottle of beer from the center of the table.

"Me too!" Kinsley agrees, and I just laugh at how my professional coworkers have suddenly turned into complete lushes.

Rowan picks up his glass of wine and holds it over the table. "Cheers to great coworkers and thank God it's Friday!"

"Cheers!" everyone yells, and we all toast. I take a sip of my drink, thankful I decided to come out.

AN HOUR AND a half and four drinks later, we're all still here. Emery made her way back to us after seeing some old friends and catching up with them for a while.

"So, Saige, talk to us. We know you're from North Dakota, we know your roommate's name is Evelyn, but what else? Give us some dirt," Kinsley says, eagerly tapping her fingers on the table. "I mean, you've been out with us only once," she questions, "and all I know are the basics. Tell me the dirt." She winks at me.

"Dirt?" I raise my eyebrows. "I don't have any dirt, but even if I did, you fools are the last people I'd tell it to!" I wink back at her and laugh.

Everyone busts out laughing, and Rowan shouts, "She's smarter than we give her credit for!"

"What's that supposed to mean?" I ask, trying not to be insulted by his comment.

He rolls his eyes toward me in an obvious way. "I mean, come on, Saige. You just graduated college. You know how lucrative Jackson-Hamilton is and how hard it is to get a job here. I didn't mean that you weren't smart. We just assumed Mr. Hamilton got a good look at you and that's why you were hired, not because you actually had the credentials."

I blink at him, offended by what he just said. "So a smart woman can't be pretty too? Not that I'm pretty," I add, more to myself. "I'm actually kind of plain—"

Zay snorts, cutting me off, and I shoot him an annoyed look.

"Look. I was fifth in my class from the university. I have a degree in interior design and an extensive background in aviation. I went to the number one flight school in the country *and* have my private pilot's license—even though my fear of heights about killed me getting it. I hate flying. I got this job because I have what it takes, not because I'm a pretty face." I swallow hard but force a smile to hide the fact that I'm obviously hurt by his assumptions.

He has the guts to look sheepish, at least. "I'm sorry, Saige, I really didn't mean it that way. I was trying to be funny and I missed the target."

"Ya think?" Emery grumbles, then turns to me. "Saige, you've more than proven you have what it takes. Ignore him." She narrows her eyes at Rowan in annoyance and he shrugs.

"No, don't ignore me," Rowan begs playfully. "I wouldn't be able to take it." He presses his hand over his heart.

I can't help but chuckle, even though I'm still slightly hurt. "I'm not upset," I tell him, only half-lying. But then Kinsley makes a face, like she knows she's about to upset me.

"It's just the way we see Mr. Hamilton look at you," she says. Ah, Kinsley. If this group is concerned about how anyone got hired here, they should be worried about her. A party girl with a filthy mouth working at one of the most exclusive aviation companies in the United States.

"Look at me?" I question Kinsley, raising my eyebrows. *What're they talking about?*

"He definitely has eyes for you," Zay chimes in with a smile. "Don't look, but kind of like the way he's looking at you right now." He drops his eyes from across the bar to the bottle of beer in his hand.

"What?" I snap my head up and scan the bar to find Holt Hamilton standing at a table with a small glass of amber liquid pressed to his lips. Our eyes meet, and I immediately flush. I'm not sure if it's his blue eyes or the heat from the alcohol finally hitting me, but my heart races and I begin to sweat. Holt nods casually at me and turns back to the man he's with and begins talking. The two men lean in to each other. From their posture and facial expressions, I can tell whatever it is they're discussing is important.

"Holy fucking shit, Holt Hamilton is at Bar 51," Kinsley says with a look of shock on her face.

"Why is he here?" I question, reaching absently for my ice water.

"How the hell would we know?" Zay answers, his voice reeking of displeasure.

I can't tear my eyes away from Holt. His dark hair stands out against the light brown of the man he's talking with. He's remarkably tall, and it's easy to see him across the bar since he's almost a head taller than everyone around him.

"Why are you blushing, Saige?" Rowan asks with a teasing laugh.

"I'm not blushing." I duck my head when I realize that I probably am blushing. "It's just hot in here."

"It is now that Holt Hotness Hamilton is here," Emery says with a laugh. She runs her fingers through her light brown bangs.

"I wish he was gay," Rowan sighs and sips his wine. "I'd climb all over that man like a spider monkey."

"Gross!" Kinsley throws a napkin at him from across the table.

"I have an idea!" Emery says, pulling her phone out of her purse. She's tapping away at the screen and pulls up an app. "Let's play Truth or Dare!"

"Oh Jesus." Zay chuckles. "With this group, I'm not sure if that's a good idea." He looks out of the corner of his eye at me before taking a sip of his beer.

"It'll be fun," Emery says enthusiastically. "And if you choose to forgo either the Truth or the Dare, you have to take a shot. That's the consequence."

"I've already had four drinks!" I remind them. I'm a responsible drinker. I hate being drunk. I like to enjoy myself but not push my limits.

Rowan taps my arm. "Well then, you better be prepared for the Truth or the Dare, sweetheart."

"You said you were going to look out for me," I mumble and narrow my eyes at him.

He grins at me. "Oh, sweet girl, I'll make sure you get home okay." Then everyone laughs.

I swallow a groan. Why do I feel like this is going to be a bad idea?

SIX LEMON DROP shots line the center of our table, and we've all refreshed our drinks and have fresh glasses of ice water.

"Ready?" Emery asks, and looks around at everyone, a hint of a challenge in her eyes.

"Let's do it," Zay says and rubs his hands together, ready to begin.

Emery beams with delight. "Okay, so we're going counterclockwise. Rowan goes first, then Saige, then Zay, then Kinsley, and I'm last. We'll ask you Truth or Dare. If you pick truth, we'll use the questions from the app. If it's a dare, we'll come up with one as a group. Rules though, friends." She looks pointedly at each of us. "It has to be safe, but it has to push boundaries."

The guys grumble.

"I refuse to kiss Rowan," Zay teases.

"You're not my type," Rowan jokes back.

"So, Ro." Emery grins at him. "Truth or Dare?"

Rowan rubs his chin and ponders his two options for a minute. "Truth."

"I knew he'd go easy on us," Kinsley says.

"Hey hey," he chides. "Let's start off nice and slow. Build our way up."

Emery taps the app on her phone, and the questions scramble. "Okay," she says and chuckles to herself as she reads the question before reading it back to us. "Have you ever cheated on a boyfriend or girlfriend?"

"Really?" Rowan raises an unenthused eyebrow. "That's the question?"

"Yep." She turns the phone to face him, and he turns up his nose.

"Yes," he answers, sounding bored. "I've cheated on both."

"What!" Kinsley screams across the table. "You've had a

boyfriend and a girlfriend?"

"Yes," he mumbles and takes a sip of wine. "It was a long time ago."

She drops her head back in laughter. "I need to hear more about this."

I glance over to where Holt stands with his guest, and we make eye contact again, sharing a brief but friendly smile before I quickly turn my attention back to my friends. Emery is smirking at me, which means she caught me looking.

"No, you will not hear more about this." Rowan raises his chin in defiance, then snatches Emery's phone. "Moving on. Saige, truth or dare?"

I glance around the table at my friends and, without much thinking, blurt out, "Dare."

Oh, shit. My stomach twists into a giant knot as those words fall from my tongue.

Everyone begins hooting and hollering, and I can't help but laugh along with them. "Remember, safe," Emery reminds us. "And, friends, let's be reasonable."

"Reasonable," Kinsley snorts. "Okay, let's put our heads together, guys." They lean in to the center of the small round pub table, and whisper-yell over the tops of empty drink glasses and finally all sit back in their chairs.

"Bad idea." Zay shakes his head and purses his lips. "I don't like it."

"Well, if one of you disagrees, then maybe you should come up with something new," I chime in and look at Zay, who looks irritated.

"Not in this lifetime." Kinsley giggles. "You ready, Saige?"

I swallow hard against my dry throat. "No."

Truth. Always choose truth. What was I thinking?

"Too bad." She grabs a shot off the table. "You are

going to go ask Holt Hamilton out for a drink."

"What?" I snap at her. I look around the table like my friends have lost their damn minds. "I can't ask him out for drinks. He'll think it's a date, and dating a superior is strictly prohibited per the company handbook. There's this thing called ethics in the workplace, people. Have you all lost your minds? Are you all crazy? Are you trying to get me fired?" They all roar with laughter and my heart races.

"First of all," Kinsley tips her head back and swallows the lemon drop shot, "it's not against company policy to date a coworker. You cannot date your direct manager. Holt is not your direct manager." She looks pleased, like she just solved a murder case.

"He owns the fucking company," I bark at her. "That pretty much qualifies as my manager."

"Pipe down, little one." Rowan pats my hand. "It's just a drink, and purely innocent."

I glower at him. "You said you'd have my back. This is not having my back, Ro." I wipe my sweaty hands on my skirt.

"It's all in pure fun." His eyebrows dance at me. "Tell him we dared you if you have to."

My frown deepens. "So I look like a thirteen-year-old? Hi, Mr. Hamilton. My friends over there dared me to ask you out. Will you have drinks with me? No thanks." I cross my arms over my chest in defiance. Then, realizing that I probably look like I'm actually thirteen, I uncross them.

Zay chimes in, "I'll bet one hundred dollars she won't do it."

"Chicken, Saige?" Kinsley kicks me under the table.

"I'm not a chicken, you assholes," I grumble. "I'm reasonable. This is not reasonable. I'd like to keep my job."

Emery nudges me. "It's all in fun, and I am dying to see the look on his face when you ask him."

I glance at Holt, feeling anxiety building in my stomach. Suddenly, he turns in our general direction to find all of us watching him. His brows pinch together in a confused look, but he offers us all a polite smile and a little nod of his head.

Ugh . . . "Fine. I'll do it." I add my two whiny cents, "This is really stupid, though, and if I wasn't already close to being three sheets to the wind, I'd just take the damn shot." I fan my face. The heat from the alcohol or the stuffy bar is getting to me.

"Atta girl!" Rowan grabs my hand and helps me down from the tall barstool. My knees wobble, and I press a hand my cheek to cool the flush crawling across my face. Between my nerves and the alcohol, my stomach is twisting and turning.

"Just breathe," Rowan whispers in my ear as he grips my hand tightly. "Just ask him if he'd be interested in grabbing a drink sometime."

"And when he says no?"

"You just smile and come back to us."

Zay clears his throat. "What if he says yes?"

I turn around to shoot him a death glare.

Emery answers, "Then just know that she asked out the hottest man alive, and he accepted. Win-win." She offers me a reassuring smile.

"Hottest man alive?" Zay mumbles under his breath and pffts into his glass of beer.

"Yes!" Emery and Kinsley say simultaneously.

"I can't do this," I say, reaching for my chair. Nerves are getting the better of me, and my knees are literally knocking together.

"You can," Rowan assures me. "Go."

He gives me a little shove and lets go of my hand. I take a deep breath and begin putting one foot in front of the other. As I close the distance, Holt turns and sees me approaching. He's leaning over a small tabletop, twirling a tumbler in his fingers. He smiles as I approach and stands up straight.

I take note of how he's rolled up the sleeves of his blue dress shirt, and his tie is loosened and hanging from underneath his pressed collar. I like—wait, no—I love casual Holt. I take a deep breath and will myself not to faint.

"Ms. Phillips," he says as I finally reach his table.

"Mr. Hamilton." I force a smile and pray it looks sincere. He tips his head to the side just a bit, and I look between him and his guest, hoping I didn't just interrupt something important.

But of course he's gracious and introduces us. "Jack Morrison, this is Saige Phillips. Saige, Jack Morrison, a longtime friend of mine from college. Jack, Saige works for Jackson-Hamilton." Jack has short brown hair and stands about the same height as Holt. While he's decent looking, Holt is stunning.

"Nice to meet you." I reach out my hand to shake his.

"You as well," he responds and grips my hand firmly. "Holt's newest protégé?" he asks me, and I look back to Holt and smile.

"Hardly," I answer Jack. "But I am enjoying my career with Jackson-Hamilton Aviation." I hope that didn't come across as ditzy, because I swear, between the higher pitch in my nervous voice and my sure-as-hell fake smile, I know I must look like the biggest airhead. "Mr. Hamilton, I'm sorry to interrupt you two, but do you think I could have a word with you in private?" I ask. I can feel my cheeks flush with embarrassment, but I hold my chin high and forge on.

Before Holt has a chance to respond, Jack speaks up. "I have to get going anyway. Great catching up with you, buddy! Golf. Let's do it before the snow starts to fall." The two men give each other that half-hug that guys do where they bump shoulders and pat each other on the back. I like seeing Holt Hamilton like this.

"You got it, man," Holt smiles at his friend. It's the most casual I've ever seen him, sleeves rolled up and guy talk with a friend. He's always so professional and perfect, nothing ever out of place and his business face always "on."

"Nice to meet you, Saige," Jack says before turning back to Holt and flashing a strange look at him. I notice Holt give his head a little shake before he turns his attention to me and leans an elbow against the tall pub table.

"What can I help you with, Saige?" It's the way he says my name, with his upper lip curling itself into a cocky grin, that gets my heart racing, but it's that dimple that I want to reach out and brush my fingers over.

"Um, hi," I stumble through my greeting, realizing I already greeted him when I first got here.

"Hi," he says, cocking his head a little as if confused as to why I'm standing here.

I turn and look back to the table where Emery, Rowan, Kinsley, and Zay sit, all of them watching us intently. Turning my attention back to Holt, I do my best to push down my nerves and appear confident. "So I was just having drinks with ah, um—"

"Yes, I saw you sitting over there." He gestures to the table behind us. His eyes dance between my friends and back to me.

"Anyway . . ." I pause. "Would you like to get a drink sometime?" I blurt it out, then add hastily, "Not tonight, or anytime soon, but maybe just sometime, I don't know, maybe after work—"

"Yes." His answer catches me off guard. It's direct, non-wavering, and decisive. While I'm a mumbling fool, he owns his confidence.

"Yes?" I question him, making sure I heard him correctly.

"Yes, Ms. Phillips." His lips twist into a smile. "I see no reason why we can't have a drink together."

I blink a few times. "Because I'm fine if you say no," I stutter through my sentence.

He chuckles to himself. "I already said yes."

I chew on my bottom lip to keep from looking like a giddy schoolgirl who just asked out a boy she likes. "Well, great then. We'll figure out a time to have drinks."

"Tomorrow night." Again, owning his confidence. "I'll pick you up at seven o'clock." His blue eyes are piercing and locked on mine.

I blink, taken aback. "Tomorrow?"

He smirks. "Do you have plans tomorrow?"

I think about that for a red-hot second, and I know the answer—no. Sorry, Drew and Jonathon. I'll have to fight over the two of you on next week's episode of *Property Brothers*. I shake my head. "Nope. No plans. I mean, I'll cancel the date I had planned with Drew—"

"Date?" he questions, his eyebrows shooting up.

"Kidding," I mumble. I'm an idiot, I swear.

"Well then, I'll pick you up at seven." He pulls his wallet from his suit jacket hanging on the back of a chair and takes out a crisp one-hundred-dollar bill, tossing it onto the table. He presses his glass to his lips and empties the contents into his mouth, setting the empty glass on top of the large bill once he's finished. "Until tomorrow, Saige." His eyes darken and his voice lowers as he says my name. He nods over my shoulder, presumably to Emery, Zay, Kinsley, and Rowan, then he steps around me.

"Tomorrow," I whisper as I watch him leave. I can't believe that all just happened. I can't believe he said yes. I'm dumbfounded and confused. And I'm about to vomit.

"OPEN THE DOOR, Saige!" Kinsley yells as she bangs on the metal bathroom stall.

"Go away," I muster out between bouts of puking. Apparently, I really did need to vomit.

"You need someone to hold your hair."

I groan and flush the toilet, watching the contents of this evening's beverages disappear with a swirl. I fan my face and dab the sweat from my forehead with a piece of toilet paper before tossing it in the bowl and flushing one final time. Straightening my skirt, I take a deep breath and release the lock on the door.

"Feel better?" Kinsley asks, stepping aside to let me out of the stall. "You didn't even have that much to drink—I'm sure it's just the nerves and the letdown from Holt declining your offer."

Emery leans against the paper towel dispenser on the bathroom wall, tapping away on her phone. She looks up and offers me a sympathetic look but doesn't say anything.

I turn on the faucet and pump my hands full of soap, inspecting myself in the mirror. I scrub my hands and cup some water from the faucet into my mouth, swishing it around. The taste of bile is still strong on my tongue.

"So how did he do it?" Kinsley asks.

"Do what?" I run my fingers under my eyes to wipe away my eyeliner that has started to bleed.

"Let you down." She looks away from me. "I saw him smirk, then get serious, then he left quickly. God, I'm sure it was super uncomfortable for both of you." She laughs. "We shouldn't have made you do that, Saige. I feel really bad." For as *bad* as she feels, her sarcastic tone says otherwise.

Swallowing down my annoyance, I run my fingers through my long hair, adjusting some of the loose curls.

"He said yes." I bite my bottom lip to hide my smile.

But she continues like I didn't just reply. "I mean, Monday at the office is going to be so awkward—"

Emery cuts her off. "He said what?" She struts over and sidles up next to me. In the mirror's reflection, I see a quirky smile tugging at the corner of her lips.

"He said *yes*," I repeat. My stomach twists like I may need to puke again, but it suddenly calms.

"Holy shit," Kinsley mumbles.

"Our girl has herself a date with Chicago's most eligible bachelor," Emery squeals.

"It's not a date, just drinks," I remind her, trying to hide my own excitement.

Kinsley stands dumbfounded and confused while Emery's excitement builds.

"Oh my god. Oh my god. Oh my god." She jumps up and down. "When? Where? What are you going to wear?"

"Stop!" I grab her upper arms to stop her from jumping. "I'm nervous as hell and you're not helping!" I laugh at her.

Kinsley snaps out of her stunned expression and joins us at the sink. "So details," she says, and I can't tell from the look on her face if she's genuinely interested or jealous.

I shake my head, still not quite believing it. I have a date—*drinks!*—with Holt Hamilton. "I asked him out for a drink, just like you guys told me to. It was so ridiculous," I admit, "but he said yes. And then suggested tomorrow night. He's picking me up at seven. That's all I know." Less than twenty-four hours from now. My stomach twists again, this time with anxiety.

"Oh. My. God!" Kinsley exclaims and begins bouncing up and down, mimicking Emery's earlier freak out. They're sweet to be happy for me, but it's just drinks. One time.

I blow out an anxious breath. "Now I need to get home

so I can try to get some sleep."

Emery laughs. "Who are you kidding? There will be no sleeping tonight."

I have to agree with her. There is no way with the adrenaline coursing through me right now that I'll be getting any sleep tonight.

THREE

Holt

T HOSE FUCKING LEGS.
They were the first thing I noticed when I met Saige. Her legs go on for miles. I thought I was hiring a midwestern farm girl; however, she is anything but. She's been a bit of a mystery to me—all of her social media accounts are locked down, and no online photos. She's almost as good at being as invisible as I am, except I paid someone a lot of money to keep me off the Internet. I hired her sight unseen and only because of her last name. Thankfully, her credentials matched exactly what I was looking for, which made it easier on me and less likely for HR to question my motives.

And then I met her. Her and her long dark hair and those fucking endless legs. She left me speechless. Everything about her was nothing I had expected. Tall and lean. Dark and fair. Kind and ambitious. Mysterious and perfect. Exquisite. She is perfection.

I stand outside Bar 51 and take a deep, cleansing breath. "What the fuck are you doing, Hamilton?" I run my hands through my hair. I cannot go out for drinks with her. I know I shouldn't, but fuck if I could tell her no.

"Mr. Hamilton?" The sound of my name pulls me from

my thoughts, and I turn around to find Saige and our other employees huddled together. "You waiting on someone?" Isaiah Gutierrez asks me. I look past him to see Saige standing arm in arm with Rowan Hansen.

"Uh, no. Was just getting some fresh air before I head home." I turn my attention back to Isaiah. "You guys headed out?"

"Yeah, it's that time." He gives a short laugh. His eyes are bloodshot and glossy.

"Well, I hope you all enjoyed your evening," I tell Isaiah, but I turn my attention back to Saige as I shrug my suit coat on.

The group of them begins to chat and laugh before they disperse. Saige gives me a small wave as she starts to walk away, her arm still looped through Rowan's. Part of me wants to rip her away from him, and the other part of me is happy she's found a friend that she can trust—a very gay friend, thankfully.

Rowan helps her keep her balance as they walk down the street, and I smile as she giggles. I catch her look over her shoulder at me one last time before they turn the corner and disappear, but not before I memorize the look of want in her eyes.

MY FEET HIT the pavement with a heavy rhythm this afternoon. Normally, I'd spend an hour in the morning working out in my home gym, but today I slept in and then decided to hit the concrete of the wild Chicago streets to kill some time before I leave to get Saige. The warm, humid lake air fills my lungs, but there is something about the burn that's full of pain and pleasure—and I like it.

I jog home and quickly shower, throwing on a black suit with a gray shirt, no tie. Dressy, but not too formal. It takes me less than fifteen minutes to maneuver Chicago's back streets to get to Saige's uptown condo. This is an area that's up and coming and, while lots of younger people are moving to the area, there is still quite a bit of crime. Strike one. I park curbside outside her building and find the secured main entrance doors propped open so anyone can enter her building. Strike two.

I take the elevator to the fifth floor and follow the numbered doors to unit five-eleven. The halls are well lit and the floor is quiet, the only positive so far about this building and location. I knock on the door, expecting to wait, but it opens almost immediately.

"Sweet baby Jesus," a woman says as she pulls the door wide open and stares at me. She's dressed in scrubs and her dark hair is pulled back into a long braid.

I smile politely. "I'm here for Saige."

"Oh, yes! Please come in." She steps aside, and I step into the condo. It's small but modern. From the front door, you walk right into the main living area. A small galley kitchen is off to the left, full of modern appliances.

"Saige!" the young woman yells but doesn't move from the doorway. Women tend to do this from time to time and, while certainly flattering, it makes me extremely uncomfortable.

In an effort to stop her staring, I reach out my hand for introductions. "I'm Holt Hamilton." I shake her hand. "You are?"

"Evelyn Lopez. Saige's roommate." She grins.

My smile deepens. At least Saige doesn't live alone. "Nice to meet you."

"Likewise," she says and fidgets with her braid.

"So how do you know Saige?" I ask. I do realize that I've been here for less than thirty seconds and I'm already prying into both Saige and Evelyn's personal history. Not that I really care, but I don't want to look creepy either.

"We went to college together," she says as she finally closes the door and steps into the kitchen.

"You went to college in North Dakota?" I ask, surprised at this information. She didn't strike me as the North Dakota type with her feisty Latina attitude. But then, neither does Saige.

"I did." She nods. "We were roommates our freshman year in the dorms. We've been friends ever since." She pulls a bottle of water from the fridge and offers it to me. I politely decline. "I moved here first," she says, twisting off the bottle cap. "Saige used to talk about how much she missed Chicago. She lived here when she was younger."

I already know Saige's story, but I'm interested in hearing what Evelyn has to say about it, so I stay quiet and nod for her to continue.

"She always talked about how she would love to move back here, so when your company expressed interest in her, I told her to jump at the opportunity." She smiles warmly to herself. Clearly, she cares for Saige. Another plus.

"Well, I'm glad you did. Saige is a phenomenal employee." Understatement of the century. "We're very pleased to have her."

Just then, I catch Saige out of the corner of my eye. She's wearing black skinny pants and a top with sheer accents on the sleeves and around the waist. Her dark hair hangs in long, loose curls and her perfect lips are painted bright red. She's stunning.

"Saige." I turn and address her, keeping it together on the outside while my insides thrum wildly at the sight of her.

"Mr. Hamilton." She smiles warmly at me.

"Holt," I correct her.

"Holt," she acknowledges, and damn if my name

doesn't sound like perfection coming from her lips. "I see you've met Evelyn."

"I have." I turn back to see Evelyn leaning against the kitchen counter, grinning at us.

Saige shakes her head, and Evelyn lets out a little laugh. "I have to get my purse. Let me show you our place." She leads me to the living room. They have a comfortable set up. A small plush sectional sits in the middle of the room, and a flat screen TV rests on a wooden stand with glass doors. "Living room." Saige gestures to the room we're standing in. "Down that hallway is Evelyn's room." She points down a small hallway off the opposite end of the living room. "And my room is down here." She begins walking down the short hallway she just pointed to and into her room. I follow, and just inside her room I notice a huge window overlooking a small city park tucked away behind their building. I guess that's another plus. "It's small, but it works for us." A queen-sized bed with a bench at the foot sits against the largest wall. The bench is covered in clothes that spill onto the bed. On her nightstand is a paperback romance novel and a pack of birth control pills.

"Sorry about the mess." She laughs and pulls her purse off her bed. She walks over to a tall chest of drawers covered in small containers of make-up and bottles of perfume, grabbing a few items off the top and shoving them into her purse.

"Your home is beautiful," I tell her. Not as beautiful as her, but I will say her condo fits her. Simple yet beautiful.

"Thanks." She smiles, pleased. "You ready to go?"

I nod and follow her out of the room. Evelyn waits for us in the living room and sees us out. "Now, Holt," she says, her voice dripping with sarcasm. "I expect you'll have our little Saige home by midnight."

Saige rolls her eyes and flicks the back of Evelyn's head.

Our Saige.

My Saige, I think to myself, but I play along and laugh with Evelyn. "I can't promise midnight, but I do promise to be a perfect gentleman."

"Aw, fine," she sighs. "I'll take that. Have fun, you two." She closes the door behind us, and I immediately notice Saige looks scared to death. She takes a deep breath and I smile at her as we leave. "Relax," I tell her and she lets out a little nervous laugh.

"LUCIA'S KITCHEN?" SAIGE'S eyes widen in surprise as I pull into the valet drive.

"You've been here before?" I ask, curious.

"No. I've heard it's amazing but impossible to get a reservation." She twists her hands together in her lap.

"It is," I admit. "But my buddy Mark owns the restaurant. Lucia is his daughter's name."

She blinks at me. "You know the owner of Lucia's?"

I grin. "I do."

"Figures," she says under her breath.

The valet opens the car door to help her out, and I jog around to meet her. Pressing my hand to the small of her back, I guide her into the fancy new restaurant in Old Town. It's just down the road from my house and one of the neighborhood's trendiest new restaurants.

"I thought we were just doing drinks," she says, raising her eyebrows at me.

"We can't very well have drinks without having something to eat. I saw the way you stumbled out of Bar 51 last night." I smirk and she blushes.

"Mr. Hamilton, your table is ready," the hostess says, and Saige falls quickly into step behind her.

The table I requested is private yet overlooks the outside

dining area below us so it doesn't stand out as isolated. The restaurant is dark with dim overhead lights and accent candles on the tables providing the only sources of light. The atmosphere is modern and upbeat, yet still mysterious.

"Would you like a drink? Perhaps a lemon drop shot? That's what I saw you indulging in last night, correct?"

Her lips twist into a smile she's holding back, and she shakes her head. "Uh, no thank you. I'll take a vodka martini, extra dirty, please."

I damn near choke when she says "extra dirty," but the waiter nods his head and looks to me. "Jameson reserve. Neat."

"Yes sir, Mr. Hamilton. I'll be right out with your beverages."

"Reserve?" She questions.

"Only the best."

She puckers her lips, and I can tell she wants to say something, but she refrains.

"So I'm curious," I begin and rest my elbow on the table. I know it goes against all forms of proper etiquette, but I honestly don't care. "Why are we here, Saige?"

Her eyes widen, but she doesn't hesitate. Good. "Because this is where you chose to bring us," she deadpans.

I throw my head back and let out an exuberant laugh. She's beautiful, smart, and funny. Everything I knew she would be and more. Our drinks arrive in record time, and I give the waiter a look to which he quickly catches on and leaves us alone. Saige picks up her martini glass and presses the rim to her bottom lip. Her tongue brushes just over the rim, easing the cool liquid into her mouth.

Her lips. That tongue. *Fuck.*

"So back to the question at hand," I say, picking up my own drink. "Why are we here?" I pull a quick taste of the smooth whiskey into my mouth, letting it settle on my tongue before swallowing.

"It's embarrassing," she says innocently, her eyes falling to her lap.

"Tell me," I demand with a smile. "I'm curious why Saige Phillips asked *me* out for a drink."

She winces after taking another sip of her martini and pats her chest as she swallows the bitter liquid. "It was a dare," she admits with a grimace. "It sounds childish, but we were sitting at the table and Emery decided we should play Truth or Dare, and they dared me—"

"To ask me out," I finish her sentence. I laugh to myself, although I don't know if I should be flattered, offended, or horrified. *Truth or Dare?* I scoff internally.

Saige looks absolutely mortified. She lifts her eyes and finally looks at me, answering quietly. "Yes. It's an app that Emery has on her phone. It's a drinking game." She looks as horrified as I felt a moment ago. I smile as she fumbles around nervously with her explanation.

I can barely contain my laughter, and I see her visibly relax. "You asked me out on a dare?" I shake my head.

She nods and grips her martini glass for dear life.

"So what would've happened if you didn't take the dare?" I ask, taking another sip of the smooth whiskey.

"I would've taken a shot."

I study her expression. She's telling the truth, but why wouldn't she just take the shot? Seems the much easier choice rather than asking out the boss. "Didn't look like you had any problem taking shots before you asked me out for drinks," I quip.

"I had already had a shot," she fires back at me. "And how would you know if I was taking shots?" She asks defensively.

I study her for a moment. "I was watching you, Saige. I enjoy watching you." I admit boldly.

She audibly gasps, her chest rising and falling with each quick breath she takes.

I fix my eyes on hers and continue, "And I saw you watching me."

Her upper lip twitches as she thinks of a sarcastic comeback. I can see the vein in her neck throbbing with the beat of her pulse before she finally whispers, "We shouldn't do this." She pulls a green olive off the toothpick floating in her martini, then she pops it into her mouth. The green olive matches her eyes perfectly.

I watch her shift uncomfortably in her chair for a few seconds before I respond, "Why not?"

"Because you're my boss." So naïve, sweet little Saige is.

"I'm actually not," I tell her.

She frowns. "You own the company I work for; same thing."

I clarify, "I'm part owner of the company you work for."

She sighs. "Holt, this is just drinks. That's all." But her eyes tell me she wants more.

I lean closer to her. "It's *never* just drinks, Saige."

Our waiter appears, interrupting us, and I see Saige take a deep breath and smile as she orders another martini.

"I'll have another as well," I raise my glass, "and could you please bring us a couple of your best appetizers?"

Our waiter excuses himself.

"What if you don't like what he brings?" Saige asks.

I smirk. "I'm pretty sure there's nothing on the menu I won't like."

She swallows hard and nervously scratches her neck.

"Aside from playing Truth or Dare, tell me something else about you."

"I heard Evelyn telling you that I used to live in Chicago." I nod as she talks. "I was born in North Dakota.

We moved to Chicago when I was four and then moved back to North Dakota when I was twelve." She swallows back some emotion and takes a deep breath before she continues. "Stayed there until I moved here for this job a few months ago."

"So how are you liking Chicago this time around?"

"Love it," she sighs with nostalgia. "I mean, don't get me wrong. There is no better place to live than North Dakota. The best people in the world live there. Also, it has some of the best schools in the country and it's safe—but I love the city. Chicago is in my veins."

I smile. "Something we have in common. It's in mine too. I'm glad you like it here." She seems to relax and settles in to our conversation.

"I've been spending a little bit of time on the weekends reacquainting myself with the city. I used to spend a lot of time exploring with my mom and dad when I lived here. It's fun to see how the city has changed in the last ten years." Her voice rises as she speaks animatedly about her past in Chicago.

Our waiter slides a board of charcuterie and a sizzling iron of pot stickers on our table, and another server removes our empty glasses and replaces our drinks.

"What is your favorite place?" I ask her, wanting to hear more about her love of the city.

She gives me a nostalgic smile. "Same as when I was little—Millennium Park. I love walking around. I don't know, I guess it reminds me of the good times when we lived here." She says it with a bit of sadness.

I don't ask if there were bad times, because I know her story. I know why her family left Chicago and went back to North Dakota, and I know that what happened here in Chicago ultimately destroyed her family.

"Tell me about you," she says, placing some assorted

meats and crackers on her plate.

"There's not a lot to know." I smile across the table at her. "I spend most of my time managing Jackson-Hamilton," I say, tossing an olive into my mouth. "I work out when I'm not working, and that's about it."

"How old are you?"

"Thirty-two."

"Obviously not married?" She eyes my left hand.

I hold up my hand and wiggle my fingers. "Never been."

She leans in and cocks her head to the side. "Why not? You're attractive and successful. I imagine you have no shortage of women lining up to become Mrs. Holt Hamilton." She grins, presses her martini glass to her lips, and takes a drink. Tipsy Saige is ballsy. I like it.

"You're right." I chuckle. "There is no shortage of women lining up to court me. However, I've yet to find one that holds my interest. One that challenges me. One that is as strong individually as she is with me."

I hold her gaze and she tilts her head, her eyes glimmering in the lights. "Well, that's unfortunate for you," she remarks. "I'm sure you've broken many hearts in your search for the perfect woman."

I laugh quietly and turn the questions back to her. "What about you?"

She raises a challenging eyebrow. "What about me?"

"I assume you're not dating anyone?" She stares across the table at me before she lets out a little laugh. "No. I had fun in college, dated a lot of guys. One relationship was kind of serious, but it didn't last long." I like hearing she's single, don't like hearing the part about having fun and dating a lot of guys. My fingers grip the edge of the table. "I'm just focusing on my career right now." I like that answer better.

Taking a sip of whiskey, I change the subject. "So I was

thinking we could go check out Azure."

"The nightclub?" Her eyes widen.

I nod. "Do you like to dance?" Not my favorite thing to do, but for the chance to be close to Saige, I'll do it.

She makes a cute but unsure face. "Not really. I need a lot of these," she holds up her drink, "before I feel comfortable enough to dance."

I beam at her. "Well, drink up. We're going dancing."

FOUR

Saige

AS WE ENTER the hot and humid nightclub, Holt reaches for my hand and laces his fingers between mine. My heart thrums nervously as he squeezes my hand in his. Dance music blares from the speakers, feeling the heavy beat of the bass thumping up my legs as we weave through the crowd. Holt leads us to a section in the back where he nods and a large man steps aside, then we take a small flight of stairs up to an area that sits about six feet above the rest of the club.

I should have known we'd be headed to the VIP lounge. Professionally dressed security stand around the perimeter of the VIP area, but do a good job of blending in with the crowd. We step into the private area full of leather seats, couches, and oversized tables to a table marked "Reserved" with Holt's name on the placard. I'm underdressed and immediately feel self-conscious as the women parading through this area are dressed in dresses that are too short, heels that are too high, and are wearing makeup that is too much work to even bother with—but they are gorgeous.

A waitress immediately appears, and Holt leans in close to her ear, giving her orders. She nods and disappears as fast as she appeared, her ass shimmying from side to side with each step in her thigh-high heeled boots. I turn my attention to the crowd below and watch the sea of bodies dance and sway to the beat of the music.

"This place is crazy!" I tell Holt, leaning in much too close to him. With the music as loud as it is, I have to practically press my lips to his ear for him to hear me.

"It is," he says back in agreement.

Our cheeks touch and I pull away, turning back around to watch the crowd again. A minute later, Holt hands me an extra dirty martini and I smile at him. Service is quick here, and then I remember we are in the VIP lounge. There's a glass on the table with extra olives, and he picks one out of the cup and tosses it into his mouth. I squeeze my thighs together tightly as I watch his full lips press together and then part when he smiles at me. Everything about this man is beautiful. He removes his suit jacket and rolls up the sleeves of his shirt, like he did last night, then he unbuttons the top button of his shirt just enough where I can see the tan skin above his collarbone.

He sips on his whiskey, his fingers gripping the glass. Finally, he sets it down on the table in front of us and takes my glass from my hands and sets it next to his. "Come on. I want to dance with you," he breathes into my ear, pulling me up from the couch.

I shake my head at him. I'm not ready yet, but he nods at me in defiance. Bossy.

"I'm not ready to dance yet," I tell him. My nerves have peaked. Holt is nothing like I expected. He's humble and sweet, yet direct and bold.

"I am." He tugs me forward gently. I can see Holt is used to getting his way. I oblige. He's so demanding.

He laces his fingers through mine again as he pulls me through the crowd and onto the small dance floor. Squeezing my hand tighter, he looks over his shoulder at me and gestures to a spot on the dance floor. We find our way to the center where bodies are colliding. Lights move across the sea of bodies as everyone moves to the beat of the music. With a couple of drinks in me, my nerves finally settle and confidence takes hold. Holt stops and pulls me to him, settling his hands on my hips. I move my hips slowly, finally finding a rhythm that matches his. *How Deep is Your Love* pumps through the speakers, and Holt tightens his grip on my hips as we move together. My body reacts to his touch in ways I never expected. My heart beats wildly, my nipples pucker, and warmth spreads from my legs up to my center.

There are people all around us dancing, but right now, it feels like it's just Holt and me on this dance floor. His blue eyes carry an intensity that makes my stomach dance with butterflies. He pulls me closer so we're chest to chest, and his arm snakes around my waist. His fingers press into my side, his grip tightening as our hips continue moving in sync like we've danced this way a million times.

Our faces come together, and his nose brushes against the side of mine. Resting my cheek against his, I feel the heat from our bodies envelop us and I wrap my arms around him. The music is upbeat, but our movements are slow, methodical, rhythmic.

For over an hour, we dance like this—lost in each other. Feeling how the other reacts to simplest of touches. Our bodies tangled, hands in each other's hair, on each other's backs—exploring. Covered in a light sheen of sweat, neither one of us wants to let go. I feel like I'm on a high, drunk on Holt.

Holt's hands roam my back, and he presses me even closer to him. I can practically feel every firm muscle against me. Our eyes have remained locked on each other's. No one else exists. Just Holt and me. His hands find my neck and their soft touch sends a shiver down my spine. His fingers press against the back of my neck, and he lowers his head, pressing his full lips against the soft flesh just under my ear.

My legs begin to shake as his tongue draws small circles against my skin. "We need to leave, Saige," he whispers in my ear.

I shake my head no. I don't want him to let me go.

Pulling away, he grabs my hand and pulls me through the crowd and back to the VIP area. Our private table has been taken over by people, and Holt greets each of them knowingly. I recognize his friend Jack from the bar last night, who notices my hand locked in Holt's and gives him a look. He leans in, whispering something to Holt, who brushes him off. Jack looks back to me before turning and walking away. Holt grabs my purse from the couch and nods goodbye to the small group in the lounge before all but dragging me to the front door.

A cool gust of air greets us as we push through the glass doors and onto the sidewalk. It's refreshing, and I take a deep breath. "Why didn't we talk to Jack?" I ask as Holt pushes past the crowd now waiting outside trying to get into the club.

"I talk to Jack all the time. I want to get you home." He's abrupt and intense.

My heart sinks when he says this. A black Town Car pulls up, and Holt opens the door, gesturing for me to get inside. He's sending me home in a Town Car? My face flushes in embarrassment as I recall how close we'd been inside the club and how terribly wrong he must be feeling.

Hesitating, I want to apologize, hoping that tonight has not jeopardized my career. "I—I—"

"Get in the car, Saige," Holt cuts me off.

Tears sting the backs of my eyes, and my heart races as I slide into the back seat of the car. I turn and look out the opposite window in the back so that if Holt looks into the car, he won't see the tears that have formed in my eyes.

The car door slams and the driver asks for the address. I take a deep breath, but it's Holt's voice that snaps me out of my daze. "Corner of Astor and Burton Place, just off Lakeshore."

And then my heart is racing for an entirely different reason. Holt is in the car with me, and we're not going to my place.

WE PULL UP outside a stunning home not far from Lakeshore Drive. The entire street is lined with homes that have been recently built, or homes that have been completely renovated, leaving some of their historical charm.

"Holy shit," I mumble under my breath when I look at the brown brick house surrounded by a custom gate.

"Right here is fine," Holt instructs the driver, who pulls up to the curb. He hands him a hundred-dollar bill, opens the back door, and slides out. Then Holt offers me his hand, and I step out onto the curb where he leads me to the large gate that opens to a lush courtyard.

"This is your house?" I ask dumbfounded.

"It is." He looks up at the enormous house.

"And you live here alone?" I glance up and notice at least three levels to this grand home.

"I do."

We take the steps that lead up to the front door, and he pulls a key from his pocket to unlock it. Just inside, he disables the house alarm and tosses the key into a large silver bowl on a small table.

"Thirsty?" he asks warmly.

"Yes, water would be great." I suddenly realize how dry my mouth is.

He leads me to an enormous modern kitchen that's

every woman's dream. It has dark cabinets accented by white marble counters and modern, stainless steel appliances. A kitchen island three times larger than any I've seen, sits in the center, and large, antique lighting fixtures blend what I imagine is the old house with the new.

Holt pulls two bottles of water from his fridge and hands me one. "Kitchen," he says, glancing around.

"It's gorgeous." Understatement.

"I love to cook," he says confidently.

"I would have never guessed that about you," I tell him and take a drink from the bottle of water he gave me. He's hot and he cooks? I try to hide the small smile tugging at my lips.

He rolls his eyes. "Yeah, yeah. Everyone thinks I'm too rich to cook, too rich to drive my own car, too rich to do anything for myself." His tone is annoyed. "But I love to cook. I just don't do it often because what is the sense for cooking for one person?"

I know what he means. Most of the time, I make EasyMac or a can of soup. I give him an understanding smile. "I didn't mean that I thought you were too rich to cook," I try to explain myself.

"It's fine, Saige. I didn't mean to take that out on you. It's just that because of who I am, everyone assumes I won't do things for myself." He waves me off good-naturedly. I wonder how many people assume things about him because of his wealth.

"I never thought that about you," I admit and smile at him.

"Well, good. Then I'd love to cook you dinner sometime." His eyes brighten.

"Offer accepted." I twist the cap back on the bottle of water and set it on the kitchen island.

"Want to see the rest of the place?"

"I'd love to." I follow in step behind him as we take a different exit out of the kitchen. I am literally in awe as Holt shows me his home. Five bedrooms, seven bathrooms, two offices, a library, a home gym, a small wine cellar in the basement, and even a decent-sized backyard. Most homes in the city have very little space for a yard, but he said a neighbor and he bought the lot that sits between their houses and divided it so they'd each have a yard.

I should say it surprises me, but when you have the kind of money to buy a house like this . . . nothing surprises me. I will say that, even though the home is exquisite, it's very comfortable. It doesn't feel stuffy or awkward.

It's hard not notice how Holt appears so at ease and laid back here. "And last but not least, I have to show you my favorite place in the house," he says as we take a narrow stairwell up a long flight of stairs to a small landing. Opening a door, we step out onto a rooftop patio that takes my breath away. You can see downtown Chicago and even Lake Michigan from up here.

"Oh my God," I say, stepping out further onto the patio. "It's breathtaking."

"I know," he says and sidles up next to me.

There are stone benches built into the perimeter of the patio, with large pots with shrubs sprinkled in to break up the seating. Outside patio furniture fills the center, and a large built-in grill and outside kitchen area complete the space.

"Look." I point to the dark sky. "The Big Dipper." My voice breaks as I say it, and I have to swallow hard. Looking at the stars brings back so many memories, good and painful. I will never forget how long it took my dad to show me where it was in the sky and for me to tell the difference between it and the Little Dipper.

"I don't see it." He tips his head backward and squints.

"Right there," I whisper, pointing right at it.

He shakes his head, his arm brushing against mine. "I still don't see it."

I sigh. I remember how my dad would point and talk me through finding it and how frustrating it must've been for him, but not once did he get frustrated with me. He was always so patient and would help me locate it time and again.

"Come here." I sit down on a large plush outdoor chaise fit for two. Holt sits down next to me, and we lean back. "See right there." I point. "Those seven stars. From the end, the stars are Alkaid, Mizar, Alioth, and Megrez. Now go to the bottom left corner. That is Phad. Across on the bottom right corner is Merak and the top right corner is Dubhe."

"I see it," he says excitedly and points his finger to the sky. "Aside from a degree in interior design, did you also major in astronomy?" he jokes with me.

"No." I chuckle. "I did spend a good deal of time taking astronomy and space studies classes, though. Is that nerdy?"

He laughs quietly. "Not nerdy, but I would've never guessed that about you," he says, turning his head to look at me. "What made you interested in those classes?"

I rest my head in my hands and lean back into the plush cushion. "My dad," I say softly. I fight down the lump that's forming in my throat. I clear my throat and hope that it masks my emotions. "Before he died, he used to spend hours showing me how to find it. We'd lie out in the grass on the front lawn at the farm, and he'd show me all the constellations he knew. I could never find the Big Dipper, though. I was always looking too high in the sky. He'd say, 'Lower, Saige.'" I can't help but smile at the memory.

He smiles with me. "He taught you well. You knew exactly where to find it tonight." His voice is soft and caring.

I shrug one shoulder. "I've pretty much mastered it by

now." Without thinking, I go on. "For a long time, I couldn't look at the sky. It made me angry, and I missed him too much. Now it brings me comfort. It's how I connect with him."

Holt rolls over on his side and faces me. "Thank you for showing me."

"You're welcome. Thank you for agreeing to have drinks with me." I try to get up from the chaise but Holt stops me. "I should get going. It's late—"

"Stay with me." His words cut me off. His eyes, full of want, search mine.

I almost don't know if I heard him correctly, so I just stare at him in disbelief. "What?" A chill sweeps through me as a breeze picks up, and I run my hands over my arms.

"You heard me, Saige. Stay with me." His voice grows needy.

"I can't do that. We can't do that." I look up at him. Because I want to do that. But I can't. I most definitely can't.

He presses his palm to my cheek, his thumb gently sweeping over my lips tenderly. "Stay," he urges again, and all logical reasoning escapes me.

I look away from him, dropping my eyes to his chest. My hair billows around us as the wind kicks up. "I can't." My heart is racing wildly in my chest, and I weigh every consequence of staying with him in my mind.

"You can."

"Holt . . ." I pause.

"I dare you, Saige. Stay with me."

I dare you. Those three fucking words will get me every single time.

FIVE

Holt

SHE SIGHS LOUDLY. I can't believe I actually dared her to stay with me. I've never begged a woman for a damn thing, yet here I am, reduced to daring Saige Phillips to stay the night with me. I'm almost ashamed of myself. *Almost.*

"Saige," I push her to answer me. I see the hesitation in her eyes, but I also see the desire and want.

"Holt, I was worried that drinks were a bad idea. Staying is a *really* bad idea."

"Staying is a perfect idea. Look at the storm blowing in," I laugh light-heartedly and gesture to the clouds rolling off the lake, moving in above us, "and I don't have my car. I wasn't going to drive after we'd been drinking, and there is no way I'm sticking you in a cab at this hour and sending you home, so it looks to me like your only option is to stay." I smile at her, hoping my charm works.

"Looks that way." She chews on her bottom lip, fighting back a smile.

She sees right through my bullshit, but I don't care. Her lips are plump, pink, perfect, and *mine*. I lean in and press a kiss to them, pulling her bottom lip into my mouth. She inhales sharply and relaxes, kissing me back. Wrapping her fingers into the front of my shirt, she holds on as I deepen our kiss. Our breaths are quick, and my cock hardens as she presses her chest against mine. But after a moment, she pulls away and presses her forehead to my chest, wrapping her arms around me.

"Stop overthinking this, Saige."

She lifts her head and looks at me through her thick lashes. Finally, she answers, "Okay."

I sigh in relief and entwine our fingers together. We walk toward the door, and I guide her carefully down the narrow stairwell to the third floor. She holds on to my hand while her other hand grips my forearm tightly as I lead her down the long hallway to my bedroom. I can feel her hesitation combined with her want, which turns me on.

She squeezes my hand tighter as we enter my room, and she stops abruptly just inside the door. Something inside me quiets any arguments that this is a bad idea, and I turn around and push her against the wall. I don't want her to change her mind, and I sure as hell don't want her leaving tonight. I have to show her what I'm feeling, what she does to me, and I need to know what she's feeling in return.

We're a flurry of tangled limbs and lips crashing. Murmurs of want and need are stuttered between passionate kisses. The sound of heavy breathing fills the space between us when our moans of desire are tempered.

Every cell inside my body wants Saige. *Needs her.* Her long fingers work the buttons on my shirt, and she pushes it off over my shoulders where it falls to our feet. Running her hands up my chest, she sends chills down my spine as she makes her way over my neck and into the back of my hair, tugging at it gently. Fuck, she knows her way around my body.

Finding the hem of her shirt, I lift it and pull it over her head, tossing it to the ground next to us. Her tits are even more perfect than I imagined, and they're held in place by a see-through black lace bra. "Jesus, Saige," I mumble against her neck as I slide the bra straps down over her shoulders.

Reaching behind her, I unhook her bra and watch as it falls to the floor in a pile next to her shirt. My cock throbs in my pants as her hands explore my stomach and stop at my waistline. I take a step back so I can look at her. Her eyelids are heavy, and her eyes full of lust. She wants this as badly as I do. It's all the confirmation I need to continue.

"Here." I take her hand and lead her to my bed. I will fuck her against my wall, and on the floor, and in the shower, and every goddamn place I can think of. But tonight, I want her in my bed. Beneath me. Soft skin and gentle touches.

As we reach the edge of the bed, I unfasten her pants, carefully unzipping them. Kneeling before her, I press my lips to the soft expanse of her stomach with my hands on her thighs. As I look up into her eyes, she inhales deeply and closes her eyes. I tug at her pants and peel them off of each of her long, perfect legs.

After a moment, she's standing in nothing but a pair of black lace panties. She's all long, thin legs and curvy hips. Every single bit of this woman is perfection. I hook my fingers into the sides of her panties, and they fall easily to her feet. Without prompting, she lifts each foot and carefully steps out of them. I can hardly control myself as I look at all of her on display in front of me. She is everything I envisioned and more. The curve of her hips, her full breasts, her long body; lean yet soft.

She reaches out her hand to me, and I take it. "Stand up," she whispers, and I do. Anything she asks of me, I'll do. Anything. "My turn," she says, her hands shaking nervously as she begins working the button on my slacks. I love that she's willing to take the lead and I'll let her temporarily.

As my pants fall to the ground, so does Saige. On her

knees, she pulls my boxer briefs down and, without hesitation, she leans in and pulls me into her mouth.

I gasp as her warm tongue guides me inside her. "Saige," I muster out as my knees become weak. She begins slowly, her lips tight as her tongue circles my cock, with her hand at the base of my shaft. I didn't think it was possible to get any harder than I already was, but I was wrong. She slowly pulls me further into her mouth and begins to slide her lips up and down my cock. It doesn't take long for her to bring me close. She looks up at me with hooded eyes, and I'm so insanely turned on that I'm about to blow in her mouth and I'm not ready for that. I pull myself out of her mouth and instantly miss the connection. Big eyes look up at me as she gently guides me back inside. I moan in pleasure at the contact, as she continues.

Once again on the verge of losing control, I stop her. "On the bed," I tell her, pulling her up by her upper arms. Her lips smack as I pull out of her mouth. She walks backward, and as we near the bed, I finally lift her and set her down on the oversized mattress. I pull her knees apart, and I can immediately see how wet she is. Her bare folds show me her arousal, and it takes all of my self-control to not slide right into her.

"Saige," I hiss as I drag my finger through her perfect pink lips and circle her clit just peeking out for me to play with. She bucks her hips up as I pull it between my thumb and forefinger. "Does that feel good?" I ask, and she nods between deep breaths. Her hips roll in motion with my fingers. With my other hand, I insert my finger inside her. There's no resistance with how wet she is.

"God," she gasps loudly and sucks in a sharp breath as I fuck her with my finger. Her eyes are closed, and she bites her lip as I bring her closer. I insert another finger, and she hums in pleasure.

"I need to be inside you, Saige. I need to feel you."

"Yes," she whispers against my lips.

I reach in my nightstand and pull out a condom. As much as I want to be inside her bare, I'm not in the mood for discussing safe sex. I just need to be inside her. I slide the condom on and position myself at her entrance. She moans and her thighs fall open wider. I push inside her, and she takes my breath away. Warm. Slick. Tight. I can barely contain myself as I fill her. I have to pause once I've settled into her so that I don't let go immediately because I'm close.

I lean over her and push myself further in. She gasps as I fill her completely. Resting my forearms on the bed beside her head, I slowly thrust inside of her, letting her body adjust to me with each motion.

"Holt," she cries out my name as she tips her head back further, arching her back. I slide deeper inside her and pull the soft flesh of her neck into my mouth, biting her gently.

Her fingernails trail lightly down my back, which is such a fucking turn on. My body responds to her touch, and a shiver trails up my spine. She hooks both of her feet over the back of my thighs, pulling me deeper into her, and I'm completely lost inside her body.

"You feel so fucking good," I tell her, quickening my pace. Her breaths become shallower with each thrust, and her back arches, telling me how close she is to letting go. I can feel her walls tighten and squeeze around me as her body brings me closer to climax. "Come for me, baby," I whisper into her ear. "I want to hear you come."

Her fingers tighten on my lower back, and I press my lips to hers. I want every part of my body touching hers with her release. A moan escapes her lips, and I capture it with mine. "That's it," I say, kissing her between words. "I want to feel you come on me." Her pelvis bucks with each thrust and she gasps.

"Holt! Oh, God, Holt," she cries out, and I feel her body tremble beneath me.

I quicken my pace and pull out of her almost completely with each thrust, then slam back into her. Sex has never felt like this with anyone else. It's more than physical pleasure; it's a different level. She moans and breathes heavily as her body finally falls limp beneath me. She's still trembling from her release as I pull out of her completely.

"Saige," I say her name as I thrust into her one last time, finally letting myself go. I pulse inside of her, and her arms tighten around my chest. Then I rest the weight of my body on top of her, and her legs slide off the back of my thighs, falling open as we both catch our breaths.

We gaze into each other's eyes, her warm breath touching my lips with each exhale. With her eyes heavy and sated, a small smile tugs at the corner of her lips. I gently pull myself from her, already missing our contact, and roll off of her. Pushing myself off the bed, I move to the bathroom.

Disposing of the condom in a trashcan, I grab a washcloth and clean myself before returning to clean her. I find Saige curled up into a ball in the center of my bed, her long dark hair splayed across the pillow. *Her* pillow, as if it's always been hers and always will be.

She's pulled the sheet over her, and one of her long legs peeks out from underneath it.

"Saige," I whisper as I check on her, tucking a piece of her long, dark hair behind her ear. The sound of her steady breaths tells me she's fast asleep. Beautiful Saige is asleep in my bed. There is nothing that could have made this night more perfect.

I slide into bed next to her, pulling her warm body to my chest. She gently rolls to her back and her long body stretches out next to me. Propped on my side, I take in all of her beauty, all while wondering how after tonight I'm ever going to be able to let her go.

I FEEL HER absence before I even open my eyes. She's left. Sighing deeply, I run my hand over my face. "Shit," I curse and push the bed sheet off of me. Throwing my legs over the side of the bed, I stumble across the plush carpet to the closet, pulling out a pair of pajama pants and stepping into them. It's when I turn around that I see her clothes still scattered across my bedroom floor and I can't help but smile.

She stayed. She's still here.

I move quietly through the dark house, flipping on lights as I begin to look for her. The kitchen, living room, and the library are empty. The den and spare rooms as well. There's no trace of Saige in my home. I'd hesitate to call it panic, but my pulse quickens when I can't find her.

Then it hits me. The patio.

I jog up the three flights of stairs and down the hall, pushing open the heavy glass and wrought-iron door. I feel a wave of relief as I see her sitting on the edge of the plush double lounger, her back to me. A large blanket is wrapped around her body, and her face is turned up toward the sky. She's even more beautiful than I remember.

"Couldn't sleep?" I ask her as I approach her from behind.

She startles and then shakes her head. "Nah. I don't sleep much these days."

I sit down on the edge of the lounger next to her, wrapping my arm around and pulling her into me. Her head falls lightly against my shoulder as the cool evening air pricks at my bare upper body, and I shiver. "Why are you having trouble sleeping?"

She shrugs. "Just this time of year. It's coming up on the anniversary of my dad's death, and every year, I struggle with it."

"How many years has it been?" I ask her, although I know how long it's been. I know the day, the year, and even the time of his death. I know everything about him, and it kills me to see how his death is still affecting her.

"Ten." Her voice is barely audible.

"Come here." I pull her into me as I lie back against the chaise lounge. Her arms are trapped inside the plush blanket, and she lays her head on my shoulder. I press a soft kiss to the top of her head, running my hand up and down her back. I'm at a loss as to what to do to comfort her, but with each exhale, I can feel her warm breath against my neck, and as long as she is breathing, I'll do anything it takes to make her happy.

"It's really late, and I should go so you can sleep," she says, trying to wiggle out of my arms and away from me.

I resist, pulling her closer. "You're not going anywhere," I whisper into the top of her head and tighten my hold on her.

"Holt," she sighs. "You don't need to stay up with me. I'll just catch a cab—"

"No," I interrupt her. "I want you here with me. And if you can't sleep, then I won't either."

She looks at me, surprised. "You don't have to do this."

"I know I don't. I want to." I clear my throat and settle into the chaise lounge.

"Why?" She looks up at me. "This was a mistake. We shouldn't be doing this." She shakes her head a little and presses her eyes closed.

"A mistake?" I question her. "How was this a mistake?" I realize my tone is bitter, but nothing about last night with Saige was a mistake.

"I mean—"

I realize how rude it is for me to interrupt her again,

but I do anyway. "We're two consenting adults, Saige. I have thoroughly enjoyed my evening with you, and I assume you have as well, since you're still here—"

She cuts me off this time. "You wouldn't let me leave." Her voice trembles as she speaks and I realize how vulnerable she looks.

"Do you want to leave?" I ask her. It's a loaded question. I know how this is going to end, regardless of her answer, and I'll show her that tonight was not a mistake. "Because I don't want you to leave, and when I touch you, your body tells me you don't want to leave." I pull the blanket down off of her shoulders, and she inhales sharply as the cool air assaults her warm skin. "Lie back," I order her and pull open the blanket.

Her soft skin immediately puckers in goose bumps, and her nipples tighten into hard little peaks. I run my hand down her chest, between her breasts, her skin still warm to the touch. Her back arches at my touch, my fingers trailing down her soft stomach. I waste no time dipping my fingers lower and into her warmth.

"Does this feel like a mistake?" I slide my finger inside her. Warm. Wet. *Definitely not a mistake*. She groans, her legs falling open and I move my finger in and out of her slowly. "Doesn't feel like a mistake, does it, Saige?"

She whips her head from side to side and bites on her bottom lip. I scoot to the end of the lounger and drop my pajama pants, my erection springing free. A cool breeze twirls around us, and the moonlight provides just enough light for me to see Saige's hooded eyes.

Aligning myself at her entrance, I press myself into her and she gasps loudly. "Does this feel like a mistake?" I ask her again as I move inside her. Bare. Skin to skin. I want to own her as much as she owns me, and she doesn't even know it. Her back arches, and I hold her knees open wide as

I fill her completely. "Because I'm pretty sure this is heaven, Saige. This is what heaven feels like."

She closes her eyes and moves her hips slowly with mine. Leaning forward, I pull one of her taut nipples into my mouth, sucking gently while I cup her breasts. Her hands find their way into my hair, and she tugs lightly with each thrust into her. She releases a chorus of gasps, and moans and sighs; all sounds of pleasure as I work myself in and out of her body. With a final thrust, I pull out of her, and her eyes shoot open, bringing her back to wherever her mind had her.

"When we're done, I want you to tell me what you were thinking," I say quietly into her ear. A small smile pulls at her lips. "Roll over," I tell her and lift her hip, rolling her onto her stomach. I press her legs together tightly and slide my arm underneath her stomach, lifting her ass into the air. From this position, I easily slide into her from behind, and she moans more the deeper I go. As I fill her, she gasps loudly and her head falls forward into the cushion.

She's unbelievably tight from this angle, and she clenches herself around me. "Feel that, Saige?" She mumbles something inaudible, and I can't help but smile. "Not a mistake," I whisper, gripping her hips as I feel her come undone all over me. As I fuck her senseless, her body shakes beneath me. I press myself in and out of her; with each thrust and every moan, she brings me closer to climax.

She suddenly shifts, lifting her ass higher in the air and pressing back against me. I fill her as deep as I can go. She groans and rolls her hips against me; she knows what she's doing to me. "You like that, don't you?" I whisper into her ear as I lean forward into her. "You love knowing what your body does to me." She looks over her shoulder at me and slowly moves. It's enough to take me to the edge. Two more pounding thrusts, and I'm spilling into her. We weren't safe this time, and I couldn't care less. Nothing has ever felt as good as being inside Saige bare. She lies on her stomach as I gasp for breaths and soften inside her. I finally pull out of her and fall down on the cushion next to her. She lies on her back and rests her arms above her head, her naked body on display for me. As our breathing settles, I pull the large blanket up over her and pull her close to me.

"Tell me that was a mistake, Saige." She rolls her head from side to side. "Because whenever I'm inside you, it will never be a mistake." Her head falls to the side and she looks at me. "And if you ever want to leave, you go . . . understood?"

She nods her head and pulls her bottom lip between her teeth. "Do you want to go home?" I can hear her swallow hard before she finally answers, "No. I want to stay." Those words put me at ease. She wants to be here as much as I want her here.

"Good, because I want you here." We lie next to each other and stare at the night sky. Finally, she rolls onto her stomach, exposing her bare back to me. I can see the faint markings on her upper back, trailing along her shoulder blade. The small marks almost look like moles, but I immediately recognize their familiar pattern. With my fingertip, I trace them lightly. "Big Dipper," I whisper.

"Big Dipper," she responds quietly before I hear the light pattern of her breathing, telling me she's fallen asleep. Without hesitation, I close my eyes and join her.

I MUST HAVE slept better than I ever have in my life, because when I wake up, Saige is wrapped tightly around me and little snores escape her mouth. She's so damn beautiful as the earliest hints of the rising late summer sun spreads across her face. Her long legs are tangled in mine, and her hand rests against my chest. For a fraction of a second, a thought crosses my mind that maybe this could be my future—our future. Together. I brush off the thought, as I've spent one night with Saige, but damn if it doesn't make me smile.

SIX

Saige

I FEEL HIS finger rubbing small circles on my bare arm, and I stretch before opening my eyes. Cool air tingles my nose as I turn and press my face into Holt's neck.

"Morning," he grumbles, wrapping his arm around me.

"Morning," I answer groggily. "Did we really sleep out here?"

"We did." I hear a smile in his voice. "You fell asleep and I wasn't about to wake you."

I smile against his chest. "I slept really well."

"I'm glad," he says, pulling me on top of him. "I don't like it that you have trouble sleeping."

"It'll pass," I say quietly. "It always does, eventually."

Holt shoots me a concerned look and runs his hand through his mussed up hair. His blue eyes stand out against his dark lashes, and I lose myself in them all over again. My legs fall on each side of his so I'm straddling him. We're both still naked under the blanket.

"Careful, Saige," he warns me as I feel his erection hardening underneath me. He always wants to be the one in control, calling the shots.

I sit up and the blanket falls off of me, bundling around my bent legs and Holt's waist. "Careful of what?" I ask, feigning ignorance. I roll my hips, already feeling him pressing against my entrance. After last night, my body wants him—needs him. I push myself up on my knees and carefully lower myself down on top of him, feeling him sliding easily into me.

"Jesus Christ," he hisses and grabs my hips, guiding me onto him. "Saige." He says my name and closes his eyes.

"Careful of that?" I ask with a smirk, sinking further onto him until I can feel him pressing into the deepest places within me.

"Yes." His eyes open, and then he closes them again as I move up and down slowly on him. We move easily together, like we've done this a million times. His fingers press into the soft flesh of my hips, controlling the speed of my movements, and he inhales sharply when I begin moving faster.

"Oh. If that bothers you, I can stop," I tell him, pausing my movements.

"No. Don't stop," he barks as his eyes snap open, and he grips my hips harder, pulling me down forcefully on him. He's so deep inside of me; it catches me off guard and momentarily takes my breath away. "There's no stopping . . . unless you want to." He moves his hips and his pelvic bones press against me, warming my entire body.

Goose bumps prick at my arms and back as the cool air assaults our warm skin. I shake my head as Holt holds me on top of him. Finally, he loosens his grip, and I begin to move again, rising up and down slowly on top of him. I know how dangerous this is—mixing business with pleasure—and I certainly know this is nothing more than sex. Anything more with Holt Hamilton just isn't possible, but I enjoy the feel of our bodies together.

In true Holt style, he takes control, rolling me onto my back without separating us. His lips crash against mine, and he moves inside me skillfully. "Every morning," he says against my lips. "I need this with you every morning." My eyes widen in surprise as he says this, because there won't be every morning, but I can't control how my heart skips a beat at the thought of it just as he brings me to climax.

"SO I WAS thinking," he says, scooping a forkful of scrambled eggs into his mouth. "We should head to Millennium Park and walk by the lake, then come back here and I'll make you dinner."

I almost choke on my coffee. Honestly, I wasn't planning on seeing Holt again after drinks last night except for in the office, and now he's planning our day. As I told him, I feel like *this*, he and I, is a really bad idea.

He must see the look of concern on my face because he immediately offers me an out. "Unless you already have plans today, of course."

I keep the oversized coffee mug pressed to my lips and study the beautiful man across the table from me. The man who's made love to me three times, the man who held me when I couldn't sleep, and the man who made me breakfast when he should've pushed me and all my crazy out the door and sent me home in a cab. I try to hide my smile behind the coffee mug, but he sees right through it.

He grins and takes a sip of his coffee. "It's settled, then. We've got shit to do today. Finish your breakfast."

"READY?" HOLT ASKS me. For the last twenty minutes, I've been curled up on his couch with my nose stuck in a book I found on his library shelf.

"Yes." I reply, setting the book on the end table. Holt has showered and changed into a pair of faded blue jeans and a dark gray sweater. Day-old stubble peeks out along his jaw line and his fiery blue eyes pop against his dark hair. He looks like he stepped off the pages of GQ.

I follow him down a hallway and through a mudroom where he opens a door that leads to an oversized garage. A black Cadillac Escalade is parked in one of the three parking spots. He opens the car door for me, and I step up into the vehicle.

As we back out of the garage, I break my silence. "I thought we left your car at the bar last night?"

He shrugs and fights off a smile. "We did. I just didn't tell you I had another vehicle in my garage." He eases out onto the street. "We'll pick up my other car this afternoon." He glances at me out of the corner of his eye, and I shake my head, letting out a small laugh.

After navigating through the downtown Chicago streets, we pull up in front of my building, parking on the street. He follows me up to my condo and pulls the key from my hand, opening the door for me. Inside, Evelyn hollers from the living room, "Saige. Get your little ass over here. You stayed the night with Mr. Sex on a Stick, didn't you?"

My cheeks flush, and Holt clears his throat as we step into the open living room where Evelyn sits on the couch, typing away on her laptop.

She looks up and her eyes go wide when she sees Holt. "You have got to be kidding me."

Holt raises his eyebrows, looking at me, amused. He mouths, "Mr. Sex on a Stick?" and smiles widely. I shrug and pretend I have no idea what she's talking about, but I'm pretty sure the grin on my face says otherwise.

With a shit-eating grin, Holt clears his throat. "Good morning, Evelyn."

"Good morning." She purses her lips at us, then asks curiously, "What do you two have planned today?"

"We're headed to the park," Holt answers, sitting down

next to Evelyn. He makes himself right at home, kicking his feet up on the coffee table. I drop my purse on the ground next to the couch and pull off my shoes.

I beam at Evelyn's questioning eyes. "I'm going to go shower and get ready. You two have fun catching up!" Jogging off down the hallway, I chuckle to myself because I know Evelyn is going to give Holt a hard time, and I know Holt is going to dish it right back at her.

FIFTEEN MINUTES LATER, I'm showered, lotioned up, and wrapping my wet hair in a towel on top of my head. I toss on a pair of white linen shorts and a navy and white long-sleeved striped shirt, perfect for the late summer Chicago weather.

I brush some loose powder on my face, line my eyes, and touch up my lashes with mascara before quickly blow-drying my hair. My dark hair hangs in long waves down the middle of my back. I line my lips and brush on some lipstick as I finish getting ready.

The bathroom door opens and there stands Holt. He smiles at me and steps into the bathroom. "You smell good," he says, pressing his lips to my neck. "I like your perfume."

I groan lightly as his soft lips press against my neck. He pulls away and reaches his hand out to the counter, snatching my toothbrush and toothpaste.

"What're you doing?" I ask, following him out of the bathroom.

"Packing your bag," he responds, matter of fact.

I frown. "What bag?"

"The one I found in your closet. You need some essentials and since I don't know your particulars yet—"

"Holt!" I interrupt him when I see the clothes he's set out on the bed. "What is all this?"

"Stuff." He tosses my toothbrush on the bed with the neatly folded stack of clothes. I reach over to see what he's set out.

"Yoga pants, sweatshirt, Converse," I list off the items and look up at him.

"For changing into after the park." He smiles at me.

I narrow my eyes at him. "Bra and panties."

He smirks at me. "Never hurts to have a spare pair unless you'd rather not wear undergarments." I roll my eyes at him and leave the underwear.

"Red shift dress and black peep-toe pumps." I raise an eyebrow. "What would I need those for?"

"For work tomorrow," he says like it's obvious, then he looks at me lustfully. "I've been dying to see you in that red dress again."

My eyes shoot open widely. "Excuse me?" Work tomorrow? He thinks I'm staying at his place again?

"You wore it the first day of work, remember?" He grabs me by the hips and pulls me close. "Oh, and don't forget to pack your make-up. Not that you need it, but I want you to have everything you need." He presses a sweet but firm kiss to my temple.

I begin laughing. I actually laugh out loud. "Holt, I am not staying the night with you again. I mean, we haven't even talked about what happened last night!" I yell it in a whisper and glance at the door, betting money that Evelyn is listening on the other side.

"What is there to talk about?" Holt steps forward and closer to me—taking charge. "I enjoyed last night. You enjoyed last night. Why can't we do that again?" He tugs at a piece of my hair and twirls it between his fingers. "I'm not ready to let you go yet, Saige," he says softly. He's a walking contradiction.

My throat dries and it's hard to swallow. "That's the

problem. I don't do casual sex, and I don't want this to end badly when you decide to 'let me go'." I use air quotes to get my point across.

He sighs loudly. "That's not how I meant it, Saige. It came out wrong." He grabs both of my shoulders and tips my chin up. "I meant I want you with me . . . today, tonight, and probably other days and nights too."

"Let's take this one day at a time," I suggest.

He smiles, satisfied. "Sounds good to me. Pack your stuff for tonight and later we'll discuss where we're sleeping the rest of the week." He leans in and presses a quick kiss to my forehead. He's insatiable. "I'll wait for you out in the living room. That roommate of yours is a spitfire."

I shake my head as he disappears down the hallway. Did that just happen? Holt Hamilton just invited me to spend the week with him. I shake my head in disbelief. I turn back to see the stack of clothes on my bed, and I brush my hand over the top of them.

After wavering for a moment, I unzip the large messenger bag and begin placing the clothes inside. I relent, just for tonight. The irresistible Holt Hamilton wins again. "Damn you, Holt Hamilton," I say under my breath.

OVERNIGHT BAG IN hand, I tiptoe down the hallway to hear a lively conversation between Ev and Holt happening in the living room. "If you hurt her, I'll fucking dis-ball you with a dull razor blade. Did you forget I'm a nurse? I've seen the injuries a dull razor blade can inflict."

I peek around the corner to see Evelyn leaning toward Holt on the couch, a very serious look on her face. I love her. I could not ask for a better or more protective friend.

He crosses his arms over his chest and raises his brows. "De-ball me? Nice, Evelyn. I have no intention of hurting her. In fact, I'm quite sure I don't like to hurt anybody—but especially not someone I'm . . ." He pauses.

"Someone you're what?" She asks, prodding him.

My heart races as I wait for him to answer.

"Someone I really, really like," he finishes, leaning back and settling into the plush couch. He's so relaxed yet confident, with his foot propped up on the opposite knee.

I pull the strap of my bag up higher on my shoulder and turn the corner. *It's now or never.* "Ready?" I ask, trying not to look at Evelyn. I can only imagine what she's thinking of me at this moment. I spent the night with my boss when I was supposed to just have a drink with him. Now I've packed a bag to spend the night again. This is crazy. *I'm pretty sure I've lost my damn mind,* I think to myself, but I push those thoughts aside.

"Ready." Holt smiles tenderly at me and stands up. "Evelyn, it's been a pleasure speaking with you again, as always." He smirks at her.

I peek at her out of the corner of my eye, and I'm positive I hear her growl as she plasters a fake smile on her face. "Ditto," she mumbles, pulling her laptop off the coffee table and setting it in her lap.

I shoot her a tight-lipped smile, and she turns her attention to her computer. Holt reaches for my hand and leads us to the front door.

"Everything okay?" I ask once we're in the hallway.

He frowns, confused. "Of course. Why wouldn't it be?"

"I thought I heard Evelyn giving you the third degree."

He waves it off. "Hardly. She's a great friend to you, Saige. She's just looking out for you. Not everyone is as lucky as you to have a friend like Evelyn." He smiles at me, and the knot I didn't realize I had in my stomach begins to settle.

WE SPEND HOURS walking the park, hand in hand. Holt only lets go for a few seconds at a time. We walk Navy Pier and blend in with the tourists. My heart is overwhelmed with happiness being back here at the pier, but a tinge of sadness lingers as I remember all the time spent here with my mom and dad. Things are different, yet so very much the same.

I glance up at the enormous Ferris wheel as it slowly spins, and Holt tugs at my hand. "Let's do it."

"No!" My heart begins to race. "I'm deathly afraid of heights."

His eyes twinkle with a challenge. "Then even more reason we should do it."

I squeeze his hand and hold my ground. "No way. I can't."

"You can." He pulls me gently toward the line. "Trust me, Saige." He looks away right after he says that.

"I'm scared," I admit, swallowing down a lump in my throat.

Holt turns back to me and smiles. His eyes are sweet and begging me to trust him. "I promise I won't let anything happen to you." And I believe him when he says this, even though my insides are screaming at me to run far away from this Ferris wheel. I remember my dad begging me to ride it with him, telling me I could see for miles from the top. After all these years, I still struggle with the regret of many things I didn't do or never got to do with my father.

So today, I will ride the Ferris wheel with Holt—for my dad.

Holt stands in line to pay for our tickets, and I step away, trying to calm myself with deep, cleansing breaths. I can't let him see me have a breakdown over a Ferris wheel, even though it's highly likely to happen.

"Saige," I hear him call to me. "Saige."

I turn around and find him waiting for me. I take in Holt Hamilton from a distance, and my heart flutters. That kind of flutter that happens when you have your first crush, except I'm not in third grade anymore, and we're not passing notes in class. He's my boss.

"Ready?" he asks.

I nod, forcing myself to be brave, and my feet finally move. "As I'll ever be." I rub my hands together nervously, and he snakes his arm around my lower waist, pulling me closely to him.

We slowly make our way to the front of the line where a car waits for us. Holt holds my hand, helping me in. I slide onto the bench seat and grip the edge on either side of my legs.

"You're fine," he says calmly as he sits next to me. The small door closes, and I hear the lock latch. "Give me your hand." He pulls my hand into his and laces his fingers through mine. The car moves slowly up before suddenly stopping to let the car below fill with occupants.

This process repeats until I'm nearly on the brink of tears. We get higher and higher, and with each stop, the rocking of the car has me nearly ready to vomit.

"Saige, just breathe," Holt says, turning toward me. He taps my knee, and I turn toward him. His crystal blue eyes are sympathetic, and he smiles softly at me. "I want you to enjoy this."

Ha. Funny. "I kind of feel like I'm going to throw up." I glance at him out of the corner of my eye before snapping them closed again. "So if puking is fun for you, then yes, this a blast!"

He laughs at me, that kind of laugh where he tips his head back and places his other hand on his stomach kind of laugh. It's deep and innocent, and hard not to laugh in response. "You're not going to throw up."

"Well, if I do, it's landing on you." I open my eyes long enough to give him the stink eye while fighting back a smile. But when we climb even higher, I close my eyes. My knees begin to knock together, and I squeeze Holt's hand so hard it has to be numb.

"Saige, open your eyes. It's beautiful up here."

"I can't." Even my voice is shaking.

"You can. I promise you, you don't want to miss this."

"Holt . . ."

"I dare you, Saige. I dare you to open your eyes and look." There it is again, the dare.

With my eyes still closed, I bite my bottom lip. "Why do you use those words against me?"

He's silent for a moment, processing. "I would never dare you to do something I believe would hurt you, and I've learned that you have a really hard time saying no to a dare." I can actually hear his smile. I sigh loudly and crack my right eye, barely enough to see through my eyelashes. "There you are," he says, and squeezes my hand back. "Look." He points. "Lake Michigan."

I turn my head and, without thinking too much, I open my eyes fully. The lake is full of beautiful sparkling blue water, and the sun bounces off the small waves, making the lake look like it's full of diamonds.

"It's beautiful," I admit before turning back to Holt.

"It's breathtaking," he says, looking at me with his eyes that match the color of Lake Michigan below. Gorgeous sapphire blue eyes stare at me and I nod in agreement. "It is."

His expression is tender. "Not the lake, Saige. You."

I blush with his admission and drop my eyes to my right hand, which is still cocooned in his. I take a deep breath.

"Thank you," I tell him. "I'm not sure I ever would've done this without you." That's not true. I definitely would not have done this without him.

"You're welcome," he says quietly as he looks over my shoulder and out at the blue sky we're floating in. My dad always tried to get me on the Ferris wheel, but I just couldn't do it. My heart flutters a little when I think about Holt Hamilton finally pushing me out of my comfort zone and getting me on this damn ride.

"But we're never doing this again," I mumble.

He roars with laughter and I can't help but laugh in return. "Deal," he says and squeezes my hand.

SEVEN

Holt

SAIGE WENT TO lie down and rest for a bit while I prepped dinner. Now baked potatoes are in the oven and steaks are seasoned. It's my go-to Sunday dinner; easy but delicious. I toss a quick salad together and set the table when I finally hear Saige bounding down the stairs.

"In here," I announce, leaning back to look down the hall.

"Smells amazing," she says as she finds her way to the kitchen. She stretches her arms over her head and yawns. Saige is fucking adorable in a pair of my sweatpants with her hair twisted up in a loose bun on top of her head. Her cheek has a crease from the pillow and she sleepily wipes her eyes. She's stunning even in sweats and a t-shirt.

"How was your nap?" I set the large bowl of salad on the kitchen island.

"Good. I was tired. Didn't sleep well last night." She winks at me. "What is that smell? Baked potatoes?" She eyes the oven.

I smile. "Yep. Hope you like steak and potatoes."

"Is the pope Catholic?" She quips. "I grew up on a farm. If I didn't like steak or potatoes, I would've been disowned." She laughs and leans back against the island's granite countertop. A few strands have fallen out of her messy bun and hang loose around her face. Her mascara has rubbed off just slightly under her eyes, making her green eyes pop against the dark outline. She's mussed up, but still the most beautiful woman I've laid eyes on. I never envisioned myself falling in love with Saige Phillips, but it's almost impossible not to.

"What?" She asks as she catches me staring.

"Nothing." I smile at her. I carry two plates and the silverware over to the table, fixing two place settings.

"What can I help you with?" She picks a small tomato out of the tossed salad and pops it into her mouth.

"Nothing. I'm going to throw these steaks on the grill and we'll be done."

"We should eat up on the patio!"

"Really? I thought you'd want to eat in here where it's more comfortable."

"You have that huge patio table, and it's beautiful out right now. Let's eat up there." She bounces excitedly as she waits for my response. How can I say no?

I grin, appeasing her. "Let's do it."

Saige begins grabbing things—the salad bowl, dressing, a bottle of wine off the island, two wine glasses—and she takes off up the stairs. I shake my head and laugh at the simple things that make her happy.

A few minutes later, I meet her on the patio. She's already opened the wine and is sitting in the middle of the lounger, Indian style, and sipping on a glass of wine.

"Hey," she says, turning her head to me. Everything feels perfect with Saige here. Just a regular night in my home, sharing my life. I fight back a smile.

"Hey." I set the tray of steaks on the stone outdoor counter and fire up the grill.

"It's so nice out," she comments, tipping her face to the

sky.

"It is. We don't get many summer nights that are this pleasant," I remark about the mild evenings we've been having.

"Do you spend a lot of time up here?"

I don't and it's a shame. I spent a small fortune having this patio updated, but it hasn't been used nearly as much as I would like it to. "Nah."

Her eyebrows shoot up. "Why? It's so beautiful up here. Even in the dead of winter, I'm sure it's amazing."

"It is. But it's damn cold." I laugh. "Honestly, Saige. I don't spend a lot of time at the house, and when I am here, I'm usually in my office or going to bed." I put the steaks on the grill and pull a beer from the mini-fridge built into the large stone island.

"Why do you work so much?" She asks sadly, pushing herself up from the chaise lounge and meeting me at the grill.

My heart rate spikes, and I fix my eyes on the steaks as I flip them. "I know what it's like to have it all and then lose it all," I say, closing the lid on the grill. "I pride myself on being honest, hardworking, and keeping everyone that's employed with me happy. The culture of a good company is only as good as its leaders."

She bumps her shoulder into mine. "You're a good man, Holt Hamilton."

I give her a small but honest smile. "I try to be." Shifting the conversation away from me, I take a deep breath. "So what do you think of your experience with Jackson-Hamilton so far? Has it been everything you thought it would be?" I wag my eyebrows at her and let out a little laugh. "But seriously," I encourage her.

She rolls her eyes at me but answers honestly. "I love it," she says excitedly. "Of course, I was nervous as hell the first few weeks. I mean, when I saw the names of some of your clients, I almost had a heart attack."

I chuckle at this. We have our fair share of celebrities, rock stars, professional athletes, and even business and political figureheads. We cater to anyone willing to purchase a private aircraft. "You'll get used to it. Pretty soon, you'll realize all of those people are just like you and me. There really is nothing different about them other than their fame."

"And their million- and billion-dollar bank accounts," she snorts.

"Ah, yes. Their money." I nod in agreement.

"It's intimidating."

I frown at her. "It shouldn't be. It's money. Doesn't make them a better person. In the end, it's just money."

Her lips tuck in, and I imagine she's thinking about her past. "I grew up poor, so money intimidates me." Poor. My heart sinks as she says this. She adds, "Well, not dirt poor. I had clothes and food and a roof over my head, but the clothes were never the latest trends, and I just never really fit in."

She tips her head back, swallowing the rest of her wine. I reach for the bottle and refresh her glass.

"You know what I appreciate about you, Holt?" She steps over to the edge of the rooftop patio, then leans forward over the short hedges that line the perimeter, giving the patio a more park-like feel.

"What?"

"I like that you have money, but you don't care. You have nice cars, this house is seriously the shit," she spins around and looks at me, "but at the end of the day, you're totally normal and not a complete dick like most rich men I've met." She smiles at me after she's done.

"Not a dick," I repeat with a chuckle. "That's a good thing."

"That's a very good thing." She smirks, then points to the grill that has begun casting a heavy smoke out the vent. "And I think you might want to check the steaks." She laughs.

I flip the lid and find the steaks actually looking perfect. I kill the gas and plate the steaks, carrying them over to the table. "I'm going to go grab the potatoes. Feel free to start serving yourself."

When I return, Saige has filled both of our plates with a steak, a dinner roll, and a small side salad for each of us. A fresh beer has been opened for me, and wine for her.

"This smells amazing!" She begins cutting into her steak. "And it's cooked perfectly. My compliments to the chef." She pulls a piece of steak off her fork with her teeth. "Mmm," she hums as she chews. I've never found someone eating erotic before, but the way her eyes roll back slightly and she tips her head, along with the sounds she's making, has totally turned me on.

"I'm glad you like it." I slide into my chair and join Saige in enjoying our dinner. We eat in comfortable silence for a few minutes before she finally pushes her plate away.

"So since all of this," she twirls her hand around the space between us, "kind of happened on a dare . . ." She bites her lip and fights back a grin. "Let's play twenty questions." I raise my eyebrows at her, and she laughs. "Except I'm the one asking all the questions."

"That's not fair," I grumble good-naturedly, taking a sip of beer.

She laughs. "It is fair. Only because I've exhausted all means of finding anything about you on the Internet. Next up is a private investigator."

My stomach turns when she says this, but I play it off because I know she's kidding.

"My Internet stalking skills are on fleek, and there is

zilch about you."

"On fleek?" I question. Jesus, I feel old.

She nods. "Yeah, like hella good."

"So you're a good stalker?" I raise my eyebrows in mock concern.

"When I need to be." She laughs and takes a sip of her wine. "So anyway, I'm going to ask you twenty questions, and you need to answer them honestly."

I narrow an eye at her. "What if I need to plead the fifth?"

She shakes her head once. "Not allowed."

"Christ," I mumble and take another drink of my beer. "Fine. Let's do it."

She rubs her hands together quickly and leans forward, resting her forearms on the edge of the table. She looks at me with a challenge in her eye. "Okay, some of these will be easy or simple, and some will make you cringe. Suck it up, but you have to answer honestly. Question number one. How tall are you?"

"Six-foot-three and a half." Boom. Easy. "Next."

She smiles mischievously, as if she knows the difficult questions are yet to come. "Number two. How old were you when you lost your virginity?"

Her cheeks go a little pink, and I smile. "Seventeen."

"Huh," she says, and I wonder how old she was. "Number three. Where did you go to college?"

My pulse quickens just a bit, but I answer honestly. "Columbia."

She nods, approving. "Impressive."

I shrug. "It's just a school. I'm sure your education was just as good as mine."

"For one-sixteenth of the cost too," she mumbles quietly. "Okay, question four. Tell me about your family."

Fuck . . . This could be bad. I clear my throat. "Well,

my parents divorced when I was in college. I no longer have a relationship with my father. I'm an only child, and my mother is the greatest." Personal enough, I think.

She takes in what I've said, spinning her wine glass between her fingers. I take a deep breath and roll my fingers on the table, hoping she doesn't press the family question any further.

"Do you like being an only child?" She asks.

"I always wanted a brother," I admit.

"I'm an only child too," she offers with a wistful smile. "It's lonely."

I can see the sadness in her eyes when she talks about being lonely, and my heart hurts for her. "It is."

"I want to know more about your family later," she says.

"Later," I respond quietly, praying we never talk about my family again.

"Favorite color?" Her expression turns light again, getting back into the game.

I grin. "Blue."

"Matches your eyes. I knew you'd say that." She taps her chin playfully, and I laugh.

"Last time you were in a serious relationship?" Her eyebrows shoot up to her hairline and she does nothing to hide her mischievous grin.

"Define serious," I ask curiously.

"Like you'd call her your girlfriend," she clarifies. "You'd remember her birthday and stuff."

"Three and half, maybe four years ago." I cast my eyes to the side, trying to remember. Honestly, none of my relationships have been that serious. I've never really found anyone that piqued my interest . . . until now. *Until Saige.*

She pinches her chin, curious. "Why'd you break up?"

"Wasn't interested in her," I say honestly. "She didn't

intrigue me. I was building a company and didn't need the distraction of a relationship that wasn't going anywhere."

"Ouch," she comments.

I shrug a shoulder, not apologetic. "It's the truth."

She moves on. "Okay, I think we're on to question eight." She counts and taps her fingers as she does so. "Favorite childhood memory?"

I smile as I think about it, feeling nostalgic. "Easy. Disney World. Just my mom and me. We spent a week there. It was the best vacation I've ever had, and I've been all over the world."

"Disney?" She acts surprised. "What made it so fun?"

"No pressure. No pretenses. We didn't have to pretend we were a happy family and put on a show for my father." *I hate my father*, I think to myself, and a chill runs through me when I think about him.

"Pretenses are the worst," she says quietly, almost to herself. Then she frowns, shifting gears. "Did you at least get Mickey Mouse ears?"

"I did." I smile. I think my mom still has them.

"Then it was for sure the best vacation." She smiles back at me. "Moving on, question number nine. What's your sport?"

I grin. "Football. Hands down."

"Did you play?" She asks, her face lighting up.

"In high school."

"What's your favorite professional team?"

"Giants."

"Oh God." She rolls her eyes. "Tom Brady is the biggest douche—"

"Saige!" I laugh at her. "Tom Brady plays for New England, not the Giants."

"Oh!" She laughs. "I still think he's a douche, though."

God, she makes me laugh. I'm not sure anyone I've ever

met would call Tom Brady a douche. Only her.

She purses her lips before asking me the next question. "Eleven. If you could go anywhere in the world, where would you go?"

I clear my throat. "Back in time." I pick up my beer bottle and press it to my lips, emptying it.

"Why?" She asks quietly.

I look away and shake my head. "We're not going there, Saige." If I could do anything to make her life different, I would. I'd do anything to go back ten years. I zone out momentarily as I take in the weight of that sentiment. "Question twelve," I prompt, and she gives her head a little shake.

Trying to bring back the jovial mood, she bounces in her chair. "What's your favorite animal?"

"Dog. Although I've never had one."

"What?" She blinks at me. "Oh my God. You need to get a dog. I have a yellow lab at home named Murphy. He's my best friend."

The way she says that, and the absolute genuine glow on her face makes me smile. "I'd love to meet him."

She shrugs. "Okay, thirteen. Biggest turn on."

"Hmmm . . . a woman's smile." I glance at her knowingly. "The way her eyes sparkle when she genuinely smiles." *Your smile, your eyes, your body. Everything about you, Saige,* is what I really want to answer.

I stand up and walk over to the fridge to get another beer. Saige taps her finger on the table as she thinks of more questions. When I take a seat across from her again, I find her biting her lip.

"So what are we at? We've got like seven to go, right?" I twist the cap off my beer bottle, tossing it in the middle of the table.

"Favorite food?"

"Italian, but I try not to eat too much pasta."

"Mmm . . ." she mumbles. "Lasagna is my forte. I'll make it for you sometime." She smiles at me. I love that she's thinking about us in a future sense. "Number fifteen. Favorite movie?"

"I don't have just one favorite. I love *The Godfather* and *Scarface*. All those old gangster movies."

"Never seen them." She shrugs.

"You've never seen *The Godfather*?" I scoff. She shakes her head. "We'll have to rectify that." I take a drink of beer and wait for the next question.

"Sixteen. Last time you cried."

"Hmm . . . my aunt's funeral. She was my mom's sister and much younger than her. She was almost more of a big sister to me than an aunt. She kept me grounded in the crazy family and world that was my life. She was probably the most influential person in my life." My aunt was the glue that held me together when everything with my family went to shit. She's the one who encouraged me to do good, instead of following in my father's footsteps.

"I'm sorry she's gone," Saige says softly, her tone compassionate.

"Me too. It was unexpected. Cancer." My voice cracks.

"I hate cancer."

"I do too." I shake my head a little.

"I'd love to hear more about her," she says, sitting up a little taller in her chair.

"I have so many stories," I tell her. "I'd love to tell you more about her sometime, but let's not bring down the mood."

"Deal." She smiles and moves on. "Favorite book?"

"Oh, gosh—" I tip my head back and think about all the books I've read.

She eyes me. "Don't tell me you don't have a favorite

book. You have an entire library in there." She gestures to the house.

I narrow my eyes in thought. "I'd probably say something by Dan Brown."

"Interesting," she remarks, but she keeps any comments to herself. "Eighteen. You're almost done with today's interrogation." She giggles. "When you were little, what did you want to be when you grew up?"

"A cop." I smile at the memory of playing cops and robbers with the kids in my neighborhood. "Until my dad told me that being a pig wasn't an option for his son." My dad. The thief. Always working against the law. I fucking hate him.

"Wow, your dad sounds like a real asshole." Immediately, she covers her mouth, looking regretful. "I'm sorry. I didn't mean—"

I reach out and touch her hand. "He is an asshole, which is why he isn't a part of my life anymore. This is a good thing."

She blows out a long breath, "Then good. But I'm still sorry I said that. I never want to insult your family."

I shake off her apology and take another sip of beer. "Next."

"Nineteen. Biggest regret."

"Ooooh, you went there." I laugh. "I believe we all have a lot of regrets, Saige. I can't name just one. I'm just trying to live my life right now to the fullest, so that I don't spend the rest of it looking back on things I could've done or should've done, or said, or did. Make sense?"

She nods gently. "I like that answer." Her smile is warm "Okay, final question," she says before taking a quick sip of wine. "It's a doozy, so brace yourself."

I raise my eyebrows. "Hit me with it."

"I don't do insta-love, Holt, so what're we doing here?"

She tugs at her bottom lip nervously.

I damn near choke on a swallow of beer. Insta-love? It hadn't occurred to me that this was so quick because I feel like I've known her forever.

She goes on, unapologetic. "I mean, we're moving at the speed of a silver bullet, but I'm not even sure what *this* is." Her eyes widen in expectation.

"Does it need to be defined?" I ask, setting down my fork and knife.

Her green eyes are still confident, but they have questions. "Defined, no. But I think we should set clear boundaries. I mean, it's weird enough that I've slept with my boss. But is this going to be a fuck-buddy thing? Do we get together on the weekends for a roll in the sheets, then at work I'm just Saige, the girl that works for you? Am I going to be your dirty little secret?" She whispers, leaning in. "I think I just need some clarification on what we're doing here. I think that's fair."

I twist my face in disgust that she'd think she was a dirty little secret. "Dirty little secret? God, no, Saige. Come on." What the fuck does she think I am?

"Well . . ." She wavers.

"You're looking for a definition."

"Clarification," she sighs.

"We're definitely not fuck buddies." I think about that for a second and frown at her. "Wait, do you have fuck buddies?" Jesus, I can't believe I asked her that, but so help me God if she says yes—

"No." She chuckles and rolls her eyes.

The relief is tangible, but I still have to ask, "When's the last time you slept with someone other than me?" If we're going to talk about this, us, I may as well go for the jugular and put it all out on the table.

"Friday night." She cringes, and my mouth goes dry.

I feel the blood rush from my head and settle in the pit of my stomach. Friday night was the night before we had drinks. The night she asked me out at Bar 51. The night before I had her underneath me. Who the fuck was she with? Rowan? No, he's gay. Isaiah?

My fists are already clenching. *I'll fucking end him.*

Suddenly, a huge cackle escapes her lips, and she presses her hand over her mouth. "Oh my God, you should've seen your face. I'm kidding! I was totally kidding." She laughs again.

"Saige," I warn her, on the verge of a real and true jealous rage. She has to know she can't mess with me like that.

She continues to laugh, but I have to say it's contagious. I fight back an angry smile and shake my head. "That's not funny."

She sighs, looking only slightly apologetic. "I know, but I wanted to see what you'd say."

"I want the honest answer," I tell her and cock my head to the side. "I think that's only fair."

Her laughter subsides quickly. She shifts uncomfortably in her chair and tucks a strand of loose hair behind her ear. "I don't know. Maybe like five months ago? Before I moved here."

"Who?" Maybe I have no right to know, but I can't help myself. The idea of someone else touching her fills me with rage. I don't want anyone touching her other than me.

She looks hesitant. "Really? We're going there? It's not like you know him, and it's not like it's going to happen again."

I don't like that answer. I don't like the thought of anyone else touching her, but she's right. It was before she even met me. "Fair enough."

She takes a deep breath and exhales slowly. "So back to the original question. What exactly are we doing here, Holt?

You have me packing overnight bags, and holding my hand in the park, and—"

"Let's just go with it," I tell her honestly. "Let's not label it."

She sighs, but nods and squares her shoulders. "Okay, but just so you know, I'm not going to fall in love with you, Holt Hamilton. It's never going to happen. We can end this here and chalk this up to a night of crazy drinking. We can walk away with no expectations for more, and no hard feelings." She swallows hard. "So if you're looking for a girlfriend that turns into a fiancée that turns into a wife, we'd best just end this here, because that's not me. I'm not that girl." She sits back in her chair and exhales a long breath. She's said her peace. She's afraid to love. She's afraid to get hurt.

And while I feel for her, understand where she's coming from, I can barely contain my smirk. "We'll see about that," I respond, pushing my chair back from the table. Standing quickly, I grab my dirty dishes and walk away.

I'M RINSING PLATES and stacking them in the dishwasher when I hear her enter the kitchen.

"Are you mad at me?" She asks and cringes.

I grab the towel off the counter and dry my hands. Tossing it on the counter, I turn around to find her standing in the entryway. "Not at all." I pretend like we didn't just have a conversation where she said she'd never be my girlfriend.

She moves toward me with concerned eyes. "Then why did you get up so quickly? Did I say something wrong?"

"No, Saige, you didn't." I sigh in frustration.

"Then what's wrong?" She keeps her distance, pressing her palms flat against each side of the doorway, filling its space.

"No regrets," I say. She twists her lips, and her forehead crinkles in confusion. I sigh again. "I've let too many dreams, too many opportunities, too many people slip away because I didn't grab on and hold on to them when they were presented to me . . . ."

She waits for me to finish. When I don't say more, she responds, "Sooooo . . . what does that have to do with what I said?"

I look away from her and out the window, reminding myself that she's twenty-three. She has her entire life in front of her, and here I am beginning to fall in love with the one girl I should have stayed far away from.

"Nothing," I lie. "Just don't count us out so quickly." I pull my lips into a tight smile.

"Then don't move too fast," she says quietly but firmly. "You've practically moved me in here after one night, although it was a good night," she quips. "Just don't rush things, okay?"

I hold back a smile and fall a little harder for her. She's fierce and independent and everything I never knew I wanted.

"Deal." I smile smugly.

Looking triumphant, she pushes herself off the doorjamb and walks across the kitchen to me. Sliding her arms around my waist, she presses her cheek to my chest. "Let's hug it out," she says, and I can't help but laugh.

"Hug it out," I repeat and wrap my arms around her, holding her tightly in return. "Do you want me to take you home?" I ask her, pressing a light kiss to the top of her head.

She looks up at me, her green eyes twinkling under the bright kitchen lights.

Please say no.

"No sense in doing that," she says, answering my silent

prayers. "I'm already here with an overnight bag. But tomorrow night," she looks at me pointedly, "I sleep at home."

Thank you, Jesus.

"What about Tuesday night?" I ask jokingly, but I don't push it.

She chuckles. "I'm staying with Rowan on Tuesday, but maybe I can pencil you in for Wednesday." She winks at me.

"Rowan, huh? I'll make sure HR gets rid of him tomorrow." I wink back at her. I've never been so glad that Rowan Benson is a gay man and for the fact that I know Saige is totally joking.

"We'll talk about Tuesday night later. Let's go to bed." But I'm confident that she'll be here Tuesday night. She wiggles out of my arms and slides her hand into mine. I let her lead and follow her through the kitchen and up the stairs to the bedroom.

WE DIDN'T EXACTLY go right to sleep, so when I finally heard the soft purrs of her breathing, it was well after one in the morning. Both of us were exhausted. Only once I knew she was peacefully asleep would I allow myself to sleep. A few times during the night she mumbled or jerked her body, but she never woke up. I'd do anything to take her nightmares from her. Thankfully, she slept restfully for most of the night.

In the morning, the alarm goes off at six, but she doesn't even budge. Saige is curled into a little ball, her arms wrapped around her knees. It doesn't look comfortable, but she's sound asleep. I slip out of bed and toss on some gym clothes, anxious to get a quick workout in before heading in to the office. I'll use the home gym today instead of jogging outside in case she wakes up.

The TV in the corner is set to CNN, and I catch up on

world news while getting a five-mile jog in. The last mile, I increase the speed and really push myself. When I'm finished, I reward myself with a piping hot cup of coffee, pouring a mug for Saige too. When I return to the bedroom, I find her on my side of the bed, lying on her stomach, her head resting on my pillow.

I set down the two mugs of coffee and slide onto the edge of the bed. As I trail a finger down her spine from neck to bottom, she slowly begins to move. "Good morning," I tell her as my finger makes small circles on her bare hip.

She twists slowly in bed, rolling to her back. Her hair falls against my pillow, and she throws an arm over her eyes. "What time is it?" She asks, her voice gravelly.

"Time for you to get up." I lean in and press a small kiss to her flat stomach. Her breasts lie perfectly on top of her chest with her nipples in hard little peaks. It takes every ounce of self-control to not join her naked body back in bed. "There's coffee for you on the nightstand. I'm going to get in the shower." I push myself off the bed and walk into the bathroom, where I undress. Tossing my clothes in the hamper, I step into the glass-encased shower.

Minutes later, I see her long, lean body through the glass shower door. She's standing at the sink and twists her hair into a messy bun on the top of her head before joining me in the steamy heat.

As she begins to lather body wash into a sponge, she asks, "So how is today going to work? Do we act like we did last week? A brief hello in the hallways and no other interaction outside of weekly meetings?"

I pull her soapy body to me and press her up against the tile wall. "Nope. You're going to go to lunch with me, and when you walk with Rowan to get your morning coffee, you're going to bring me one." I kiss her nose. "Just be *you*."

Her lips part, and she pulls her bottom lip in between

her teeth. "Just be me." I can see the hesitation in her eyes, her concern, and her worries. She'll never be a dirty little secret and I'll prove it to her.

"Yes, Saige. Just you. There's nothing to worry about."

"There is everything to worry about," she disagrees with a little shake of her head. "I was supposed to go have an innocent drink with my boss. That turned into a weekend of fantastic sex, and now I'm standing naked in his shower."

I ignore everything she just said. "Medium roast, splash of cream, half packet of raw sugar."

She blinks as droplets run down her beautiful face, her cheeks reddening from the steam. "Excuse me?"

I smirk. "That's how I like my coffee."

She's stunned for a moment. "I can't bring you coffee to your office, Holt. I've never brought you coffee before, let alone walked into your office. Everyone, and I mean everyone, will know we're sleeping together."

"Good." I feel the smile spread across my face.

"Good?" She asks, confused.

"Yes. Everyone will know you're mine." I smile at the thought. At her stunned silence, I shrug one shoulder and rub the shampoo into my hair. "They'll talk for a day, then they'll move on to the usual gossip like what big celebrity is buying our next plane." I really don't see what the big deal is, and I honestly don't give a shit if everyone talks about Saige and me, but Saige stands quietly, a concerned look on her face. Her lips are tight, and she feigns a weak smile.

"Okay," she says, not convinced.

I give her ass a little smack, and she yelps. "Now shower up. We're leaving in forty minutes. Wouldn't want your boss to have to reprimand you for being late." I wink at her, and she shakes her head, bewildered. I simply press a kiss to her lips. She'll understand soon enough that I'm serious. Serious about her and serious about not giving a shit if the world knows she's mine.

I could really get used to this. Saige in my bed, in my shower, in my life.

EIGHT

Saige

"YOU GO UP the elevator first. I'll wait and take another one." I wipe my sweaty palms on my dress and look around the lobby to see if anyone saw Holt and me arrive together.

He rolls his eyes at me amusingly. "There are security cameras everywhere in this building. I can guarantee you that more than fifty people have seen us arrive together. And they'll see us leave together too."

I sigh loudly, and Holt presses the call button for the elevator. "Relax. No one is going to say anything. No one will even notice us."

The car arrives, and we step inside. I take a deep breath and glance at Holt, who is his usual calm, cool, collected self. The doors close, and we ride quietly to the floor staring at the closed doors. I replay our weekend over and over in my head and can't believe how a couple of drinks turned into this. I glance at Holt and my stomach twists as the elevator slows to a stop and the doors open.

Holt slides his hand into mine and gives it a gentle squeeze. "Relax." He leans in and presses a quick kiss to my cheek.

"Relax," I repeat to myself with a curt nod. Stepping

out of the elevator, I turn right and Holt turns left, each of us walking to our respective office spaces. Glancing back over my shoulder, I find Holt does the same and he smiles at me. That perfect smile, the one that melts my insides and makes my heart race.

I slide into my cubicle as quietly as possible, docking my laptop and powering it up. I hear Kinsley across the hall, talking on the phone, and I silently pray that Rowan went for coffee without me today.

"Spill it." The words come out as a whisper-yell as Rowan sticks his head in my cube. "Grab your purse. You're telling me everything."

I stifle a groan. "I was hoping you already left for coffee," I admit with a grin.

He looks at me with a sarcastic expression. "Not this morning. I want the juicy details. Did you kiss him?" He holds a hand up. "Wait, don't answer. I want all the details." He studies me for a moment, and his eyes widen. "Oh God, you did! Tell me about it!"

"Ro, shush." I press my finger to my lips and he laughs.

"Did you go any further? Please tell me he doesn't have a small peen." He fans his face as if he's overheating. "With that body, I'd be so disappointed if he undressed and there was a lil' smoky instead of a bratwurst."

I stand up and smack Rowan on the shoulder and laugh. "You are so gross." I shudder animatedly. "And none of that is your business." God, we're talking about Holt's penis and I want to die right now. I rub my forehead in disbelief.

His eyes widen even more with certainty. "That means you slept with him. You saw it! Sweet baby Jesus, Saige, you slept with Holt Hamilton." His eyes are wide and he covers his mouth in surprise.

"Shut up!" I whisper loudly and grab Rowan by the elbow, dragging him down the hallway to the elevators.

He grabs both of my arms as we wait for the elevator and looks me square in the eye. "You don't have to tell me everything, just tell me if the dare was worth it." He's being the typically overdramatic Rowan.

I glance down the hall where I last saw Holt and remember the smile he flashed at me just minutes ago, then look back to Rowan. "Totally." I can't fight back my smile any longer.

"Atta girl!" He pulls me into a hug just as the elevator arrives. "You know I'm nosy as fuck, and I'm going to want all the details." He chuckles as the doors close behind us.

I turn to Rowan and demand his attention and plead with him. "You've heard more than I'm going to tell anyone else. Keep your mouth shut and don't fuel rumors. And please, Ro, do me a favor. If anyone, and I mean anyone, starts talking about us, or if we are brought up in conversation, please let me know. I value my job. I like it here. I love working with you, and the last thing I need is for this *lapse in judgment* to ruin my career."

He reaches out and gives my hand a little squeeze. "I've got your back, girlfriend."

I give him a trusting smile. "This is why I love you. You know that, right?"

He beams at me. "I know, buttercup."

We push through the glass doors and out onto the bustling city street, weaving through the morning crowds of people to get to our little specialty coffee shop. Rowan places our order and, instead of taking it to go as we normally do, we sit at one of the small bistro tables and sip on our addiction.

As I begin dishing my dirt to Rowan, my phone chimes from my clutch, interrupting me. I pull it out to see two messages from Evelyn—that I ignore—and a new text from Holt.

Don't forget my coffee and please tell Rowan good morning for me.

Rowan pops the plastic lid off his coffee cup and tosses it on the table to let the steam out. "Saige, why do you kind of look like you're going to be sick, but you still kind of have a smile on your face?"

I look out the window before turning back to him. "I don't know what you're talking about."

He narrows his eyes, not believing me. "What has you so distracted, woman? You're all over the place."

"Nothing," I insist, but my voice is weak.

He shakes his head. "You're so full of shit; it's coming out your ears." He laughs. "We should probably get back to the office. I have a call at nine with a prospective client. Some Hollywood heartthrob bullshit."

"Oohhh." I wag my eyebrows at him. Rowan hates the celebrity clientele, where I, on the other hand, love them. "I have to grab a coffee to go," I mumble as I slide off the stool and balance myself on my heels.

"A coffee to go, for your *lapse in judgment?*" He smirks, making air quotes.

I nod and smile. "Oh and my lapse in judgment told me to tell you good morning."

He sighs. "Good God, I love that man. Either you grab onto him like a spider monkey or I'm going to." Rowan fans his face and grabs his coffee from the table.

After ordering Holt's coffee, we hustle back to the office to arrive by nine. Rowan nudges me in the shoulder, and I take a left to head toward Holt's office.

"Proud of you, girl." He winks and takes off down the other hall where our offices are.

I stand and square my shoulders, lifting my chin confidently, except I'm terrified. I whisper to myself, "I'm just delivering a coffee. His secretary does this every day. This is *not* a big deal." My little pep talk does nothing to calm my nerves, but it's now or never. My feet carry me past a wall of small offices—finance, accounting, all the numbers people. I nod and force a stiff smile at a man who passes me in the hall.

At the end of the hallway is Holt Hamilton's office. His administrative assistant, Joyce, sits at a small desk just outside his office door and types away quickly at the computer. The glass walls of the office allow me to see him. He sits with his back to the wall, his attention focused on the Chicago cityscape just outside the exterior office windows.

I stop at Joyce's desk and take another deep breath. I try to still my racing heart, but it's no use, my voice cracks. "Mrs. King? I have a coffee delivery for Mr. Hamilton."

She looks up from her computer and over the top of her glasses and smiles at me. Her salt and pepper hair is perfectly trimmed into a blunt bob, and her face looks like it's seen every plastic surgeon in town. It's pulled tight and not a wrinkle to be found. She's very attractive and put together for a woman who looks as though she should be retired.

"Ah, Ms. Phillips. Yes. Mr. Hamilton mentioned you'd be stopping by."

"Here." I shove the paper cup at her, and I notice my hand shaking. "It's just as he requested."

Joyce looks at me and pushes her chair away from the desk. Standing up, she rounds the desk and taps lightly on Holt's door. He spins around in his large leather chair and gestures for Joyce to send me in.

She slowly opens the door to the sound of the speakerphone, and a man's gruff voice fills the large office. There's a small conference room table off to the right and Holt sits behind a large cherry wood desk. "Go on," she urges me inside the office, then smiles at us and closes the door quietly behind me.

"Mr. Marquez. Unfortunately, I have an emergency that I need to tend to. Let me call you back as soon as I get this resolved." Holt is speaking to the man on the other end of the line, but his eyes are fixed on me. Before Mr. Marquez even has time to reply, Holt cuts the line and sits back in his chair, his hands resting on the edge of his desk.

With a smirk, he pulls his hands in front of his face and steeples his fingers, pressing them to his bottom lip. "Ms. Phillips, thank you for delivering my coffee this morning."

"Mr. Hamilton," I cock my head to the side, "it's been a pleasure." I walk over to the desk and set the coffee down in front of him. "Is there anything else I can get you this morning or shall I get back to work? I have two high-priority clients waiting on me to customize their aircraft."

He grins at me. "That'll be all for now, but please make sure your calendar is free at twelve-thirty. Block about ninety minutes."

My eyes widen in surprise, and I smack my lips. "Very well. Enjoy your coffee." I spin around on my heel and walk toward the closed office door.

"Ms. Phillips?" He stops me in my tracks, just as my hand grips the door handle.

"Yes?" I ask over my shoulder, turning slightly so I can see him.

"That dress is my favorite. It leaves very little to the imagination." He picks up his coffee and presses the plastic lid to his mouth, but it does very little to hide his devious smile.

I shake my head and purse my lips while rolling my eyes. "Goodbye, Holt." I close the office door behind me and offer a brief wave to Mrs. King as I head back to my side of the floor.

Finally sitting down at my desk, I begin sorting through my emails and putting together recommendations for my client meeting this afternoon with Sergio Perez, a Columbian politician. Many South American politicians are involved in under the table "activities" to provide additional income. Most of these activities are illegal and involve drugs and/or guns. The idea of working with this man is causing my nerves to act up, and my stomach drops momentarily. I have to remind myself that this is a purely legal business transaction, and this is my job, regardless of how Mr. Perez made his money.

As I'm reviewing a list of "must haves" and requests from Mr. Perez, my interoffice instant message pings on my computer and alerts me to a new message.

> Holt: That wasn't so bad, was it? I'm going to have you deliver my coffee every morning.

I huff, trying to think of a witty comeback as my fingers hover over the keyboard.

> Me: Mrs. King would be devastated. Getting your coffee in the morning is the highlight of her day.

> Holt: I can't stop thinking about you in that dress . . . red suits you.

I can see that he's still typing a message, but I respond anyway.

> Me: Holt!

> Holt: What?

> Me: I have work to do. See you at 12:30.

> Holt: I like distracting you. I want you in that dress . . . bent over . . .

> Me: STOP! Goodbye, Mr. Hamilton.

> Holt: Goodbye, Ms. Phillips.

I shake my head and laugh to myself. How in the hell am I going to explain that to HR if they're monitoring our instant messaging? I close out the message and return to my work.

As I complete my client folder for Mr. Perez and hit send on an email to another client, my instant messenger pings again, this time a group message. These are almost as bad as group text messages. I grumble to myself and open the message.

> Kinsley: Rowan is holding out on us, Saige. Dish it up. He knows everything and won't share.

> Me: There's nothing to tell.

> Kinsley: You're such a liar. We're doing lunch out of the office today. We're holding you hostage until you spill it.

> Me: Uh, I have lunch plans today. Going to have to take a rain check.

> Isaiah: With Holt?

I don't immediately respond as I contemplate what to say.

> Emery: Saige?

> Me: Fine. Yes. I'm having lunch with Holt. It's not a big deal. I'm sure he just wants to talk about the two new clients I have.

Emery: He wants to talk about getting in your pants!

Kinsley: He's probably already been in her pants. He wants more.

Me: STOP!

Emery: #HowHotIsHolt

Kinsley: Quick drink after work? Just the girls.

Rowan: I take offense to that.

Kinsley: You're one of the girls, Ro. You're more of a chick than I am.

Isaiah: LOL!

Rowan: Yeah, but seriously, #HowHotIsHolt

Me: OMG you guys. What if they monitor our messages?

Isaiah: They don't.

Emery: Who cares if they do? So drinks?

Me: Fine. One.

Isaiah: Do ever feel like our group messages are a bit like having ADHD? We're all over the place.

Kinsley: Yeah, but we all follow along.

Me: Some of us have to work, people. I'm out.

I click the small X in the upper right hand corner of the message and close it out. Then I gather my folder, my list of recommendations, and notebook, and head to the conference room where I'm scheduled to meet with Mr. Perez. I'm surprised to find him already waiting for me when I arrive, as I wasn't expecting him for another ten minutes.

"Mr. Perez." I smile at him and reach out my hand. "I'm Saige Phillips. It's a pleasure to meet you."

He immediately stands up and pulls my hand into his, shaking it. "Please, call me Sergio." His accent is thick, but he speaks English very well. He's dressed in a gray tailored suit, no tie, with a white dress shirt. His dark hair is short and styled back off his face, and from the looks of him, he can't be over thirty. He's the spitting image of Enrique Iglesias, right down to the five o'clock shadow.

"Can I get you anything to drink? Coffee? Water?"

"Scotch." He grins; his white teeth stand out against his tan skin. "On the rocks, please."

I manage to keep my face straight. It's early for alcohol. I normally offer that to my afternoon clients, but scotch on the rocks it is. If he's going to be spending more than fifty million dollars with us, who am I to deny the man a scotch?

There is a small mini-bar at the end of the conference room. With the clientele we keep, it's important that we have all the amenities, including a fully stocked bar. I deliver a glass of scotch to Mr. Perez, who has since returned to his seat at the head of the conference room table. A power move. I see it all the time with these clients.

I smile and take the seat to the right of him, pulling out my recommendations. "Mr. Perez—"

"Sergio," he interrupts me as he adjusts his sleeve and plays with his watch. A Rolex, of course.

"Sergio." I shift my eyes from his watch to his eyes and smile at him kindly. As I've stated before, I'm very good at my job. "I've had a chance to go through your requirements and requests. I agree with all of them, but did want to show you a few additional options for this aircraft."

Pulling sketches from my folder, I proceed to show him alternative interior color choices, accent metals, and woods, as well as additional custom technology packages outside of his initial needs.

He smiles, nods, and listens carefully as I walk through every option. I'm obsessive about documenting every detail so that we can place the needed purchases and get his plane customized as quickly as possible. He accepts every recommendation I present, and I fight back a smile as I silently pat myself on the back.

As I finish my notes, he leans back in his chair, propping his left foot onto his right knee. "You're very beautiful, Ms. Phillips."

My heart thrums, and I take a deep breath. I keep my eyes cast down on my notebook and don't look up to him. I'm asserting my power now. "Thank you," I respond politely.

"You do good work. But a beautiful woman like you shouldn't be working." I now raise my head and look at him. He rubs his chin with one hand while strumming his fingers on the table with his other. "You should let your man take care of you. I'm assuming you do have a boyfriend, Ms. Phillips." His dark eyes twinkle as he flirts with me.

"It's Saige, and I do have a boyfriend," I tell him firmly, although I'm not entirely sure I do. Truthfully, I would've said it whether Holt and I were together or not. I'm not giving this asshole an inch of me. I keep my smile professional and as warm as I can muster. "And I disagree with you. I enjoy my job very much, and the last thing I need is a man taking care of me." My voice hitches nervously. I can feel his eyes on me as I stand up and begin to gather the papers that are spread out across the conference room table, shoving them back into the project folder.

Sergio follows my lead and stands up quickly, adjusting his suit coat. He leans in, and I can smell his cologne. It's spicy, but light. "Well then, I'm glad you've found a career that makes you happy." His pink lips twist into a devious smile and I swallow hard. With my papers in hand, I step forward and extend my arm, guiding Mr. Perez toward the conference room door. He leans in to me again, the smell of scotch heavy on his breath. "Because there is nothing you couldn't have sold me today." He wraps his fingers around my forearm.

"Thank you," I say nervously, pulling my arm out of his grasp.

"Please, you first." He ushers me in front of him. "It's been a pleasure working with you, Ms. Phillips. I hope to continue this relationship."

My stomach turns. *Relationship?* "Likewise." I offer a tight smile as we step out into the main hallway of the Jackson-Hamilton offices. "I'll be in touch with an updated estimate, and we'll proceed from there." I reach out my hand to shake his again. Even with clients that I don't like, or that upset me, I always remain professional. Always. His dark eyes slowly take me in from head to toe and he licks his lips before he grins.

"Very well." He nods and pulls my hand into his. Instead of shaking it, he pulls it to his lips and presses a kiss to the top. I manage a smile and tug gently, trying to release my hand from his grasp, but he's stronger. He holds it just long enough to let me know that he's in control, and I submit. I stop fighting him. He smiles when he realizes he's won. Finally releasing my hand, he turns quickly and walks toward the elevators. Normally, I walk clients to the elevator to send them out, but not today.

"Send my greetings to Mr. Hamilton, please," he tosses over his shoulder.

"Fuck off," I mumble under my breath and return to my desk.

TWELVE THIRTY SNEAKS up on me, and I quickly give my face a onceover in the small mirror of my compact. I've really never given much consideration to how I've looked before; I've always felt secure with my simple appearance. I wear very little makeup and the only thing I do beauty wise is get my eyebrows waxed. But for Holt, I want to feel more than simple; I want to be attractive.

I brush a light coat of taupe lipstick across my lips, rub them together, and tuck a loose strand of hair behind my ear. With a deep breath, I grab my clutch and shove my cell phone into the inside pocket. My legs feel like Jell-O, much like they did last week when I walked across the bar to ask Holt out for a drink, only this time, I'm walking across the office—his office—for lunch. My, how things have changed in only a matter of days.

My heels click along the travertine tile, announcing my arrival. Mrs. King looks up from her computer and smiles at me again. "Mr. Hamilton is waiting for you. Go on in." She gestures toward the door but doesn't get up to let me in like she did this morning.

"Thank you." I tuck my clutch under my arm. This morning, Holt's glass office was on display for anyone walking by to see. This afternoon, the opaque privacy glass doesn't allow anyone to see into his office. His office has glass that goes from clear to opaque, providing immediate privacy.

I open the door quietly and find him sitting at his desk, shuffling through a stack of papers. When he looks up, I nearly gasp when I find him wearing dark-rimmed glasses.

"What?" he asks, pushing the stack of papers away from him.

I blink. "I didn't know you wore glasses."

He grins and sits back in his chair. "Now you know. You should've asked me when we were playing twenty questions." He tips his head to the side and steeples his fingers.

"What other secrets are you keeping from me?" I tease him and close the office door behind me. I expect him to continue the playful banter, but almost immediately, his face falls flat and he looks odd, almost pensive. "Are you okay?" I ask, suddenly wondering if I've upset him.

He shakes his head a little and smiles. "Sorry." He rubs between his eyebrows. "Just got distracted for a minute. You ready to go?" He pulls off his glasses and tosses them on his desk.

"Yes. I have a two o'clock meeting, so we have to be back by then."

He glances at the large watch on his wrist and stands up, reaching for my hand.

I shake my head, a spike of panic surging through me. "Not in the office, Holt," I tell him quietly, pulling my hand away from his.

He pulls both of my hands into his, lacing our fingers together, then he pulls me to him, our noses almost touching. "I'll respect your wishes for now, Saige. But we're not doing anything wrong. I won't hold your hand today, but I will tomorrow," he says certainly.

I try to hide my wince. "Maybe we should just keep this on the down low—"

"Why?" he interrupts me, his face twisted in annoyance.

"I'm new here," I remind him. "I'm still navigating my

way, building relationships, and trying to prove I'm a valuable employee. I don't want anyone thinking that our spending time together is going to advance my career."

He smirks at me. "Do you think I'd promote you or give you special attention based upon you sleeping with me?"

His words have me flustered. "That's not what I said, but I don't want my coworkers to think that."

He shrugs, annoyed. "Who cares what they think?"

"I do," I argue. "I like my job. I like the people I work with. I like the owner of the company I work for." I look pointedly into his perfect blue eyes. "I just don't want to screw that up."

"You won't." He sighs, relenting. "But I understand, and I will respect your wishes outside of this office. Inside this office, that's another story." He snakes his arm around my waist and presses a light kiss to the side of my neck. I feel my breath catching as chills shoot through me and goose bumps erupt on my skin. His touch has that affect on me.

"Do you see that conference room table?" he breathes into my ear. I nod and look at the smooth wood table behind him. "You're going to find out what it's like to be fucked on that table." I swallow hard and inhale sharply. "And my desk," he says, turning me gently by my chin to look at his large executive desk. "You're going to be bent over the edge of that desk with your perfect ass in the air, trying to not scream my name." His blue eyes darken as he speaks.

"Holt," my voice hitches, and I have to hold on to his biceps to keep my unstable legs from giving out.

"Wait, I'm not done yet." He presses a gentle kiss to my lips before he turns and looks out his office wall of windows. "And then I want you naked . . . against that wall of glass, overlooking all of Chicago while I'm inside of you. I want your perfect tits pressed against that cold glass while I fuck you."

"Jesus," I mumble under my breath as I envision my naked body pressed against the window overlooking all of downtown Chicago. My knees shake lightly and there's a gentle throbbing between my legs as I replay what he's just said he wants to do to me.

"My two favorite things in the world: Chicago and you," he says tenderly, then snickers.

I can now barely contain the throbbing between my legs, let alone form a coherent thought at this moment. Holt trails a finger from my temple, down my cheek, and over my lips. I close my eyes and drink in his touch.

"Let's go eat lunch, sweet girl," he says, pressing another kiss to my lips while I try to catch my breath. "Because I want dessert back here in my office."

I take a deep, cleansing breath and determine it's better not to say anything. Sometimes there are no words adequate enough to describe how you're feeling. This is one of those moments.

NINE

Holt

I PRESS MY hand to the small of Saige's back as we leave my office, and I catch Mrs. King fighting back a smile as I guide Saige down the long hallway to the elevator bank. Her long legs poke out from her dress, and her heels make her legs appear even longer. Fuck me. I can't stop picturing her propped on the edge of my desk with those long legs wrapped tightly around me.

I hear Saige say something, but I'm so caught up in visions of her naked in my office that I don't actually hear what she says.

"Excuse me?" I ask, shaking off my impure thoughts.

"Where are we going?"

"I have reservations at Prime Grill."

Her eyes widen. "Holt, you don't always have to take me to these insane restaurants. It's lunch. I'm fine with soup from a deli."

Soup. I almost laugh at her. "They have everything there. Salads, burgers, steak, and even soup, Saige. Whatever your heart desires, I'm sure they'll be able to make you happy."

I want to make you happy. I want to be what your heart desires.

"Mr. Hamilton," Mr. Jones greets us. Mr. Jones is a driver that Jackson-Hamilton has at our disposal, mostly for dropping me at the airport, or driving me around town for meetings, but today I'm using him to take us to lunch.

"Mr. Jones," I acknowledge his greeting. He opens the back door of the Town Car and holds it open for Saige.

She looks back over her shoulder at me before she slides into the back seat. "A driver?" She raises her eyebrows at me once I'm settled next to her.

"We pay him handsomely. He needs to earn his keep."

"A cab would have been fine." She rolls her eyes at me and blows out a puff of air.

"Saige." I shake my head. She's going to have to get used to enjoying some of Jackson-Hamilton's perks once in a while. "Why do you question everything?" I try not to sound annoyed. As much as I love her banter, I want her to appreciate some of the amenities I can offer her.

She chews on her bottom lip. "I'm sorry. I don't mean to question or argue. It's just that . . ." She pauses. "Some of the extravagance makes me uncomfortable."

"Extravagance?" Is she serious? It's a Town Car, not a limo.

"Yeah. The VIP status. The private cars. The exclusive restaurants."

"Saige," I whisper, running my thumb across her soft cheek. "Trust me. That is far from extravagant. You want extravagant, let me fly you to Rome on one of our private jets or shower you in diamonds. That's extravagant. This is lunch. And the other night, I took you to a nightclub. Far from extravagant."

She raises one eyebrow. "The most exclusive nightclub in Chicago, Holt. That is extravagant."

"Would you rather eat at McDonalds? I can arrange for Mr. Jones to deliver us there instead."

She sighs and lets out a small laugh. "That's not what I'm saying."

"Then what are you saying?" I snap at her, having difficulty keeping my annoyance at bay.

"I just want you to know that I don't need the private clubs, the VIP, or the extravagant meals," she says softly.

"I know you don't. But I like giving that to you." I pull her hand into mine.

She shakes her head and swallows. "It's too much, Holt. Too fast." She pulls herself away from me just slightly.

Shit. I slide over to her, pulling her to me. "Don't pull away from me, Saige."

"Then slow down," she begs.

"I don't know how," I blurt out, feeling reckless and unlike myself. That's what she does to me.

I run my knuckles over her soft cheek, and her eyes flutter closed. "But I'll try," I promise. Her head falls to the side and into my palm. Goddamn, she's so beautiful. Leaning in, I press a kiss to her soft mouth, gently tugging on her bottom lip. Her body reacts to my touch as it always does, and I feel my cock stir.

Lunch. I'm taking her to lunch, I remind myself. *Get yourself together, Holt.*

"Jones," I call to the front seat.

"Yes, sir," he answers.

"Change of plans. Please take us to McKinney's instead."

He nods at me in the review mirror, and I pull Saige's hand into mine. If normalcy is what she wants, I will oblige.

WE'RE TUCKED AWAY in a booth in the back of the dimly lit Irish pub. The place is normal, not extravagant, just as she asked.

Saige squeezes a lemon into her iced tea, and I have to admit, she looks much more in her element. "I love it here." She smiles across the table at me.

I lean back against the wooden booth. "I'm glad," I answer her. "I used to come here all the time when I returned to Chicago after college." I think about how quickly my tastes grew more expensive over the course of a few years. It wasn't long ago that McKinney's was high-end for me.

She sips her tea and sets it down on the cardboard coaster. "Speaking of college, tell me about Columbia."

My entire body tenses as she begins to ask more questions about my past. "What do you want to know?"

Her eyes are wide and inquisitive. "What was it like going to college in New York City?"

I contemplate what to say and what I should hold back. "You went to college, Saige. You have to believe those four years were some of the best of your life, right?"

She nods. "Oh yeah."

I smile at her. "That was the same for me. Only I was in New York City. I was away from my family, having the time of my life, but it was also hard. I took school seriously. I had fun, but I did it in moderation."

"That's so you," she says, twirling the straw in her drink.

I frown. "What do you mean?"

She sighs and looks around before her eyes meet mine. "You're like this anomaly. You're serious yet totally fun. You're handsome yet boyishly cute. You're controlling yet sweet. You're a walking contradiction, Holt."

I laugh. "It's all about balance, my dear."

She grins, then cocks her head, looking thoughtful. "I think that's what makes you so successful."

I raise one side of my mouth in a smile. "Thank you for the compliment, but I'm hardly successful."

She scrunches her face and narrows her eyes at me. "What do you mean? You own a private aviation company. You manage a multi-billion-dollar business. What's not successful about that?"

"You're wrong. Well, partially wrong. I do own *part* of a private aviation business. But I'm only as successful as the people that I hire." I tip my head to her. "I wouldn't make money if I didn't have the best sales team, the best finance team, and the top people in this industry working their asses off for me and my company. They are the success in my business, not me."

Her lips twist into a soft smile.

"What?" I smile back at her.

"I like that answer."

I study Saige's face and think to myself that finding Saige was the best thing I ever did. "Good."

"OH MY GOD, I'm so full," Saige groans and rubs her belly. "That was hands down the best soup and bread bowl I've ever had."

I chuckle. "I knew you'd like McKinney's."

"Thank you for taking me to lunch," she says, leaning in and pressing a light kiss to my lips. I love when she kisses me. I know she has hesitations about us, but when she tosses her inhibitions aside, her playfulness comes out.

"I plan to do it often." I kiss her back. Mr. Jones weaves through the busy Chicago streets, delivering us safely back to the office. "You're back twenty minutes early for your meeting."

"Good. I need to freshen up and look at my project file again."

"Which client is this?" I ask as we step into the open lobby.

"Richards," she says, and I outwardly cringe.

"Word of advice with that one, Saige. Nothing you do will be right. He'll haggle over every option and threaten to take his business elsewhere. He won't, but please don't let him intimidate you."

"Who is he?" She asks as we wait for the elevator.

"Jeremy Richards. CEO of MegaMusic entertainment."

"Aww," she says, tipping her head back in recognition. "Rowan hates the celebrity clients. Says that for people that have money coming out of their asses, they're the cheapest—" She stops abruptly.

"What?" I prod, holding back a laugh.

She blinks, trying to look innocent. "Nothing."

"Saige, say it."

"No. I shouldn't repeat what someone else says."

"Saige." I raise my eyebrows.

She twists her lips in a pout. "I feel bad. I shouldn't have said anything. I don't want to get Rowan in trouble."

"You're not, and he won't."

She mumbles, but I hear her clearly. "He says they're the cheapest motherfuckers around."

I toss my head back and bust out laughing because it's the truth. "He's right," I admit. "They will nickel and dime us over every last detail. But you know what? They keep coming back. I'm confident you'll handle Mr. Richards just fine," I tell her and squeeze her shoulder reassuringly. "Don't let Rowan or anyone tell you anything about our clients that'll intimidate you. You're very good at what you do and you're well respected for it."

She smiles at me as we step into the elevator. What I don't tell her is that Jeremy Richards is the biggest asshole I've ever met. But when he drops over twenty-five million dollars annually with us, I deal with his bullshit with a smile on my face. Still, I feel guilty knowing that Saige is going to have to deal with him now as well.

When the doors slide open, Saige offers me a tight smile before stepping off the elevator. I can tell she's focused on this next meeting, as she's distracted and didn't even say goodbye.

Three hours later, I hang up from my last conference call and wander out of my office. Most of Jackson-Hamilton has left for the evening, except for a few of the guys in accounting who make it their job to stay late every night. I swear it has something to do with numbers; those guys always work late into the evening, usually leaving around the time I do.

"Mr. Hamilton," Joyce says as she pulls her purse straps up onto her shoulder. "Everything you asked for has been done."

I nod to her. "Thank you, Joyce."

"See you tomorrow, sir. Oh, and your mother called. Asked that you please call her right away."

I nod again. "Goodnight."

As I walk the perimeter of the office, I find the place damn near empty, most everyone including Saige is gone for the evening. I settle in and begin making business calls to three potential clients in Australia, where it's nearly eleven in the morning. All three clients are interested in our most popular and most expensive aircraft, the Bombardier Global Express.

For the rock bottom price of fifty million dollars, I can get them a brand new Bombardier. For a more reasonable thirty-five million, I can get an almost new plane that we can essentially make new with customizations. With the uptick in the economy, many foreign businesses are finally putting stock into private aircraft and our business is booming.

I dial Lawrence Ward, the CEO of the largest private utilities company in Australia. Pushing the button on the speakerphone, I pace the floor of my office, looking seventy-nine stories down onto the bustling Chicago streets. Cars look like ants from this distance.

As Mr. Ward's administrative assistant connects us, I quickly pull the client file that Isaiah put together for me, outlining the client's needs, wants, budget, and essentially a full background check, including assets, liabilities, and the company's credit rating. I scan the important information and, just as I finish, Mr. Ward answers.

"Hello, Mr. Hamilton," he says, his voice jubilant and thick with his Aussie accent.

"Mr. Ward. I'm glad we are able to connect." For the next thirty minutes, we trade pleasantries and discuss what Jackson-Hamilton has to offer in terms of a private aircraft for Mr. Ward's company. I hang up pleased with the discussion, and with Mr. Ward anxious to speak with Isaiah to move forward with a sale.

As I'm dialing James Powers, the head of a telecommunications company, also in Australia, I catch a glimpse of vibrant red walking directly toward me. Long legs stride forward from down the hall. I hang up the receiver before the call connects, just as Saige reaches the door to my office.

"Mr. Hamilton," she says with a hiccup and a giggle.

I smirk at tipsy Saige. Her eyes are glossy and her cheeks are flushed. "Ms. Phillips. Whatever has you in the office this late?"

She smiles at me and holds on to the doorframe to balance herself. "I forgot my phone in my desk. When I saw your light was still on, I thought I'd stop by and say hi. So hi." She wiggles five fingers in the air.

I practically growl. "Come here," I order her.

She hesitates and her green eyes widen before she finally walks over to where I sit behind my desk. I pull her closer to me, positioning her between my legs. I grip her hips, my thumbs pressing gently into her flat stomach. Her head tips forward and her dark wavy hair falls in front of her.

"Where were you?" I ask.

Her beautiful green eyes shine in the office lights, and the whites of her eyes are bloodstained with the slightest shade of pink. "Bar 51."

I grin. "You like that place, don't you?"

"It has some fond memories for me," she whispers. Reaching out her hands, she brings them to my shoulders, rubbing them gently.

"Does it?" I ask. It does for me as well.

She nods sloppily, biting her bottom lip. "It does."

I raise my eyebrows and smile up at her. "Tell me about these memories."

"This one time," she starts before suddenly stopping and pulling her bottom lip into her mouth.

"Go on," I encourage her.

"This one time . . . I met this guy." Her eyes widen and her lip curls into a smirk.

"Tell me more."

"He sat across the bar, watching me while I was with my friends. He had this mystery about him . . . and I wanted to discover it. He has these piercing blue eyes, and I was insanely attracted to him."

"Insanely, huh?" I love hearing her describe her attraction to me.

"Yeah. Like the kind of attraction that takes your breath away. Have you ever felt that?" I have. The minute I met you.

My right hand falls from her hip, and it slides down the curve to her outer thigh. I find the hem of her dress and slip my hand underneath it. My fingers trail just under the bright red fabric, crawling up the front of her leg.

Her breathing hitches as my fingers crawl higher and she wobbles on unsteady legs. She turns her head to look out of the glass office where most of the lights have now been turned off. Coming to the apex of her thighs, I push the soft piece of satin between her legs to the side and slide my finger underneath, running it between the soft folds of skin.

"Holt," she gasps as my finger trails over the soft skin of her pussy, dipping and rubbing her wetness around.

With my foot, I nudge her legs apart just a little more. Dipping my finger inside her again, I feel her warmth . . . her wetness . . . and I'm instantly hard. I stand up quickly and turn her around, pressing my chest to her back. Brushing her long hair back and over one side of her shoulders, I breathe into her ear from behind her. "Remember all the things I told you I was going to do to you, Saige?" I can hear her swallow and she nods quickly. "I'm going to fuck you against my desk right now. I need to be inside you. I need to hear you call my name as I'm inside you."

I feel her entire body shudder, and she drops her head back against my shoulder. Without concern that anyone is left in the office, I push her dress up over her perfect ass. Saige is wearing a pair of satin thong panties, and I pull them down. They fall to her feet, and she steps out of them.

I guide her forward just a few steps and place her hands on the desk. "Bend over," I whisper, and she follows my commands. She reaches forward and presses her breasts to the hard wooden desktop, her perfect ass on display in front of me. I pull my cock from my pants and run the thick tip against her wet entrance, teasing her. Inserting just the tip, I pull out before pressing into her, this time further. She mumbles something inaudible as I push further into her, finally filling her.

"Feel that, Saige?" She nods and pants as I plunge in and out of her. "I want to fuck you like this every single day. Every morning. Every night. Me and you, Saige. There is no better feeling in the world than being buried deep inside of you." I twist my fingers into her long hair and pull her head back. She gasps when I pull harder and twist her head to the side so she can see me. I press a kiss to her temple, and she closes her eyes, moaning with each slow thrust. "Feel that?" I whisper and she nods.

"Holt," she breathes heavily. I can feel her walls tightening around me as she moans and rocks her hips back against me.

"Not yet, baby." I slide in and out of her easily. She fits perfectly around my throbbing cock. Releasing her hair, I grip her perfectly round ass and dig my fingers into the soft flesh. She falls forward onto the desk, and her fingers grip the edge.

I press my thumb into the soft, puckered skin of her backside, and she yelps when I push in further. As my cock works in and out of her wet pussy, my thumb works in and out of her tight ass. She gasps and moans and tosses her head from side to side with each thrust of both my cock and thumb working in rhythm together.

"You like that, huh, baby?" I smile as I watch her legs shake and her pussy clench around me as she climaxes. Her forehead rests on my dark wood desk, and she nods against the wood as I slow my pace. "Turn over," I tell her, pulling out of her.

She pushes herself up and rolls her hips. Her body twists and she's now perched on the edge of my desk. Her cheeks are flushed, and her eyes are heavy, sated. I spread her legs wider and shift her dress higher. She's bare and glistening, and I invite myself back inside her.

She gasps as I fill her, her eyes rolling back and her teeth biting her lower lip. There is nothing sexier in the world than how Saige looks when I'm inside her. Content. Satisfied. *Mine.* I reach behind her and unzip the back of her red dress. The straps fall over her shoulders, leaving behind a red satin bra. Sliding my fingers under the straps, I guide them down, exposing her full breasts. Leaning in, I pull a tight nipple into my mouth, and Saige yelps in pleasure. Her entire body shudders around me, and I bring her to the brink of pleasure once again.

"Holt," she pants wildly.

"Just feel it, babe," I mumble against her breast, and I feel my own climax coming. My balls ache as I pound into her. Pulling her closer to me, there is not a part of our bodies that isn't touching. My fingers grip her back tightly as I spill my release into her, and she moans against my chest. Loosening my hold on her, she falls back against my desk, her naked torso on display. She shifts her hips, and I move inside her. A smile pulls at her lips.

I chuckle. "Keep doing that and you'll have me ready for round two." I actually feel myself harden slightly inside her.

"Promise?" She teases, lifting her hips again and pulling me further into her.

"Saige," I warn her. I close my eyes and will myself to keep it together.

"There's no better feeling in the world than you inside me," she whispers, and I agree.

I look at this beautiful woman splayed across my desk, legs wrapped around me, and I feel weak. Anything she asks of me, I'd do it. Anything she wants, it's hers. Never have I been so powerless in all my life. She's different. I don't know what it is about her, but I'm utterly obsessed with her.

"Sit up." I pull her up by the elbows and slide her bra straps back on her shoulders, positioning the bra over her breasts. Next, I replace her dress and lean into her so I can zip it from the back. The bottom of her dress still sits high on her waist and, when I finally pull myself from her, I lower it a bit.

My hands grip both sides of her face, and I press my lips to hers. "What are you doing to me?" I whisper against her mouth.

She kisses me back, not answering my question, as she wiggles out of my embrace and slides off the edge of my desk. Her dress falls back into place, and she runs her hands over the wrinkled mess. "I'm going to go use the restroom," she says, turning toward the door.

"Over there." I point to a door in the corner, and she looks over her shoulder to see where I'm directing her.

She walks across my office and disappears through the large wooden door. Minutes pass and she finally emerges. Her hair that was once wild is now pulled back into a low ponytail. Her smudged lipstick has been cleaned and reapplied, and her sated eyes are now full of life.

I sit at my desk and watch her as she approaches with those legs that never end—my weakness. "Come home with me," I tell her softly. I don't ask. I don't order. I want her to choose to come home with me.

"Too fast," she says quietly, reaching for her clutch, which is resting on the edge of my desk. And my heart sinks in disappointment.

"Saige. I'm not asking you to marry me. I'm asking you to come home with me. I like having you there. I like going to bed with you and waking up with you. I like knowing where you are and having you within my reach."

"You know where I'm at when I'm at my place," she counters.

"But you're not within my reach, and I'm surely not waking up next to you."

"Another night," she says, leaning in to press a kiss to my lips. "I need to sleep in my own bed tonight."

I sigh in frustration but don't want to push her. "Let me

at least drive you home."

"Deal," she says with a smile and nods.

I grab my wallet and keys, and lock my desk while Saige waits for me just outside my office.

She smiles when I catch up to her. "I'll never look at your office the same again," she says, laughing.

I smirk. "I'd hope not."

"How many other women have you done that with?" She asks, her eyes dropping from mine.

"Zero."

"I find that hard to believe." She sighs.

I answer sincerely. "That's the truth, Saige. I have never mixed business and pleasure."

"Until now." She nudges me with a hesitant smile.

"Until now," I repeat. "But the next time, I want you against the window," I whisper to her as I press a kiss to her forehead.

"Who says there's going to be a next time?" She chides.

"Oh, there'll be a next time. Trust me." I smack her bottom, and we step into the elevator.

TEN

Saige

HOT WATER PELTS my skin as I breathe in the steam while thoughts of Holt assault my mind. "Too much, too fast," I keep reminding myself. "This is supposed to be fun. Not serious." It's not uncommon for me to talk to myself—it's a coping mechanism my therapist taught me to use. I coach myself and this is good. Except everything I'm telling myself, I'm feeling the complete opposite.

Drinks with Holt was only supposed to be drinks. Nothing more and definitely not sex. But every time I see him, every time I let him touch me, I feel myself slipping into thoughts, possibly hopes, of something more. "Dammit," I curse at myself.

The hot water helps to relax my tired body as I finish showering and wash my hair. When I'm done, I plug the drain and fill the tub. The water is so hot it's almost uncomfortable. Almost. Sliding in, I rest my head on the back of the tub and close my eyes, trying to rest my mind, except my mind never rests. Ever.

I sigh in defeat and blow a puff of air from between my lips. My red toenails peek out from the water at the end of the tub, and I notice how wrinkled my skin is. Unplugging the drain, I push myself up and wrap my body in a large bath towel while wrapping my long hair in another towel. I lotion myself, pull on a pair of comfortable cotton pajama shorts and a white tank top, and dry my hair.

As I heat a kettle of water on the stove, I realize I'm still alone in the apartment. Evelyn should've been home about an hour ago. I dig my cell phone out of my purse and send her a quick text, checking in on her.

As I pull out the tea bags and a jar of honey, my phone chimes. Evelyn is working late and picking up overtime. She does this often, as the hospital always seems to be short-staffed.

I fix my cup of tea and make my way down the hall to my bedroom. Propping pillows against the headboard, I slide into bed and pull my book off the nightstand. Page after page, I lose myself in the romantic suspense. Sex, love, and mystery; every page is a gripping tale that I don't want to stop reading—except that it's almost eleven thirty and I have to be up for work.

My mind races between the story, Holt, Evelyn, work, home, and my dad. I sigh heavily, knowing this is going to be a night that I'm going to need to call on my old friend Ambien. I hate taking drugs to sleep, but I know from recent history that I won't sleep for a minute tonight if I don't.

I pull the small prescription bottle from my nightstand and take two tablets, swallowing them down with a swig of my tea that has long gone cold. Then I shut off my bedside lamp and snuggle under the covers. It doesn't take long before I can feel sleep beginning to take over, and I whisper a quiet prayer of relief.

WHEN MEDICATED, I rarely dream, but when I do, they're much more vivid. I can describe every detail, including color, smell, and even touch. It's almost if my dreams are a reality. I swear I feel cocooned in Holt's arms. I can smell him and feel the slight brush of his stubbled chin across my cheek. With his soft lips pressing to my forehead, his voice urges me to sleep. I like when my dreams are of Holt.

After a bit, Holt fades away and the farm slides in. The smell of fresh cut grass and the evening's damp air hang all around me. Uncle Brent pinches my side and calls me Piglet, and I stomp away from him in anger.

My dream-turned-nightmare always starts the same—with this scene. I'm lying in the grass, staring at the sky. The Big Dipper comes into view, and I'm temporarily happy. Good memories. But good memories are always replaced by bad ones. The smell of grass turns to the smell of gunpowder. It's a distinct smell: bitter and full of sulfur. The light green grass clippings are replaced by a pool of blood.

I can always hear my younger voice screaming in my dreams. It's sharp and shrill, and I'll never forget how long I screamed until nausea takes over, in which case I usually wake up. Only this time, I don't, and in this dream, Brent isn't with me when I find Dad.

I kick the shotgun aside and lie down on top of him. It doesn't matter that half his head is gone. I cling to him like I used to when he'd try to leave for work. I was little and I'd wrap my scrawny arms around him, laughing when he'd try to shake me off him. Except I'm not laughing now; I'm crying. I twist my fingers into his shirt and scream for him to stay.

My hair is covered in his blood, and I hope that if I scream hard enough, he'll sit up and laugh at me, telling me how he tricked me. But I know it's not a trick because his blood is warm and real, not fake. The smell of the gunpowder hangs in the air, and I finally stop screaming when I feel strong arms squeeze the air out of me.

"Saige!" The voice is concerned. Suddenly, I'm pulled

away from my dad and brought into reality. "Oh my God, wake up!" Hands grip my head and pull me toward the voice. "Saige!"

"Evelyn," I mumble. She always comes to help me. She pulls me from the darkest corners of my mind and talks to me. "Ev," I mumble through my tears as I feel myself coming to.

"No, it's me," he says, his voice trembling. Holt.

Abruptly, my bedroom door flies open and bounces off the wall behind it. The large overhead light turns on, and then I hear Evelyn's voice. "Saige!" she yells, running to the bed. I feel the mattress dip; only I'm still wrapped in someone's arms. "Holt's here," she says, brushing my hair away from my face. "Open your eyes."

I wiggle out of Holt's arms and slide away from him in embarrassment, not turning around to look at him.

"Saige, are you okay?" he asks, and I step out of bed on wobbly legs.

"Sit down," Evelyn urges me as she wraps her hand around my wrist.

I yank it from her and storm to the bathroom. "I'm fine. You can both leave," I bark before shutting the bathroom door. Turning on the faucet, I let the water run cold before I lean in and scoop it from the tap and drink it. I twist my wild hair into a messy bun on the top of my head and sit down on the cool tile floor, pressing my back against the vanity. I can hear Evelyn whispering just outside the bathroom door, and I know she's talking to Holt.

"Leave!" I holler at them through the door. The whispering stops, and then I hear heavy footsteps. My bedroom door closes before there's a light knock on the bathroom door.

"Saige, open the door." It's Evelyn.

I wipe tears from under my eyes and take a shaky

breath. "I'm fine."

Her voice is low and angry. "Open the goddamn door before I kick it in and make you pay to replace it."

At that, I don't hesitate to lean in and twist the lock on the door because she is serious. When the door opens, I find Evelyn in a pair of yoga pants and t-shirt holding my bottle of Ambien.

"When did you start taking these?" She asks, her eyes full of anger.

I shrug. "I've had them. I hate taking them, and I usually don't. I just wanted to sleep tonight."

Her face is severe. "How many did you take?"

"Two?" I think . . .

Her eyes narrow. "The bottle says one is your dose. Do you realize what happens when you don't follow medicine the way it's prescribed, Saige?"

I try not to roll my eyes. "Evelyn, it's a sleeping pill. I took two. Not eight. I want to fucking sleep for an entire night. No dreams. I want to wake up refreshed for just one morning," I yell at her.

She cuts me off and throws the bottle at me. They bounce off my crisscrossed legs and roll across the bathroom floor. "Therapy, Saige. You need to talk to someone, not medicate yourself. I love you more than I love my own family, but this shit has been going on too long." She crosses her arms over her chest. "I'm tired too," she admits, her voice breaking.

Guilt overcomes me when I see how my life is affecting hers. Evelyn has always been the one to pick up the pieces of broken Saige. "I'm sorry," I manage to say before tears begin to fall.

"I'm so worried about you," she admits, kneeling down next to me. I nod and try to choke down the giant lump in my throat. "And so is he." She reaches out and pulls my hand into hers.

"Why is he here?" I'm embarrassed that Holt saw me like this.

"He was standing out in the hallway when I got home from work looking pathetic. He told me he dropped you off earlier and that you didn't look well. He said he tried calling, and from the eighty-seven missed calls on your cell, he wasn't lying. I let him in. We both checked on you and you were sleeping. He told me he was staying. As much as controlling men annoy the hell out of me, I wasn't about to tell him no." She chuckles.

My head drops into my hands. I'm mortified. "He hasn't seen one of my nightmares before."

"You scared him," she admits. "Maybe now would be a really good time for you to look into that therapy I keep telling you to get." She raises her eyebrows at me.

"I've had therapy," I argue. "That's where I got the Ambien."

She sighs loudly. "Saige. You've been in Chicago for almost three months. You need a therapist *here*."

I can't argue with her because she's right. She's always right.

"And you need water. A shitload of it. We need to flush some of that Ambien out of your system. What time did you take them?"

"Eleven thirty."

"Shit," she says. "You're going to feel like hell tomorrow."

I nod my head knowingly. "I'm going to go lie down." I push myself up from the floor, and Evelyn stands up at the same time. She fills a glass with water from the bathroom faucet and hands it to me. I take a deep breath before tossing back the entire glassful. Setting it on the counter, she takes it and refills it following me to the bed and placing it on the nightstand.

"You need to talk to him," she says with a sympathetic look on her face. "If you care about him, he deserves to know why this happens to you. Don't push him away."

"I don't care about him," I lie. I'm not sure who I'm trying to convince, Evelyn or myself.

She sighs. "Keep telling yourself lies, Saige, but you're not fooling me." She shakes her head, leaving me alone.

I WAKE TO sounds of pots and pans clanging together and glance at the clock. Nine o'clock. "Fuck!" I yell, jumping from the bed. Yanking open my bedroom door, I run to the kitchen and find Evelyn standing at the stove, stirring something in a small pan. "Ev! It's nine! Why didn't you wake me up?"

She turns to look at me, but it's not her that answers. It's Holt. He's behind me, sitting on the couch in a pair of black track pants and a gray t-shirt. "Because you're not going to work today, sweetheart," he says, not even bothering to look up at me. "You've officially called in sick."

"What?" I answer him, my tone snarky.

"You're sick. You're taking today off, end of discussion, Saige."

"Says who?" I prop my hands on my hips, feeling my blood pressure rising.

"Says me." His voice is equally snarky. He folds the newspaper he was reading and sets it on the coffee table, cocking his head to the side.

"I'm going to make a quick phone call," Evelyn says, skirting past us and jogging down the opposite hallway to her room.

I narrow my eyes at him. "You're not my doctor, or me. I'm not sick."

His eyes hold mine in a standoff. "You need rest."

"Holt, give it up."

"Give what up, Saige?" He stands up quickly and walks toward me. "The fact that I care about you and want to make sure you're happy, and healthy, and sleeping well? I won't give that up." He grips my shoulders, forcing me to look at him. I turn my head away from him and roll my eyes in annoyance.

He goes on, "Or the fact that you won't talk to me about what's bothering you and causing this. I won't give that up either."

"It's none of your business," I sneer.

"You're my business," he says quietly. "Personally and professionally."

I snap my head back to him. "Professionally, I'm your employee . . ." I pause.

"And personally?" he asks, his eyebrows cocked and his eyes begging for answers.

"I don't know," I blurt out.

Silence fills the space between us, and I can see the vein throbbing in his neck. A flush crawls up the side of his face, and he clenches his fists together.

I can't help but remind him, "You're the one who didn't want to label us. So let's leave it at that, okay?"

His blues eyes seethe with anger. With a nod, he finally responds, "Great. We don't know anything other than that you work for me."

I raise my chin, feeling obstinate. "Yep, that's about right."

He shakes his head. "Why do you shut me out, Saige?"

"Why do you care?" With every bitter word, I feel him slowly beginning to withdraw.

"Because I care about you. I think I've made that pretty clear." His face goes from angry to hurt. I can see the confusion and pain. Even sad, he's the best-looking man I've ever seen. His face is cleanly shaven and, even without his smile, I can almost see the indent of his dimple. He speaks before I have a chance to respond. "It's also abundantly clear you don't feel the same as I do."

I don't know what to say in response to him. The hard lines of his jaw move as he clenches his teeth. I want to tell him that he does mean something to me, but I'm too afraid to even admit that to myself, let alone him.

Stepping around me, he grabs his cell phone off the kitchen counter where it was sitting next to mine. "Get some rest today, Saige. We'll see you in the office tomorrow." Then he storms off toward the door and, before I even register what's happening, he's gone. Only seconds later, my heart sinks to my stomach, and I feel tears stinging the backs of my eyes.

"It's for the best," I tell myself, grabbing my phone and heading back to my bedroom. Evelyn wasn't lying when she said I had eighty-seven missed calls from him. In fact, it was eighty-nine and twenty text messages. I don't bother reading them before I shut down my phone and toss it on the nightstand. Avoidance. It's what I do best.

MORNING TURNS INTO afternoon, which turns into evening. A lightning show outside illuminates my dark bedroom as I lie in bed and watch the rolling clouds move in. Summer storms are my favorite thing and remind me so much of home. My heart still aches for those summer nights on the farm in North Dakota.

I pull my phone from the nightstand and power it on. No new text messages or voicemails. I hover over the contact titled *home* and press it. Three rings before I hear the click. A deep breath, and finally I hear my mom's voice.

"Hello?" Her soft voice fills the other end of the line.

"Hi, Mom," I say, trying not to get choked up. Just hearing her voice has me wanting to cry.

"Saige!" I can hear her smiling.

"I wasn't sure if you were working tonight, so I thought I'd chance a call. I'm glad I did."

"I miss you so much, baby girl. How is everything in Chicago?" In the background, I hear the dining room chair scrape against the wood floor of the kitchen. She must be sitting down at the dining room table like she always does when she talks on the phone.

"It's going." It's falling apart is what I really want to tell her, but I'm not sure telling her that I'm sleeping with my boss and the owner of the company would go over well. In fact, I'm positive it wouldn't.

"You don't sound very convincing." She knows me. "What's wrong, Saige?"

My voice cracks as I bite back my emotion. "I miss you, the farm, and Murphy so much."

She sighs. "That old mutt is sitting on his dog bed in the corner. He misses you too, and so do I." What I wouldn't do to curl up in my old bed with Murph snuggled up next to me like he used to do. Every hurt, every pain, and every heartache I ever had Murphy tried to take away as we lay in my bed together.

"What else, Saige? It's more than missing home."

The lump forms instantly, and I choke back tears. It doesn't do me any good trying to fight them.

"Saige," she says quietly.

"I'm not sleeping well again. I miss him so much, Mom." A loud sob escapes and the tears begin to fall.

Her voice is concerned yet comforting. "I know you do, honey. So do I. You were doing so well before you left. What happened?"

"I think it's just being here. In Chicago. This was his city. This place was his dream." My voice cracks as I try to explain myself.

She sighs loudly and lowers her voice. "Then live his dream for him—for you. Don't be sad; be happy that you get to experience the city he loved so much."

I nod as if she can see me and take a deep, cleansing breath. "I love you, Mama."

"I love you more, sweet Saige, and I miss you so much. Tell me something good."

"Hmm . . . I'm still loving my job and I get to work with such interesting clients, Mom."

"That's fantastic. Loving your job makes it so much easier to go to work every day. Are you dating anyone?"

Thank God she can't see me because I almost choke before I blurt out, "No. No dates here."

"That's too bad. You're young. Have fun, Saige. Get out and meet people."

"I will. Right now, I'm focused on just getting settled into the city and my job. That's my priority. Will you tell Brent I said hi?"

"I sure will, sweetie. Thank you so much for calling. I miss you every day," she says tenderly.

"I miss you too, Mom. I'll call again soon."

"I love you, Saige. If your sleeping doesn't improve, please let me know. We'll get you some help."

I swallow hard, not wanting to worry her more. "I will, Ma. Love you."

I hang up before she says goodbye. I hate hearing her say those words. Crawling out of bed, I wander down the dark hallway to the living room, hoping to find Evelyn. Only I find an empty apartment. I turn on the TV and find *The Breakfast Club* is showing, and I curl up on the couch and fall asleep to one of my favorite movies.

"Saige. Wake up." Evelyn nudges me.

I groan and stretch. "What time is it?"

"Midnight. You need to get to bed. I'll shut off the TV." She picks up the remote control from the coffee table.

I squint at her in the dim light. "Where were you?"

"Out. Go to bed. We'll talk tomorrow." She folds the blanket that I had pulled over me as I walk toward my bedroom. Stopping, I turn around and watch her picking up after me.

"Ev?"

"Yeah?"

"Thank you for always taking care of me."

She sets the blanket on the back of the couch but doesn't say anything. "Night, Saige."

"Night."

ELEVEN

Holt

I TAKE THE stairs two at a time. Someone is frantically ringing the doorbell and knocking rapid-fire on my front door.

"Coming," I yell. Before I open the door, I look through the peephole and see Evelyn on my front porch. I pull the door open quickly, and she takes a step back. "Evelyn?" I'm surprised to see her on my front step.

She wrings her hands together nervously and releases a deep breath. "Hi, Holt. I'm really sorry for this, but do you have just a few minutes to talk?"

"Of course, is everything okay with Saige?" I step back and hold the door as she steps into my house, my heart still racing from the surprise of someone at my door, but now because I'm worried something is wrong with Saige.

"That's a loaded question," she mumbles. "And holy shit . . . this house, Holt." She looks impressed, briefly sidetracked.

"Thanks," I mutter, closing the door. Evelyn stands with her head dropped back, staring up at the coffered ceilings. "Let's go in the sitting room," I offer and lead the way. She drops her purse on a small loveseat and sits. I sit opposite her on another loveseat. She sighs and looks at me.

"Tell me what you know about Saige," she says, maintaining eye contact with me. She's a straight shooter and doesn't dance around subjects. I appreciate this about her.

"First, just tell me everything is okay, please?" I rub my hand over my tired face.

"She's fine," she exhales loudly.

"Good. So what do I know about Saige?" I start. "I know that she works for me." I tilt my head to the side and look at her coyly, wondering what she's fishing for. "I know that I'm really enjoying spending time with her." I narrow my eyes slightly to see if I'm heading in the direction she wants me to go.

"Holt, what has she told you about herself?" She wrings her hands together in her lap.

"Well, we played Twenty Questions—"

Her face twists in a combination of frustration and confusion. "Jesus Christ! I don't care about twenty questions. I don't care if she told you her favorite color was blue. Personally, Holt, what has she told you about her *personally*?"

"Blue is personal, Evelyn." I smirk.

She purses her lips and glares at me. "I'm not here to entertain you or to listen to your jokes. I'm here because Saige is hurting—really, really hurting—and she pushes people away when she's hurting. And except for right now, I like you, so I'm trying to help her so she doesn't screw up whatever it is that's happening between you two. Because for the first time in a very, very long time, I've seen a glimpse of happiness in her—and I know it's because of you." She exhales sharply.

I sigh. It feels good to know I'm making Saige happy, because she's damn near impossible to read. And I love that my being in her life is changing her, possibly, but the idea of her hurting kills me . . . I prop my elbows on my knees, my face serious. "I'm not trying to be funny. I honestly don't know what to do. I care about her . . . in fact, I more than care about her," I pause at that revelation, "but she really knows how to push me away—so you know what I'm left with? Nothing but questions." I sigh and rub my temples.

Evelyn jumps right back in where she left off, and I lean forward, resting my elbows on my knees as I listen to her. "I'm almost positive she won't tell you what's going on, and she's going to keep pushing you away, and then she's going to slip further."

"Slip further? " I question. "Tell me what's going on, Evelyn."

Her eyes are sympathetic, and she lowers her voice as if she's telling me a secret. "Her father died when she was thirteen."

I nod my head. "Yeah, she told me this."

"He killed himself." She didn't tell me that, but I knew from the news articles and research that I have. I swallow hard and take a deep breath. She adds gravely, "She was there when it happened, Holt."

I feel the blood rush from my head. This part I didn't know. "What do you mean?"

Evelyn looks pained as she starts. "It was her thirteenth birthday. He killed himself in the barn on their property. She heard the gunshot and found him on the floor of the barn. She saw everything. She was there when he stopped breathing. He was everything to her. Everything . . . and she watched him die."

I inhale sharply and my stomach drops.

Evelyn finishes, "She's afraid to love anyone or anything because she's afraid of losing them, like her father."

"Back up," I demand. "She told you all this?"

Evelyn makes a slightly offended face. "I'm her best friend. I'm the only person that knows about this other than her family and her therapist back in North Dakota." She pauses a moment and sighs. "She's struggling, Holt. It's almost the anniversary of his death. She's in a new city. She hasn't been talking to a therapist since she moved here, and she's starting to crumble."

"Then I'll pick her back up," I answer easily. Because I will. I'll do anything for her.

Evelyn shakes her head, sad. "She's not going to let you."

"She doesn't have a choice," I tell her with determination. "Pushing me away isn't an option."

Evelyn nods now. "She's going to do everything and anything to sabotage this. She's a good person, Holt. She really is. But she's afraid, and she *will* let go of you."

"Well, when she lets go, I'll be sure to hold on tighter. I'm not letting her go that easy, Evelyn."

Tears fill Evelyn's eyes then, and my stomach turns as I replay the details of what she's told me over and over in my mind of Saige witnessing her father's suicide.

"Does she know you're here?" I ask. She shakes her head no. I nod once. "Thank you for telling me this."

"Holt." She takes a deep breath. "Saige is my best friend. She's smart, and beautiful, and an amazing person . . . but she's so lost right now. On the outside, she has it all together, but on the inside, she's a mess. I'm begging you not to hurt her, because I'm so afraid she won't be able to handle it—and I promised myself I wouldn't let anything happen to her."

I look Evelyn in the eye. "Nothing is going to happen to her. I promise I won't hurt her."

She stands up and runs her hands along the front of her jeans. "Thank you for talking to me. I know you weren't expecting me."

"Evelyn." I shake my head in frustration. "You're welcome anytime."

"Thank you," she says, forcing a stiff smile and glancing at the time on her phone. "I need to catch the train back. Please don't tell Saige I stopped by. She'd be angry."

"I won't say a word. But wait here just a minute." I hold my finger up to pause her. I jog up the stairs and throw on a pair of tennis shoes and a baseball hat. Meeting Evelyn near the front door, I grab the keys from the side table. "I'll drive you home. I don't like you ladies taking the train this late at night."

"I do it all the time." She crinkles her forehead in annoyance.

I'm not taking no for an answer. "Not when I can take you home. Let's go." I guide her out the front door to my car, which is parked in the drive. It only takes a few minutes on the quiet streets to get back to Evelyn and Saige's place. From the street, their condo appears to be dark except for the flicker of the TV that you can see through the large glass window. I wonder if Saige is watching TV or is sleeping, and as much as I want to go up to see her, I send Evelyn in alone.

I HARDLY SLEEP thinking of everything Evelyn told me. Saige losing her father, I knew about. His suicide, I knew about. Her finding him . . . seeing him . . . holding him, I knew nothing about. I finally give up on sleep around four thirty in the morning. Frustrated, I throw off the covers, pull on a pair of jogging pants and a t-shirt, lace up my tennis shoes, and hit the streets. I want a nice long run this morning. I'm hoping it clears my head.

It's still dark and the streets are eerily quiet. I've always found that the time between four and five thirty in the morning to be the most desolate hours outside. Life seems to literally stop between these ninety minutes. My feet carry me mile by mile down the Chicago Lakefront path. I run for miles, feeling my lungs sting with the cool Lake Michigan air. At this hour, I only pass a few other runners.

Turning around after five miles, I push myself harder on the way back. While I feel exhaustion begin to set in, the adrenaline from running keeps me moving, and I make it back to the house at about five forty-five. That clocks me at just over a seven-minute mile. While I should be happy about these running times, all I can think about is Saige. I need to give her space while still letting her know that I have no intention of going anywhere.

I shower and head into the office, finding it fairly quiet at seven o'clock in the morning. I catch up on the work I put off yesterday, and I make a few client calls to some of our past and prospective clients in the United Kingdom. By the time my calls are done, the office is abuzz with activity and I walk the floor, anxious to see Saige.

My stomach drops when I find her desk empty, but I glance at my watch to see that it's eight fifteen. She's out getting her coffee with Rowan. Suddenly, my stomach calms, and a small smile tugs at my lips.

On my way back to my office, Joyce shoots me a look of annoyance.

"Yes, Joyce?" I wait for her to respond.

Joyce has worked for me for more than ten years. I can read her moods like a book, and she's in a doozy of one this morning. I shove my hands into the front pockets of my suit pants and wait for her to dish out her disappointment in me. I'm curious what it is today. Yesterday, it was that I needed a haircut. The day before, it was that I hadn't returned my mother's calls. Last week, it was that I needed to start dating. If she weren't such a damn good administrative assistant, I'd fire her for being too much like a mother instead of an employee.

"I need ten minutes to meet with you regarding the

client cocktail party."

"Throw some time on my calendar."

Her voice grows agitated. "No. I've tried that. You're too busy. I need you this morning. Now! I need to finalize details, and I won't take no for an answer."

I chuckle. She's feisty, which is why I like her. She gets shit done, which is why I keep her employed. "Fine. Let's do it." I nod toward my office. After I take a seat at my conference table, Joyce follows me in with her notebook and folder. We very quickly decide on the invitation, the catering menu, and the open bar. I trust her to make these decisions on her own, but she's more comfortable believing that I've made the decisions, so I let her tell me what she thinks, and I agree with her. It's how we work.

Fifteen minutes later, she smiles, satisfied with my answers, and proceeds to leave. As she reaches my office door, she quickly turns around. "Oh, Mr. Hamilton, I forgot to tell you. Mr. Perez would like you to call him; something about his meeting with Ms. Phillips last week." She raises her eyebrows and offers me a concerned look before exiting and closing my office door behind her.

I stifle a groan. Mr. Perez is the neediest of all our clients, which is why I assigned Saige to his account. His desires and the level of attention he needs are beyond what I would call normal, and Saige is the only one I know who would make him happy. Annoyed, I make a note to call him later.

I click on the company instant messaging system to send Saige a message to come and see me. But when I see her profile, I find that she is still offline. Frowning, I glance at the clock on my screen. It's after ten in the morning. She's always online immediately after she returns with her coffee. I dial her extension from my desk and there's no answer. Pulling my cellphone from my suit pocket, I dial her mobile, waiting impatiently while the call rings, but again no answer.

"Dammit," I hiss under my breath. I pound out a quick text message asking her to call me as soon as she can. Without a second thought, I grab my car keys and shut down my computer.

"Joyce! Please clear my calendar this afternoon. I have to take care of some unexpected business, and I'll be out of the office."

"Yes, sir," she answers calmly, clicking away at her computer. "Is everything okay with your mother?" She looks over the rim of her glasses curiously. She's knows damn well this is about Saige.

Shit. My mother. I still haven't returned her call from last week, and she's left me multiple voice messages. I nod once. "Yes. Everything is fine with my mother. This is work related." I shoot her a stiff smile and leave quickly, anxious to get to Saige's condo.

Traffic is a bitch, and I'm on edge as I keep glancing between the road and my phone, hoping Saige will respond to my text. Thirty minutes later, I pull up to the curb outside her place. The door to enter her building is propped open again, and I growl in disbelief that the residents here are this careless, but I'm also thankful because it allows me access to the building.

I jog down the hall to her door and knock, shifting from foot to foot while I wait for her or Evelyn to answer. I knock again, growing more impatient with every second that passes. I try calling her again, and again the phone rings with no answer. I run my hands over my face in frustration and lash out, punching the wall next to the door.

Instantly, my hand begins to sting, but the sound of her voice numbs my pain. "What're you doing?" She gasps as she strides down the hallway toward me. I cradle my right hand in my left and open and close my fingers as I watch the knuckles almost immediately turn from a shade of red to a light purple.

"Punching a wall. What does it look like I'm doing?" I reply with a snarky tone.

"Holt . . ." She pulls my hand into hers.

"Saige . . ." I say, sighing before pulling my hand away. "You didn't come into the office, and I was worried—"

Her face softens and she speaks quietly. "I had an appointment this morning. I was coming back to change and head in to the office. I made the proper call to my manager, so that they knew where I was . . . I didn't think I needed to tell you—" She suddenly stops and pulls her bottom lip into her mouth. "I mean, it's not like we're . . ." She pauses.

My stomach drops. "We're what, Saige?"

"I don't know." She shrugs, pulling her keys from her purse. "I mean, we're not anything, you know . . ."

I stare at her and see a totally different Saige than the one that walked into Jackson-Hamilton a few months ago. Her confidence is gone. The life in her eyes has faded. She's not the confident girl that strutted across the bar and asked me for drinks. In a matter of days, the girl I knew has vanished—but I know she's in there, and I'm dying to peel back the layers and find her . . . if she'll let me.

"Saige," I mumble, leaning my shoulder against the wall. "Let me in. Let me help you." She inhales sharply and closes her eyes as she nods slowly. I pull her into my arms and hold her. "Baby steps," I whisper.

"Baby steps," she whispers back.

I FUMBLE AROUND with the Keurig, making two cups of coffee while Saige changes her clothes and meets me back in the living room. I hand her a mug, and she turns it in her hands, blowing at the steam coming off the top. "I don't want you to think I'm crazy—" she starts before I interrupt her.

"Saige. Stop. I'd never think that, there's no judgment here."

She swallows hard and tucks a piece of hair behind her ear. "I went to see a therapist this morning." She looks at me as if I'm going to say something, but I don't. All I can see is the sadness in her eyes. Her chin trembles, and her hands shake as she clears her throat. "I told you before about my dad having passed away."

I nod in confirmation and set my cup on the coffee table in front of us.

"It's more than him being gone," she says, her voice breaking. I reach out and pull her hand into mine, giving it a gentle squeeze. "A lot of people lose parents, and I know I'm far from the exception." She takes another deep breath. "He killed himself on my birthday." Tears threaten to spill over the bottom lids of her beautiful green eyes. "I was there, Holt. I heard the gunshot. I found him on the floor of our barn, the hunting rifle next to him. You could still smell the gunpowder, and he was missing half of his head."

My eyes widen in horror. Evelyn told me the details, but with Saige's emotion, it's almost as if I'm hearing them again for the first time.

She swallows hard. "I remember every vivid detail. The shirt he was wearing, the watch on his arm, the way he kissed me before he walked down to the barn. I'm so sad at having lost him, but I'm so fucking pissed at him at the same time." There's a spark of anger in her tone. "I needed him, and he quit. He fucking quit."

"Saige . . ." I search for something to say, but she stops me.

"No." She firmly shakes her head. "Don't tell me suicide is a mental illness. He wasn't mentally ill, Holt. He lost all of our money, his entire life savings, and every tangible item he owned, in some ridiculous money scheme with his coworker. This man was supposed to be his friend, his mentor, and he robbed him blind and essentially left us homeless. He killed himself because he felt like he failed us."

I swallow hard against my dry throat. Seeing Saige shuffle between hurt and anger kills me.

Her tone hardens again. "We moved back to North Dakota because we didn't have a dime to our name, and he took the easy way out. He killed himself . . . on my birthday." Her voice cracks and tears spill down her cheeks. "I miss him and I'm so angry with him all at the same time," she barely chokes out.

"I'm so sorry," I whisper and rub her hand. There's so much I want to tell her, but right now is not the time. I need to just be here for her and listen.

Her face twists in disgust and she closes her eyes as she speaks. "I saw his brains, Holt. I will never forget—" Her voice cuts out, and she stops talking as she's overcome with emotion.

"Come here." I pull her into my lap, and she buries her face in the crook of my neck. Her body shakes as she sobs uncontrollably, clinging to me like a little child. "It's okay," I whisper repeatedly as I comfort her. It takes her some time, but she finally settles down and pulls herself out of my lap.

She positions herself next to me on the couch and pulls my hand into hers. "I don't sleep well because I dream of everything I saw in the barn. My therapist says it's PTSD, and that with regular therapy, I should be able to cope and deal with this—but with me moving to Chicago; I haven't been going to a therapist until now."

"And the session this morning was . . . ?"

"Intense." She exhales loudly. "Digging up every little detail I can remember and rehashing it all over again with a new therapist."

I nod in understanding.

She continues, "But good, I guess, too. The more I talk about it, the more I seem to process everything. I'm hoping that someday, I'll be able to tell the story and it won't send me into a tailspin." She forces a small smile and takes a sip of her coffee. "I need to apologize to you for what happened the other night. I took more Ambien than I should have because I just wanted to sleep—I wanted my mind to shut off and it had the opposite effect. Then when I woke up and you were there, I was hurting, but I was also embarrassed." She looks away from me.

"You never have to be embarrassed with me," I tell her, rubbing my thumb across her soft cheek.

"I know. But it's humiliating, and I should've never treated you the way I did, and I'm sorry," she says, regret filling her eyes.

"What can I do to help you?" I would do anything to take away her pain, her fears, and her anger.

"Just be patient with me. All of this is new. Chicago . . . my job . . . you." She looks at me and her face twists in concern as if she's just offended me.

I squeeze her hand. "I'll be as patient as I need to be, Saige. I'll do whatever it takes to make sure you're happy and healthy."

"And stop being so perfect." She smiles and nudges me with her foot.

I chuckle and run my hand through my hair. "I'm hardly perfect."

"Holt. You are the epitome of perfect. You own your own aviation company, you could be a body double for Henry Cavill, and grace the cover of *GQ* tomorrow. But more than that . . . none of that defines who you are." Her eyes soften and her lips hint at a small smile. "You are caring, and kind, and amazing . . . and sexy." Her eyes sparkle when she says that.

"Say it again." I love when she opens up.

"Say what?"

"What you just said."

She grins. "You're sexy."

"Come here." I reach for her hand and pull her closer. "Kiss me." And she does. She presses her full lips to mine and kisses me like I've never been kissed. It's soft and sweet and everything Saige encompasses rolled into a perfect kiss.

"So, Holt Hamilton. What are the skeletons in your closet?"

I literally hold my breath when she says that. If she only knew my past, or my background. Those are some skeletons I never intend to let her see.

She winks at me. "I'm waiting to find out you have a wife and three kids that you keep in another house—"

I literally laugh out loud at that. "No. No wife and no kids."

She quips playfully, "Then what? There has to be something wrong with you."

I swallow hard but don't respond. "Saige. What you see is what you get." If only that were the truth.

But she doesn't see it. She doesn't see the lies in my eyes or my hesitation. She simply puts her trusting hands over both of my cheeks and peppers my face with kisses.

I BROUGHT SAIGE to my house to rest for the afternoon. There was no sense in her heading back to the office after her session this morning, and it's easier for me to work from my home office than from her couch. It's late afternoon and I dial the international number, pressing the speaker button on the phone. It rings three times before Sergio Perez's voice fills the room.

"Mr. Hamilton," he says. "Thank you for returning my call."

His greeting and tone immediately sets me on edge. "Mr. Perez. What can I help you with?" I pace the wood floor of my office and glance out the window that overlooks the backyard.

"I met with Ms. Phillips last week," he says with his heavy accent.

"Yes, I heard the meeting went very well."

He musters out a menacing chuckle. "It did. I enjoyed my trip to Chicago. So much so that I'm interested in coming back."

I nod. This is nothing unusual. "I assumed you'd be returning upon delivery of your plane. I'd have to look into the work order to see when that is expected, but as with most aircraft, it'll more than likely be three to four months."

"I have an important party to attend in a couple of weeks in Washington DC. I'd like Ms. Phillips to accompany me as my guest."

My heart stills. Sergio Perez wants *my* Saige to accompany him to a party. "I'm not sure how I can assist you with that." I chuckle, knowing there is no way in hell Saige would ever agree to that or that I'd let her agree to that.

His voice deepens and all sense of friendliness has disappeared. "This is where I need you, Mr. Hamilton. It appears I have fifty-two million dollars that says you'll help me secure this date."

I punch the air in front of me and I can feel my blood pressure rise before I rub the back of my neck and try to remain calm.

"I've left Ms. Phillips two voice messages, but she appears to be too occupied to return my calls."

I snap at him bitterly. "She's been out of the office,

unwell for a few days this week. Upon her return, I'll ask that she contacts you right away." I can hear my back teeth grind together as I clench my jaw tightly.

"Very well," he says with a chuckle. "I look forward to hearing from her and continuing my business with Jackson-Hamilton Aviation, Mr. Hamilton." I can hear his low laugh as he disconnects the call without a farewell.

Thankfully, I hear the dial tone because the slew of curse words that fly from my mouth is anything but professional, and I don't respond well to threats.

"Everything okay?" Saige's voice pulls me from my murderous thoughts. She rubs her eyes with the palms of her hands, her hair wild from her nap.

I rake my hands over my face and sigh deeply. "I just got off the phone with Sergio Perez," I say, pushing myself away from my office desk.

Saige leans against the doorjamb and her eyebrows furrow. "Okaaaayyy," she drawls.

"He's interested in securing something very important to me." I stare at Saige as she stands innocently in my doorway.

"He wants your plane?" She asks, her eyebrows shooting up.

I turn and look out the window at the gray sky. "No. Something more important than my plane."

She frowns, confused. "Holt, you have nothing more valuable than your plane. This house would be next, but I highly doubt Sergio Perez is moving to Chicago and wants your house," she snickers. She's clueless that she is what he wants.

I shake my head. "Not my house. He wants you."

"Me?" Her voice shoots up an octave and her eyes flutter with fear.

"Yes. He wants you to accompany him to a party, and

he wants me to make it happen. He basically threatened to pull his business if it doesn't happen."

Saige blinks, thinking it through. She steps into the office and walks over to the desk. "Then I'll go to the stupid party. It's one night. He drops millions with you every year, Holt. I can manage that asshole for one night." She places her hand on my shoulder and gives it a gentle squeeze. "I'd do that for you—for Jackson-Hamilton."

I scoff. "It's not happening. I don't trust him. And while I find it noble that you'd be willing to sacrifice your personal time to attend a party with Mr. Perez, I'm not comfortable allowing that."

She rolls her eyes at me. I hate when she does that. "Holt—"

I give a firm shake of my head. "Not open for discussion, Saige. He's dangerous."

"He's dangerous in his country. Here . . . not so much." I can still see the fear in her eyes, even though she's pretending it's not a big deal. I can see she hates him.

"Still not happening," I bark at her.

"Fine." Her shoulders slouch in defeat.

I take a deep breath and exhale it slowly. "But you are going to have to call him."

"I planned to call him tomorrow when I get back to the office. I checked my voicemail and he's called twice."

I give her a pointed look. "Just keep it professional."

"I will. I always do." She looks at me pointedly. "But I still don't see the big deal—"

"Saige!"

"Fine . . . fine." She turns around and struts away, throwing her hands in the air in frustration.

TWELVE

Saige

HOLT AND I quietly arrive at the office together, each of us going our separate ways once we get here. Traffic was a bitch, and we got here just after Rowan's cutoff time for coffee, so I'm not surprised to find him waiting for me in my cube with two cups in hand and an annoyed look on his face.

"Morning, sunshine," he says sarcastically as I toss my purse on my desk and slide my laptop into the docking station.

"Morning, Ro. Sorry I was late. Traffic."

He leans in and whispers loudly, "Don't blame traffic. You were getting a piece of that fine ass this morning, weren't you?" I smile and shake my head at him when he narrows his eyes. "Don't lie to me, Saige. You had the best mind-blowing morning sex of your life, didn't you?" He grins like a thirteen-year-old boy, his annoyance long forgotten.

"I didn't," I whisper back and wink at him. I'll keep him guessing.

"Liar."

"It was the second best mind-blowing sex of my life," I say, throwing myself into my office chair and spinning around to face Rowan.

"Good God, woman, I want the details, all of them. That man is what dreams are made of." He fans himself.

"Ro." I chuckle and shake my head at him in mock disgust.

"I know, I know. It's weird that I'm talking about your man that way, but seriously, Saige . . ." He gives me an expectant look.

"We're taking things slow," I say, sipping the piping hot coffee. "As slow as you can for sleeping with him on the first date, I guess." I roll my eyes at myself. I'm still surprised that I did that, but I quickly dismiss it. Nothing I can do about it now.

"You're taking the relationship part slow," Rowan says. "I get that. No need to muddy the waters with crap no one needs." He crosses his leg and bounces his foot.

"Actually, he's the one pursuing something a little more serious than just a roll in the sheets," I admit surprisingly.

"What?" he gasps. "He wants the real deal? Sweet baby Jesus, Saige, what are you hesitating for?"

"What're you two talking about?" Isaiah asks, coming into the cube and taking a seat next to Rowan.

Rowan spares no seconds dishing. "Mr. Sex God is wanting to pursue a relationship with little Miss Saige here, and she's giving him the brush off."

Zay's eyebrows shoot straight up. "Isn't that what every girl wants? The successful millionaire to fall in love with her, and here you are settling for just sex?" Rowan tsks.

"I'm not settling," I explain. "It's just that this is what works for us right now."

"You mean works for *you*," Zay corrects me, rolling his eyes. He crosses his arms over his chest and leans against the cube wall.

I sigh to myself. "Yes. For now. That doesn't mean

things won't progress into something more in the future." I smile at the thought of Holt and me in a real relationship.

Zay shakes his head and sighs, frustrated. "I now know why you're gay, Rowan, because women are fucking confusing as hell. Ninety-nine-point-nine percent of them are marrying themselves off in their minds to a man they'll never have, but then when one of those men wants an actual relationship, she's fine with a quick lay. I'll never understand you." Zay drops his arms from across his chest.

I just smile at him. "I'm not meant to be figured out. I'm just enjoying the moment, not labeling anything . . . yet." I lift an eyebrow at him and smile.

Zay scoffs and rolls his eyes at me.

Things are definitely tense, and I decide to change the subject. "But, you guys, I have good gossip." Leaning in closer to the two, I whisper, "Sergio Perez called Holt, and he wants me to accompany him to some party." My heart races at the thought of being alone with Sergio Perez.

"Whoa!" Rowan holds up a hand. "Don't do it, Saige. That man is scary shit."

I shrug. "He is," I admit. "But he's threatened to pull his business from Jackson-Hamilton if I don't do it. Like fifty-two million dollars worth of business."

Rowan's face twists in concern. "I know how much that man is spending here," he says bitterly. "I see the invoices. But I will also say that it's dirty money, and Holt knows better than anyone that losing Sergio Perez is hardly going to break the Jackson-Hamilton bank."

He's not wrong. Still, I can't imagine losing this account. "I know, but I don't want to be responsible for Jackson-Hamilton losing a client—regardless of where his money is coming from." I know Holt said it's not about the money, but I'd never forgive myself if losing this account was because of *me*.

Isaiah shakes his head. "Saige, I'm with Rowan. Don't do it. It's not worth risking your career for some d-bag."

"I'm not worried about my career," I explain. "I'm worried about losing Mr. Perez as a client."

"What does Holt think?" Rowan asks.

I look between Isaiah and Rowan before I answer. "He doesn't want me to do it either."

"Then there's your answer," Zay says, mollified.

I sigh loudly in frustration at all the men in my life. "You know I'm capable of making a decision for myself, don't you?" I swing my chair around and open my email, shooing them off. "Now go away. I have work to do."

"Yes, ma'am," Rowan says as he leaves, taking Isaiah with him.

I spend the better portion of the day catching up on work that I missed while I was out the last few days. Joyce, Holt's administrative assistant, has checked on me three times to make sure I'm feeling all right and has offered to bring me tea and lunch. I politely declined all of her offers, but she finally just showed up at two in the afternoon with a hot tea and a Greek salad.

No talking, no asking. She just drops the tea and salad on my desk and walks away, but not before giving me a sly smirk that tells me she's won this battle of wills. I'm grateful for Joyce, because the salad is divine and the tea is delicious. I inhale both as I write up invoices for Sergio Perez's plane so that the custom interiors can be ordered. As I hit send on the final email, my instant messenger pings. It's a message from Kinsley.

> Kinsley: OMG! Rowan told me about Sergio. How the hell do you do it? Holt and a goddamn corrupt Colombian politician both trying to get in your pants.

Me: Shut up.

Kinsley: It must be really rough to be you.

Me: Sergio Perez is all yours, Kinsley. He's just tacky enough that you'll find him charming ;)

Kinsley: God, I love your snark.

Me: Back at ya.

Kinsley: #HowHotIsHolt Have you seen your boyfriend today? He's smokin' in that fitted suit.

Me: He's not my boyfriend.

Kinsley: Bullshit.

Me: Goodbye, Kinsley.

And I close out of instant messenger, although I can hear her laughing to herself over the cube wall. I decide that I'd like to thank Joyce for thinking about me, and I walk the perimeter hall around to the other side of the floor where Joyce's desk sits just outside Holt's office. I smile at coworkers I've never met before but occasionally see in passing. I find Joyce nose down, glasses on, writing frantically in a notebook.

"Ms. King," I say quietly as not to startle her. "Thank you for bringing me lunch and tea. I've been so busy catching up from being out the last few days that I didn't realize how hungry I was or how much I needed that tea until you set it in front of me."

She looks over the top of her glasses at me. "Don't

thank me. Thank Mr. Hamilton. He insisted that I don't take no as an answer from you . . . and you make it very difficult." She laughs.

"You wouldn't be the first person to tell me that," I laugh back with her. "Is Mr. Hamilton available? I was hoping to catch a few minutes with him." I try to look in his office, but the privacy glass doesn't allow me to see in.

"He's in with Jack Morrison. Let me call him." She reaches for the phone.

"No, that's okay. I'll stop back later."

Just then, the office door opens and I hear a familiar voice. It's Jack, the man who was with Holt at Bar 51 the night I asked Holt out for drinks.

"I knew I recognized her at the bar. Getting involved with her is a huge mistake, Holt. How you managed to get yourself into this one is beyond—" Jack's voice cuts out the second his eyes meet mine. "Saige," he says with a forced smile. "Nice to see you again." My stomach drops and I swallow hard against my throat.

Holt's office door opens all the way, and I see him standing behind Jack, a horrified look on his face.

"Nice to see you as well, Jack." I look between him and Holt.

"Saige, come in," Holt says, practically shoving Jack through the open doorway and into the small space in front of Joyce's desk.

I take a step back. "I was actually just heading back to get on a conference call." I look to Joyce, and her eyebrows are raised in amusement at my lie. "I just stopped by to thank Ms. King for bringing me lunch and tea. It was very thoughtful of her." I smile at Joyce, whose eyes are narrowed in confusion.

I nod to Jack out of politeness. "Jack. Nice to see you again. Holt," I say with a curt nod, dismissing myself. As I quickly walk to my desk, I wonder why in the hell Jack is talking about me.

WHEN I RETURN to my desk, I dial Mr. Perez's phone number and wait while the phone connects.

"Ms. Phillips," he answers with his thick accent.

"Mr. Perez. Please accept my apology for the delay in responding. I've been out of the office, unexpectedly."

"Thank you for returning my call." I can almost hear the smile in his voice.

My heart thumps in my chest as I do my best to keep this conversation steered in the professional direction. "I wanted to let you know that everything has been ordered for your plane. If deliveries are on time, we should have your aircraft finished in three to four months."

"That is excellent news," he says with a long exhale, which sounds like he's blowing a cigarette into the receiver of the phone.

"I thought you'd be happy to hear that," I say, trying to wrap up the call. "I'll keep you posted if there are any changes or delays—"

"Ms. Phillips," he interrupts me. "The purpose of my call was personal, not professional."

"Excuse me?" I sigh in frustration.

"I'd like for you to be my guest at an industry event," he begins.

"You're in Colombia," I jump in, hoping to end the conversation.

"The event is in the States. Washington DC."

Shit. "I'm sorry, Mr. Perez," I stammer. "I just don't think this is a good idea. I'd like to keep our relationship strictly professional."

Silence fills the phone line, and I can feel my heart

beating wildly as I wait for him to respond.

"I won't take no for an answer, Ms. Phillips." My ears burn as blood rushes through them. That's twice today that two different men won't take no for an answer, and I grow more agitated and less friendly.

I sit up a little straighter and feel a rush of confidence settle in. I'm going to agree to Holt's wishes, even if I regret it. "I'm sorry, Mr. Perez. My answer is no. Have a wonderful day. I'll be in touch when I have more information about your aircraft." I disconnect the call and rest my head in my hands as I calm myself down.

"Are you okay?" Holt's voice startles me.

"Yes," I say quickly, turning around to find him just behind me in my cube. "Just had an awkward conversation with Sergio Perez."

"And how did that go?" He raises his eyebrows, scrutinizing me.

I give him a shaky smile. "I politely declined. He's not happy."

A giant smile spreads across his face. "I didn't expect him to be."

I sigh loudly. "Holt, I should just go."

"Not happening." He steps in closer and grips my chin, lifting my head so our eyes meet. "Saige, there are very few things in life that are non-negotiable. Sergio Perez is one of those things." His eyes are serious but caring. He's adamant, and I'm glad I respected his wishes.

I close my eyes and lean into his touch. "I understand," I whisper, feeling safe in his touch.

He brushes my cheek with the back of his knuckles. "Now wrap up here. I'd like to leave within the hour."

I miss Holt's touch the second he pulls his hand away, After he leaves, my instant messenger pings almost immediately.

Kinsley: I just heard everything. #HowFuckingHotIsHolt

Me: So hot.

Kinsley: I'm actually jealous of you . . . and I don't do jealous. That man is so into you.

I find myself smiling at Kinsley's observation as I type out a response.

Me: Remember, it's just fun.

I know we've crossed the line from fun to something more serious, but my coworkers don't need to know that.

Kinsley: Fun my ass. That is love, girlfriend. Deny it all you want.

Me: Oh stop.

Kinsley: Fine. But I want sordid details . . . soon!

Me: Sordid, no. Update, yes.

Kinsley: Sigh. Talk to you tomorrow. Shut down. Lover boy wants to get you home. LOL.

Me: Bye.

I close instant messenger and shut down, glad to put today behind me.

"OH MY GOD, that smells amazing!" I say as I enter the kitchen, finding Holt at the kitchen island in a pair of jeans and a tight gray t-shirt, cutting up carne asada.

"It's Tuesday. I thought we'd do Taco Tuesday for dinner." He winks at me.

"I love tacos," I tell him enthusiastically, picking up the head of lettuce to wash it.

He shoves the plate of chopped beef to the center of the island and begins slicing tomatoes and onions, adding them to the bowl of cilantro that has already been cut.

"You know you don't always have to cook for me," I tell him as I dry the lettuce with paper towels and begin chopping it up.

"I know, but I like cooking for you, Saige." I look over at him where he stands watching me.

"I like it too," I admit. "But I'd like to cook for you sometime."

"I'd like that." He smiles at me, and I practically swoon. My stomach twists with excitement every time he unknowingly makes future plans for us.

Five minutes later, we sit down to eat at the small kitchen table that sits in a bay window nook. It's less formal and more comfortable than the dining room, perfect for the two of us. Holt shakes up margaritas while I plate us tacos and rice.

"Thank you for handling Perez," Holt says as he takes a bite of his taco. I nod and scoop some guacamole on a tortilla chip. He swallows and wipes his mouth with a napkin. "I should warn you, though. He'll be at our company cocktail party in a couple of weeks."

"What cocktail party?" I lick some salt from the rim of my glass before taking a sip of margarita. The tequila burns as it travels down my throat to my stomach.

"Every year, Jackson-Hamilton hosts a cocktail party for our clients," he begins. "We do it this time of year instead of around the holidays because Chicago weather is so unpredictable. Years ago, it started out small, just an open bar and casual atmosphere, but over the last couple of years, it's turned into something much more formal."

I raise an eyebrow. "What do you mean by formal?" I stuff a chip in my mouth.

"Everyone dresses up; we have drinks of course, and food. Last year, we had heavy appetizers, but Joyce has insisted on a buffet dinner for this year. All of this happens in the penthouse."

"I've never been to the penthouse," I say, wondering what it looks like. If it's Jackson-Hamilton's, I can imagine it's probably extravagant.

He jerks his head toward the ceiling. "It's one floor up. We rarely use it. The entire floor was converted into an amazing meeting and gathering space. If we're hosting numerous clients or holding events, we use the penthouse."

"So Sergio will be there," I say, pushing my rice around my plate as an unsettling feeling creeps in.

"He will. But it won't be a concern," he says matter-of-factly.

"How do we know that?" I ask skeptically. My stomach twists when I think about coming face to face with Sergio.

"Because I'm not leaving your side the entire night." His blue eyes lock on mine, sealing his promise.

I wipe my mouth and smile at him. "Do you honestly think that's realistic?" I take another bite of my taco.

"Absolutely. When it comes to you, I'd do anything to keep you safe." My stomach settles and my heart flutters.

"Holt," I whisper, and he leans in and presses his finger to my lips, shushing me. "Okay, changing subjects," I say. The tequila from the margarita has warmed my belly, and I'm feeling just brave enough to dig for information.

"Go for it," he says.

"I've seen Jack Morrison three times. The first time you introduced him to me, everything was fine. The second time, when we were at his nightclub, I got a bad feeling. And then today, I could've sworn he was talking about me." I hate how insecure I sound as I ask about this.

Holt scrunches his face in confusion but drops his eyes. "I'm not sure what you're talking about."

"Holt," I say plainly, "girls know when something is up. It's our intuition or something. He doesn't like me—and I'd like to know why." I push my plate away.

Holt sighs. "Jack doesn't know you well enough to like you or dislike you, Saige. And honestly, the only person you should be concerned about liking you or not liking you is me." He grins and leans forward, pressing a quick kiss to my cheek.

"No." I shake my head. "Something is up." I twist my napkin around my finger as I question him further.

"Nothing is up, Saige." He sits back in his chair confidently.

"Then who was he talking about this afternoon at the office?" I ask, trying to not sound upset.

He purses his lips and shrugs. "I don't even recall the conversation." With that, he quickly stands and clears our plates. My gut tells me he's trying to protect my feelings, and for the time being, I decide to drop the subject.

"So back to the cocktail party." I steer the conversation back to a safer topic. "I need to go shopping. I can't say I own a formal dress."

He snaps his head to me, his blue eyes beaming. "I may have just had the best idea ever."

I head over to the sink and start rinsing the dishes, stacking them in the dishwasher. "What?"

"How do you feel about New York City?" He wags his eyebrows at me.

"I don't know. I've never been to New York City." I dry my hands on a dishtowel and set it on the island as I search his eyes for answers.

"We can kill two birds with one stone," he says excitedly, pulling his phone out of his back pocket. "My mom has been begging me to visit, and you can shop. We can go this weekend."

Shopping? His mom? A trip to New York?

"Fine. Let's do it." I crack a smile.

"Pack your bags, Saige. I'm taking you to New York."

WE LEAVE STRAIGHT from the office on Friday and I grow excited as Holt's driver pulls right up to the private jet at the airport just outside of Chicago. Holt helps me out of the backseat of the sedan and walks me to the plane owned by Jackson-Hamilton. As I step inside, I'm in awe. I expected it to be nice, but this is exquisite. Anything you could think of, this plane has. A bathroom with a shower, a bedroom, a conference table, a small entertainment area, and even a small dining area.

Holt greets the attendant and the pilots, then they talk briefly while I get lost in the plane's luxuries. The velvety soft leather seats, the sandalwood table, and other wood accents have me planning ideas for other Jackson-Hamilton clients.

"Saige?" Holt says, pulling me from my thoughts.

"I'm sorry, what?" I glance at him, still hazy from taking in all the plane's insane details.

He looks pleased to see how much I like it. "Take a seat. They're ready to depart." He points to a large leather seat, and I sit down, buckling myself in. "What do you think?" he asks as I run my fingers over the soft leather and lift the window shade to look outside.

"It's truly amazing. I think this is the most beautiful plane I've ever seen. Even the ones we design aren't like this," I remark. I've only been in a coach seat on an airplane three times in my life, so this pretty much tops my list of luxury, and I've designed luxury.

"Me too. I designed every square inch of this plane," he says proudly, leaning over me to glance out the window.

I'm completely relaxed as we taxi down the runway and begin to accelerate. The takeoff is smooth, and Holt rests his hand on my thigh. "What're you thinking?" He nudges me in the shoulder. "You've gotten quiet."

"I'm thinking flying makes me very nervous."

His eyes widen in disbelief and a small smile pulls at the corner of his lips. "Saige. You work for an aviation company—one of the top private jet manufacturers in the world—and you're telling me you're afraid of flying?"

I wince at him, trying not to laugh. "Was I supposed to disclose that in the job interview?"

He chuckles. "I guess not. I just find it an odd choice of business if this is one of your fears."

I shrug. I don't think it's that odd. "I got my degree in design. I never anticipated working for an aviation company—you found me, Holt. Remember?" I smile softly at him.

He nods and looks out the window. "I did," he says quietly, pulling my hand into his. "Best thing I've ever found."

The words were meant to be happy, but his voice was laced with sadness. If he wasn't holding my hand and I couldn't feel our connection, I almost wouldn't have believed him.

THIRTEEN

Holt

SAIGE DOESN'T BUDGE as we land in New York City. The flight was smooth, and she dozed off a few minutes into the flight. She curled up in her chair and rested her head on my shoulder, falling into a deep sleep. I could tell this week has taken a toll on her. Between her breakdown and dealing with Sergio Perez, I was glad she agreed to let me bring her to New York. This is the best place in the world to get lost and distracted—and I couldn't wait to have her all to myself for an entire weekend.

We taxi to the small hangar off the main airport where they park private aircraft. I can see our SUV waiting. As we come to a stop, I kiss Saige gently on the lips to wake her. With groggy eyes, she jumps out of her chair and grabs her purse.

We deplane and Saige stretches when we finally step off the plane, with her long arms high in the air, her back arched, and her face to the sky. "I can't believe how fast that was," she says with a yawn.

"Time flies when you're sleeping." I nudge her playfully.

As our driver loads our luggage into the back of the SUV, I hold the car door open and Saige slides into the backseat. I take a seat next to her, and we're on our way. Saige is quiet as our driver navigates the busy New York City interstate, delivering us to Manhattan. Even at this time of night, traffic is crazy.

"Holt," she points at the Manhattan skyline as we get closer, "it's amazing!"

"This is nothing," I tell her. "Wait until we're in the middle of the city. Honestly, though, Chicago reminds me a lot of New York City."

She turns and looks at me with a giant smile on her face. "But it's New York."

"That it is," I respond. The look of excitement on her face makes me smile.

It takes us about forty minutes to arrive at the Four Seasons from the airport. When we step out of the car, Saige pulls her phone from her purse to take pictures of the city while I arrange with the bellman to deliver our luggage to our room. Once the arrangements are made, I send our driver off for the evening.

We're greeted upon entering the massive lobby and I'm immediately handed an envelope with our keys. Saige grips my hand tightly as we walk through the stone lobby, and she tugs on me to slow me down as she takes in its beauty. All stone and glass, it's classic yet modern. "This place is amazing," she mutters as she takes it all in.

I escort her to the elevator, where we quickly ascend to our secure floor. "Wait until you see the room," I tell her as we walk to the end of the hallway.

She audibly gasps when I swing the door open and we step inside the dark room. The shades are drawn and our room is nearly floor to ceiling windows that overlook Central Park. "Holy shit!" she says, dropping her purse on the large round foyer table that sits just inside the suite. "That's Central Park."

"It is," I tell her, delighted. "We'll be sure to go for a

walk through there. Or a horse-drawn carriage ride," I say, closing the hotel room door.

"No way. Emery would kill me. She made me promise we wouldn't ride one of those carriages. Animal abuse." She shrugs and I laugh. She turns around and gives me a look. "Emery is very serious about this."

"I don't doubt it," I tell her. Emery is our office's happy little hippie. I shake my head and stifle a laugh.

Saige has her fingertips pressed against the glass as she takes in the city. Lights, buildings, Central Park. What should be overwhelming for a small farm girl from North Dakota transfixes her.

"Holt, is that the Freedom Tower?" She points to the large building in the distance.

"It is. We'll be sure to stop by while we're here."

"I'm worried we won't get to see everything in two days," she says, finally walking away from the window.

"Then we'll come back," I promise.

"Presumptuous." She smirks.

"Determined," I respond, smirking right back.

She laughs just as a knock sounds at the door. The bellman has arrived with our luggage, and he stacks it in the large walk-in closet.

"Holt!" Saige yells from the bathroom. The door is wide open and the light is on, so I let myself in. "Is that the tub?" She asks, bewildered. She's standing over a sunken tub the size of a hot tub and could fit six people.

"It is." I'm in awe of the things that excite her.

"I'm taking a bath three times a day while I'm here!" she squeals.

"Whatever makes you happy, Saige."

She spins on her heel and wraps her arms around my waist, pressing her mouth to my neck. "You make me happy," she says quietly.

I swallow hard, pulling her in tighter to me. "You make me happy too."

"I was thinking," she says, looking up at me with glowing eyes. "Maybe we should order some wine and celebrate our first night in New York."

"I think I like that plan," I reply, walking us backwards out of the bathroom.

"I also think we should draw up a bubble bath and drink our wine in the tub."

"I think I also like that plan." I press a kiss to her forehead, and she smiles.

"And then when we're done with our bath and our wine, I think we should see how comfortable that bed is." She tilts her head over to where the large king-sized bed sits inside another room off the main living area.

I feel my cock twitch at her suggestions. "You're really good at this planning thing," I mumble against her lips.

"I know." She giggles. "Now go order the wine. I'm going to get the bath ready."

FIFTEEN MINUTES LATER, two bottles of wine, a cheese and cracker tray, and an antipasti plate arrive in our room. I find Saige relaxing in the middle of the oversized tub, her hair piled on top of her head in a messy bun, and I hand her a glass of white wine.

"To New York." I raise my glass in a toast.

"To New York," she repeats, raising hers.

We toast and I strip, joining Saige in the hot water. I sink into the bubbles and pull her to me. She instinctively wraps her long legs around my waist and, as she rubs her center against me, I instantly grow hard.

I groan as she pulls herself even closer, aligning my erection at her entrance. Licking her lips, she takes a slow, long sip of wine, tipping her head back to swallow. I watch the muscles in her slim neck constrict as she swallows, and I instantly want to press my dick to those plump pink lips, but instead I slide inside of her. Her muscles constrict and fight my invasion momentarily until she relaxes, and I easily press myself further inside her. She inhales sharply, her wine glass shaking in her hand as I fill her completely. Setting the glass on the edge of the tub, she presses her lips to mine and slowly begins to move her hips.

"I love when you're inside me," she whispers against my ear.

"It's my favorite place in the world to be," I tell her, grasping her hips and guiding her up and down slowly. The bubbles float on top of the water lapping against the side of the tub as Saige moves on top of me.

A low mewl escapes her lips as we move together in unison. "I'm going to come," she mumbles between sharp breaths. Just the sound of her ragged breathing is a turn on.

I quicken my pace and reach down between us to find her clit.

"Holt!" she hisses as I work her with my fingers.

"I love what my touch does to you," I tell her and she leans forward, resting her forehead against mine. "Come for me." She nods against my forehead and closes her eyes. Her breathing hitches and I can begin to feel her descent. Then her hips shake and she tightens around me. With two gasps, she collapses on top of me and works to regain control of her breathing. Reaching behind her, she grabs the base of my cock, squeezing gently as I still move inside her. "Saige," I scold her as I'm instantly brought to my release. I grip her hips tightly as I spill into her, hearing her giggle against my ear.

"I love what my touch does to you." She uses my own words against me.

I chuckle, feeling out of breath as I lay my head back against the edge of the tub, coming down from my own release. "What're you doing to me?"

"The same thing you're doing to me," she says quietly, wrapping her arms around me. I want to read so much more into it than what she probably means, but instead, I'll take this as a small victory, and I wrap my arms around her in return.

We take our time showering with each other, and I wrap Saige in an oversized robe when we're done. I can see the exhaustion in her eyes, so I tell her, "As much as I'd like a repeat of what we just did, we need to rest. You have some serious shopping to do tomorrow, and I need to meet my mother for lunch." I lean in and press a kiss to her lips. "You're welcome to join us if it's not too soon for you," I tell her and tighten the tie on her robe.

"Let's see how shopping goes tomorrow," she says, running her fingers through her long, damp hair, settling into her pillow. I try to hide my smile, because where I expected hesitation, there was none. Saige rests her hand on my chest and I finally relax and fall into an easy sleep as soon as I hear the sound of her breathing settle, knowing she's fast asleep.

MY EYES CRACK open, and even though it's dark, I can still see her tall, statuesque silhouette in the window. Even sixty floors up, the Manhattan lights still cast a glow through the wall of windows. Her right hand and forehead are pressed against the glass, her eyes tilted down to the New York City streets below.

The clock reads three forty-two in the morning, and Saige being awake means only one thing—nightmares. I slide out of bed and pad across the soft carpet to where she stands. I wrap my arms around her waist from behind, pressing myself to her. The soft cotton robe is warm against my skin.

Saige tenses as my arms tighten around her, but she doesn't move. Over her shoulder, I can see the small specks of light below as cars move slowly through the early morning Manhattan streets. After a few quiet minutes, I finally feel Saige relax and she leans back into me.

"You okay?" I press a kiss to her temple.

"Yeah," she answers, her voice groggy and weighted with emotion.

"I was hoping with how tired you were that you'd be able to sleep through the night."

"Me too," she answers softly and wraps her hands around mine, which are resting on her stomach. "New York really is the city that never sleeps," she says. "There has been non-stop traffic down there for the last hour."

"Manhattan is always a zoo," I tell her as I recollect the memories of my years spent here in college.

"I wonder what it would be like to be alone here," she starts. "Not alone, as in by myself, because there are more than eight million people that live here, but what would it be like to live here and know no one. To just exist in a city where no one knows who you are. To just wander. To just be lost."

"I think it would be very lonely," I answer her honestly and wonder why she's having these thoughts.

"I think it would be perfection," she says softly and almost longingly. "To have no one know who you are. No one to see your scars or your flaws or your worries."

"Is that what you want, Saige? Someone to hide all of who you really are from?"

"I don't know," she admits honestly.

I press my nose into her long hair, breathing her in. "Because I find your flaws and your scars beautiful, and whatever worries you have, I'd like to put them to rest." If she'll let me.

I can feel her heart thrumming in her chest as she turns slowly in my arms. Draping her arms over my shoulders, she stares at me. "Why me, Holt?" Her eyes beg me for answers, answers I'm not sure she can handle.

I shake my head, swallowing. "I don't know." Because I don't. I hired her for a job. That was all this was supposed to be, a way to help her. This was never supposed to be more. But it became more, and now I can't let her go. I reach out and run my thumb over her lips. "Because when I think about life without you, it's boring—lonely. I don't want to be lonely, Saige."

"I don't want to be lonely either," she whispers, pressing her lips to mine.

I drink in the feel of her soft lips against mine. Deepening our kiss, I untie her robe and push it from her shoulders, letting it fall in a pool around our feet. I walk her backward, and then she gasps when the warm flesh of her back presses against the cool, glass window.

Her nipples harden as I brush each thumb pad over the tight little buds before leaning down and pulling one into my mouth. Her fingernails press into my shoulder as I suck harder and she moans in response. Reaching down, I slide my fingers between her soft folds, finding her slick. I rub gently, finally pressing a finger inside her. Her head falls backward against the glass, and she bites her bottom lip.

"Turn around," I order her and she obeys. "Press your hands against the glass."

She places both of her hands on the glass, on either side of her head. Grasping her hips, I pull them back toward me, tilting her ass in the air just slightly. I rub my hand over the soft skin of her behind, wanting so badly to take her in the ass . . . but I know she's not ready for that, yet. Positioning myself at her entrance, I'm sure to wet myself before sliding into her with one deep thrust. She yelps but instantly begins to moan in pleasure as she adjusts to me.

I place my hands over hers on the glass window, lacing my fingers between hers. "I'm not going to be sweet, Saige," I warn her, and she tenses.

She turns her head to the side, and I can see her lips twist into a smirk. "I never asked you to be sweet with me," she says, pressing her ass back against me, causing me to slide even deeper into her. Jesus Christ. Hearing her say that turns me on and I can feel myself grow harder.

I raise my hand, slapping her ass, hard, and feel it instantly warm beneath my hand. She gasps, and I don't give her time to collect herself before I begin fucking her . . . hard and deep, aggressive and rough. I want to fuck the feelings out of her. I want to fuck away the memories of her father killing himself. I want to fuck away all the fucked up images she'll never get out of her head, but mostly, I want to fuck away all of her pain. I want her to need me as much as I need her. I need her to want me as much as I want her. I want her to love me as much as I love her.

"Holt!" she screams.

"Tell me what you want, Saige," I breathe into her ear, gently biting her earlobe.

"I don't know," she cries out as I pound in and out of her. I've never been more turned on in my life.

"Tell me, Saige."

"Holt," she cries my name, pressing her forehead against the window again.

"Now, Saige!" I yell at her as I feel my cock hardening inside of her. I pull my hands from hers and grab both of her ass cheeks, pressing my fingers into the soft flesh of her perfect ass. I've never been so fucking turned on by anyone in my entire life.

Only the sounds of her heady breaths escape her lips, and I grow angry, wanting to hear her say she wants me. I fuck her harder, growing angrier with each thrust until I finally lose it, releasing my anger into her. Then I growl loudly and pump myself into her before hastily pulling out.

Turning, I stalk toward the bathroom. Why can't she say it? What's holding her back? I sigh in frustration as I think that maybe she'll never want me, love me, need me the way I need her.

But as the door slams behind me, I hear her meek voice mumble the words I've been dying to hear. "You. I want you, Holt."

FOURTEEN

Saige

THIS MORNING'S EARLY sex session against the glass wore me out. I fell back asleep with little effort and now that I'm awake, I see that it's closer to lunch time than it is breakfast. Holt is nowhere to be found, but I did find a note on the nightstand.

I hope you slept well.
XO,
H

I dress quickly in a pair of black skinny jeans and a gray oxford shirt. I pair this with red jewelry and red flats for a pop of color. Running a large curling iron through my hair, I create big, natural-looking waves, and I apply simple make-up of a light foundation, eyeliner, mascara, and red lipstick.

Within thirty minutes, I'm out the door and headed to Fifth Avenue; this is where Holt told me I'd have the best luck in my shopping endeavors. I have an idea in mind of what I'd like for a dress, but as I hop from boutique to boutique, I'm coming up empty handed. Everything is too glitzy or too glamorous. I need chic but simple.

In between boutiques, I tap out text messages to Holt,

but an hour later, he has yet to reply to one. While I walk the busy New York streets toward my last stop of the day, Barney's, I stop and get a New York hotdog from a street vendor. From a corner street cart with a little yellow umbrella on top comes this amazing hotdog topped with sauerkraut, grilled onions, and spicy mustard. It's divine.

I enjoy the walk, taking in all of the sights that I can. I'm in awe of the buildings, the traffic, and the hustle of people in a hurry to get everywhere. However, even if I had a week here, I'd never be able to see everything I want to see.

As I make my way through Barney's, I'm taken aback at its opulence. Everything is pristine and perfect. Every rack, every display, every single employee from top to bottom. I find a sales associate, Deb, who is over the top helpful, which I'm thankful for because I don't look like I belong in a store like this. I describe what I'm looking for, and in no time, Deb is shoving me into a fitting room with five dresses that all look exactly like I've described—simple, chic, and elegant. Within minutes, I've narrowed it down to two, and I stand in front of a mirror with the dress that is my favorite. It fits perfectly, hugging every curve, hiding every flaw, accentuating all my assets. It fits my tall frame perfectly, as I pace back and forth in front of the mirror.

"It's stunning," Deb says of the olive green dress. "I can't believe how perfectly this color matches your green eyes."

"It's my favorite color," I admit.

"Shall I wrap it up for you?"

When I look at the price tag, I swallow hard against my dry throat and almost choke. Over four thousand dollars for a piece of fabric I'll most likely never wear again. Sweat forms on my forehead, and I begin debating the pros and cons of spending more than one of my entire paychecks on this dress. I've always been a girl of common sense, rational and levelheaded, but today I throw that out the window. I smile and nod at Deb. She hangs the dress over her arm and disappears with my credit card.

After I put myself back together, fixing hair that's out of place and slipping on my shoes, Deb meets me outside the fitting room with a garment bag, my card, and receipt. Then I step outside, feeling pleased as I blend into the masses of people on the streets, everyone bustling about to get somewhere. I love the energy New York has, and like Holt said, it's very much like Chicago, only better.

Arriving back at our room, I find Holt sitting at the small oval table, his cell phone pressed to his ear. A smile pulls at his lips when he turns around. He's talking, but his eyes follow me as I walk back to the attached bedroom to hang up my dress in the closet.

Not wanting to disturb him, I kick off my shoes and lie down on the bed to rest for a few minutes. Minutes later, I hear him come into the room, but I keep my eyes closed. "Shopping is exhausting," I mumble and let out a small laugh.

"Do not let my mother hear you say that," he says, laughing in return.

"Speaking of your mother, how was lunch?" I push myself up and sit cross-legged on the bed.

He frowns. "She had to cancel, but we're having dinner with her tonight."

"Who's we?" My eyebrows shoot up.

"You and me, Saige. It's just dinner, nothing serious, so don't read into it." His tone tells me he's annoyed.

"I wasn't," I lie. I mean, shit, sleeping with your boss on the first night . . . that's fast. Meeting his parents a couple of weeks later . . . that's warp speed. I try to picture meeting her, but I instantly begin to get anxious and try to think of an excuse as to why I can't go.

Pushing off the bed, I blurt out, "I mean, I'm pretty tired; maybe you should just go. Plus, she hasn't seen you in ages. She's not going to want to spend her time worrying about including me in conversation."

"Saige." He walks over to me, placing his hands on my upper arms. "She wants to meet you."

"I don't have anything to wear. I only packed casual clothes." I play nervously with the small diamond that dangles from a chain around my neck.

He rubs his thumbs softly on my skin. "Well, it's a good thing we're eating at her house. Nothing fancy required." He's making it difficult for me to get out of this, I think to myself.

"I have a headache. I had a really brutal day shopping." I nod toward the closet and close my eyes to show my exhaustion. When he doesn't respond, I finally crack an eye, catching him watching me. He sees right through my bullshit.

He rolls his eyes. "Yes, Barney's can be so tiring. Personal shoppers running around while you wait for them to return is now classified as a high-intensity cardio workout." He smirks at me. He can be such an ass, but I can't help but chuckle. Clearly, he's a seasoned Barney's shopper.

"Holt—" I'm about to whip out another lame excuse when he interrupts me.

Exasperated, he finally snaps. "Saige. Stop. What you're wearing is fine. You look beautiful. I promise, my mother is much more casual than what you're thinking. She lives in Brooklyn in a beautiful brownstone. She's married to a normal guy, and they have a dog. She's the least pretentious person you'll ever meet, and if you decided to show up in pajamas, she wouldn't bat an eye. In fact, she'd probably run upstairs and change into hers."

From everything he just told me, I think I already love her. "What kind of dog?" I ask, as if this will be the deal breaker.

His eyes soften and I can hear his tone relax. "A basset hound. He's a real pain in the ass, but he's the cutest damn dog—"

"Fine. I'll go." I toss my head back in defeat.

"It was the dog, wasn't it?" he jokes.

"Yeah. A cute dog will always get me." I wrap my arms around his waist and hug him.

"Noted." He laughs.

LESS THAN AN hour later, Holt's driver weaves through the Manhattan streets with ease, merging onto the Brooklyn Bridge. It's every bit as beautiful as the images you see online and on television. My face is pressed to the glass as Manhattan disappears behind us, and I feel Holt lacing his fingers through mine.

"Don't be nervous," he says, giving my hand a small squeeze.

I narrow my eyes at him briefly before smiling. He knows there's no talking me out of being nervous. But I'm instantly fascinated with Brooklyn. The buildings, the shops, the more low-key way of life. It feels like another world, and it's just over a bridge from Manhattan.

"Here we are," Holt says, leaning down to look out the window.

We pull up in front of the most gorgeous brownstone I've ever seen. The building is tan brick, with a huge staircase leading up to the large door. There is a small yard encased behind a brick and iron fence just off the stairs to the left, and this brownstone has a single car garage off to the right. It's the only one on the street with a garage. Two large carriage lights sit atop the end of the brick stairs, welcoming us.

Holt comes around the side of the car to open the door for me, and I stand in awe as I glance up and down the street.

"You okay?" he asks.

"Holt, this is seriously the cutest neighborhood I've ever seen."

He looks around and inhales deeply, a sense of pride crawling across his face. "I know. Wait until you see the inside. They remodeled everything after Dan retired. The house was built in eighteen ninety-nine," he says as we walk up the concrete steps. "My mom helped me redesign my house after she did theirs. She knew what original features should be left and what could be updated."

I nod in response as we reach the top of the steps. Suddenly, the front door flies open and there stands the sweetest looking lady I've ever seen.

"Holt!" she says, bounding through the door and into his arms.

He drops my hand to catch her as she throws herself at him. She's thin and stands much shorter than him. She has dark hair cut into a long bob that just brushes the top of her shoulders.

Pulling out of her hug, she instantly turns to me and opens her arms. "You must be Saige," she says warmly. "Holt has told me so much about you." My eyes widen in surprise at her statement.

I smile and lean in, letting her embrace me while shooting Holt a look over her shoulder. He grins sheepishly and shrugs, looking away from my scowl before stepping through the large wooden door and into the foyer.

"I'm Janice," she says, holding my arms to stand back and look at me. I assume she's giving me the motherly once-over. "Come in," she says, hooking her arm through mine.

I shoot Holt another look and this time he laughs out loud. He knows I'm uncomfortable, and I had no idea his mother would be this outgoing. "So nice to meet you," I greet her, trying to return her warm welcome.

We step into the foyer next to Holt, and he closes the door behind us. The house is narrow but stunning. Much like Holt's, it is modern and contemporary but not over the top. It's luxurious but homey. The kitchen, dining room, and a formal living room are all on the main level. There is a split staircase, which I assume leads down to the garage and up to the other levels.

"Can I get you something to drink?" She asks, leading us into the large kitchen. There are three bottles of wine in the middle of the large center island. "Dan will be joining us in just a minute." She smiles and uncorks a bottle of white wine, pouring a glass for herself.

"I'll take a glass of white, please." I'm anxious to sip some alcohol and hopefully relax a little.

"Beer?" Holt asks, striding across the kitchen to the large double door refrigerator.

"Bottom shelf," she says. "Dan has all those microbrew beers, Holt. I don't know what they are, but there's got to be something you'll like." She gives him a fond smile, then she turns to me. "So Saige, tell me about yourself." She presses the large glass of white wine to her lips and takes a sip.

"What has Holt already told you?" I tip my head in curiosity.

"Hardly anything," he interrupts. "I told her I was bringing my friend Saige to dinner." He walks back over to join us around the island. "My nosy mother is reading way more into this than she should." He shoots her a look across the island, and she laughs.

"Holt!" A boisterous man's voice fills the air just as his presence bounds through the entrance of the kitchen. He walks over to Holt and shakes his hand before pulling him into a half hug. Saved by Dan. Thank God.

"Dan, how are ya'?" The two men catch up and not far behind Dan comes a slow-moving dog.

"This is Winston," Janice says, leaning down to rub the short dog's long ears.

I walk around the island over to where Janice stands. "Holt told me about Winston." I bend down and rub under the dog's chin. He instantly rests his long muzzle on my knee. "Hey, buddy." I smile and rub the top of his nose.

Janice chuckles. "He's the laziest dog alive, which is exactly why Dan loves him."

"Hey, I heard that!" Dan hollers over his shoulder.

Holt joins all of us, fawning over this adorable basset hound. "Ladies, ladies . . . give the guy a break," he jokes with us.

Janice stands up and smacks Holt on the arm before going over to wash her hands. "I'm going to prep dinner. Holt, why don't you show Saige the house?"

"Excuse me," Dan says, walking over to me. "Maybe I'd like to meet this beautiful young thing." He grins as he pulls me into a hug, much like Janice did, and everyone laughs. "You must be Saige. Beautiful just like your name. You scored yourself a looker, Holt." I can tell Dan is a joker and trying to make Holt uncomfortable, so I laugh along with him. "Really glad you could join us, darlin'," he says, letting me go. Dan is tall and thin with gray hair and dark brown eyes.

Holt looks over at me and nods toward the door. I stop to top off my wine glass first and Holt shakes his head at me before we begin the grand tour.

"They're really nice," I tell him as he walks me through the formal living area.

"I asked them not to make it uncomfortable," he says, starting up the narrow staircase.

"It's fine. The wine is helping." I hold up my wine glass

in appreciation.

Holt shows me the impressive brownstone, and I'm in utter awe of its beauty. Original white crown molding stands out against the dark gray neutral walls and large window coverings accentuate the tall windows. Everything is stunning. By the time we make it back to the kitchen, Janice has dinner almost ready and Dan is waiting in the dining room. Holt sits down to the right of Dan, who is at the head of the table, Janice directly across from Holt, and I sit down next to Holt.

Janice outdid herself preparing baked salmon, asparagus, and homemade scalloped potatoes. My stomach growls as Holt heaps a generous portion of each dish on my plate. We fall into easy conversation over dinner, listening to Dan tell stories of his days as the owner of a transportation company. He owned cargo ships that transported goods back and forth across the continent, and I can tell that Holt got much of his entrepreneurial drive from Dan.

While wealthy, I'm impressed at how down to earth and normal Dan and Janice seem, and I can tell that was woven into the fabric of who Holt has become. I smile as I watch the three of them interact casually, acting lighthearted with each other. Well into the meal, my nerves have settled, and I finally take a deep breath and try to just enjoy the rest of the evening.

After everyone has finished, I help Janice clear the dinner dishes and offer to help her wash them, but she won't hear of it.

"How did you meet Holt?" She finally asks as she scrapes leftover food into the trash.

I'm rinsing the dishes, stacking them in the other side of the sink. I smile at her and answer honestly. "We work together."

She looks up at me with curious eyes. "What exactly

do you do there? I always think of aviation as being such a male-centric field."

I laugh. "It kind of is, but you'd be surprised how many women there are these days. Aeronautical engineers building planes and even pilots. But my degree is in interior design. I was hired to sell and build all the custom design elements for Jackson-Hamilton's clients."

"Interior design," she says, her eyes widening. "I never would've thought that could apply to airplanes before. That's really interesting."

"It is," I respond. "I noticed all the amazing work done in your house. You have an eye for design yourself."

"Oh, this old house." She brushes it off. "There were a few things that I really wanted to keep, but for the most part, it was a complete overhaul."

"Well, you kept the important things," I tell her. "The doors, the crown molding, and the wood floors. Everything was restored beautifully."

She smiles at me, appreciative. "Thank you. Not many notice that. So are you from Chicago?"

"I lived there for a few years as a little girl but moved back to North Dakota, where I was raised and went to college.

She looks at me curiously out of the corner of her eye and sets the final dish in the sink. "I'm not sure Holt told me what your last name was."

I smile. "He knew I was nervous about coming, and he promised to keep tonight casual, so he probably didn't mention it. It's Phillips."

I notice what I think is the smile falling from her face as she turns quickly and pulls a cheesecake from the fridge. "Well, I'm not sure anyone will be hungry for dessert, but I have this amazing New York Cheesecake." She smiles stiffly. Pulling a knife out of the knife block, she begins slicing pieces. "Dear, would you mind serving this? I need to run to the restroom." She drops the knife on the counter and she quickly leaves the room.

I take over, plating four pieces of the thickest, creamiest cheesecake I've ever seen. Dan joins me in the kitchen and begins a pot of coffee while talking my ear off about the ins and outs and intricacies of my job. I really like how at ease he makes me feel.

As he pours cups of coffee, Holt joins us in the kitchen. He puts his hands on my shoulders and stands behind me. "I think we're going to have to call it a night. Mom isn't feeling great and has gone to lie down." He looks at Dan, who nods and places the coffee pot back on the warmer.

"Did you want me to pack some dessert to go?" Dan asks. "Your mom will be disappointed you didn't get some. She knows it's your favorite."

Holt shakes his head and purses his lips. "No thank you," he answers Dan.

"Everything okay?" I ask quietly.

"Yeah," he says, rubbing the bridge of his nose and pinching his eyes closed.

"This happens," Dan cuts in. "She overworks herself, then she suddenly needs rest." He pats me on the shoulder. "I know she loved seeing you, Holt, and meeting you, young lady." He smiles at me genuinely. "And that goes for me as well. It's been a pleasure getting to know you."

As we head out, I say goodbye to Winston and Dan gives me a brief hug. Holt's driver is waiting for us and Holt helps me in the car before turning back and walking over to Dan. Through the window, I watch them exchange words, and Dan grips the top of Holt's shoulder, a concerned look across his face as they speak. Quickly regaining his composure, Dan looks over to the car and offers me a tight smile and a small wave. Holt shakes his hand and quickly walks back to the car, where I wait for him.

"What happened?" I ask as soon as Holt joins me in the back seat.

He sighs deeply. "Nothing. We were just talking about my mom. I wanted to make sure she was okay." He stares out the window, his hand resting on top of mine in the space between us. He's lost in thought and I can tell something is bothering him, but I don't press for details.

The rest of the ride is silent as we cross the Brooklyn Bridge and head back into Manhattan. A million questions swirl through my mind, I can tell something is bothering him and he doesn't want to talk about it. I'm usually one to push, to insist he share what's on his mind, but something tells me not to press this issue.

I take my time getting ready for bed, giving Holt some space. I wash my face, moisturize, brush my teeth, and put my hair up before I find Holt fast asleep in bed. I crawl in next to him, careful to not wake him. Whatever he isn't telling me is eating him up. I've never seen him so distant. He is always the comforter, the protector, the strong one, but tonight I feel the urge to pull him close to me, wrapping my arms around him in an attempt to comfort him.

BETWEEN MY NIGHTMARES and Holt being restless, neither of us really sleeps. I watch the minutes tick by on the alarm clock situated on the bedside table. It's three fifty-seven in the morning when I finally break the silence. We've both been restless for hours.

"I wish you'd tell me what's bothering you," I say lightly, my voice cracking from not speaking for so long.

Instead of answering, he rolls from his back to his side, facing away from me.

"Holt." I reach out and press my fingers to the warm

skin of his back, trailing my fingernails over the wide span of skin between his broad shoulders. "What happened tonight? Everything was fine one second, then it wasn't the next, and I'm not sure what the hell happened."

"Nothing happened, Saige. Let it go," he snaps.

"No," I say defiantly. "If we can't be honest with each other and talk about things, then this won't work."

He flips over quickly, startling me. "Well, if that isn't the pot—"

"Stop!" I yell at him. "I know. I promised myself I would be honest with you about everything, including the nightmares. Be honest with me, Holt. What is going on?" I slide over closer to him. We're both lying on our sides, face to face. I reach out, pressing my hand over his heart, yearning for his touch in return. "Talk to me. I dare you." Fuck it. If he can use those words, so can I.

He sighs loudly and leans forward, pressing his forehead to mind. "I love you, Saige." He stares into my eyes, looking for me to respond. I close my eyes and exhale slowly, letting those words sink in. I avoid responding, but I feel the weight of his words on my heart. I swallow hard and can hear my own heartbeat; it's beating so fast.

He sighs disappointedly. "I know it's too soon for you, Saige. But you wanted honesty, so there it is." His voice is desperate. He's clinging to hope that I'll validate what he's feeling and I want to, I so desperately want to, but I can't. His lips hover next to mine, so close that I can feel the warmth of his breath as he speaks.

I'm at a loss for words. I knew it would eventually come to this, one of us admitting our feelings for the other, but I didn't expect it here—now. "Is that what's been bothering you?" I ask. "You're in love with me?"

He rolls to his back and kicks the sheet off him. "Be careful what you ask, Saige. You might not like the answer."

He jumps up from the bed and disappears into the bathroom, the door closing behind him with a loud thud.

I follow him to the bathroom, where I twist my hair into a knot on top of my head and yank the glass shower door open. Holt is standing under the steady stream of water, his hand on the wall and his head dropped forward. I step into the shower and close the door behind me. As seconds go by and he doesn't acknowledge me, I begin to shiver as the light mist of warm water hits my skin. I walk up behind him and wrap my arms around his waist, my fingers pressed against his hard abdominal muscles. I press my lips to the back of his shoulder and pepper him with soft kisses.

I pull him tighter to me, finally speaking. "Just because I can't say it yet, doesn't mean I don't feel it," I muster, giving him honesty. "In fact, I think I felt what you're feeling first." I can feel his back tense, and his head drops further forward. "Look at me," I tell him and turn him around.

His eyes find mine as I hold his beautiful face in my hands. Water drips from his dark hair onto his pain-filled face as I lean in and kiss him.

He swallows hard. "Say it," he whispers.

My heart is racing, and I try to form the words on my tongue, but I can't. I press my lips to his, wanting him to feel what I can't say. "Let me show you," I whisper against his lips. My hands fall from his face to his shoulders and down his chest. I press a soft kiss to the firm plane of his chest where I can feel his heart beating just underneath.

His eyes never leave me as I explore every inch of his chest, finally falling to my knees in front of him. I can see his jaw muscles working as he fights back whatever he wants to say. Water runs in a small river down his abs into the short stock of dark hair just above his cock.

I reach for his firm erection, running my hand up and down his length, making him even harder. He moans at my touch. Pulling the soft head into my mouth, I run my tongue around it slowly, savoring the taste of him, while my right hand works the base of his cock simultaneously.

My sweet man comes unglued as I work him in my mouth. His legs tremble and his hands tighten into fists as he fights against his pleasure. Pulling himself free from my mouth, he reaches down and pulls me up by my arms. Shoving me against the glass shower wall, he reaches behind me, lifting me by my bottom.

"Let *me* show *you*," he says, pressing himself into me. It's fast and hard, and I yelp in shock at his sudden movement before he slows, using his mouth to kiss every inch of my face and neck and chest before he loses himself in me. In between every kiss, every lick, every touch, he tells me he loves me—and I believe him. I savor his touch and drink in his love, even if I'm unable to verbally express the same in return.

I come fast and hard with my arms wrapped around his neck. Every part of me is sated, and I rest my head on his shoulders. With two last thrusts, he finishes, filling me. I'll never have enough of this man.

"I love you, Saige," he whispers against my lips before setting me down, his eyes shifting from angry to compassionate. "And I'm going to show you again, and again, and again just how much I love you until you're able to say it in return."

I WAKE TO find Holt in the living room area of our suite, balancing his laptop on his lap while sipping a cup of coffee. CNN is on the large-screen television in the background.

I clear my throat, drawing Holt's attention to me. "Good morning." I shield my eyes from the bright sun streaming through the large windows of the hotel room.

His mouth twists into a small smile. "Mornin'."

I tighten the belt on my robe and sit next to him on the couch. "What time are we leaving today?"

"Anxious to get back?" he asks, setting his computer on the coffee table in front of him.

"No." I rub the back of my neck. "But if we have time, I'd like to check in on your mom."

He smiles at me. "I appreciate your concern," he starts, setting his hand on my thigh, pushing the end of the robe aside. "But I've already spoken with her. She's feeling better and apologized about last night." His hand slides further up my inner thigh, pushing my legs apart.

"I'm glad," I respond, my breath hitching.

There is a hunger in his eyes, and the corner of his lips twist into a grin. "We're not leaving until this afternoon, and I plan to spend all morning *showing* you how I feel about you." He leans in and presses a kiss to my lips as his fingers find my center. I gasp as his finger swirls my clit, and I instantly find myself sinking back into the couch to give him better access.

"Oh no, not here," he says, standing up. He reaches for my hand and pulls me to a standing position. He walks me backwards slowly, back toward the bedroom. "I plan to spend all morning exploring every inch of this perfect body," he says, pulling the tie on my robe so that it falls open. "When you think of New York, I want you to remember how tired and sore you were and not from walking around the city."

He guides me into the bedroom, stopping me just as the back of my legs hit the mattress. Then he slides the robe off my shoulders, letting it fall into a pile at our feet. Reaching between my legs again, he gently rubs back and forth, and I gasp at his touch. "You're wet," he observes, sliding a finger inside me. "And so fucking tight. Lie down." He guides me onto the bed, my back pressed into the soft mattress.

My skin pricks with goose bumps as he runs his hands over the soft flesh of my stomach and up to my breasts. He pinches my nipples, and my back arches at his touch. I lose myself in Holt as he takes his time touching me. His fingers and lips mark every spot on my body, and he claims me through his words and his touch.

With each kiss, I allow the walls I've built to crumble, brick by brick, allowing Holt access to my heart, a heart I once thought was dead.

After a nap, I awaken sated, wrapped in Holt's arms, the late afternoon shining in the window. Holt's soft lips press against my temple, and he pulls me closer to him.

"Hey there," he says quietly. "Time to get up." He presses another kiss to my cheek. "Car will be here in an hour."

I roll over and wrap my arms around his neck. "I could lie here with you forever." I pepper his chest with light kisses.

"I think I'd love that," he says tenderly, running his fingers through my hair.

I wrap my legs through his and can feel his heart beating against my own chest. "Thank you for bringing me to New York. I had an amazing time."

His eyes search mine, and he smiles softly. "I had an amazing time as well." He presses one last kiss to my forehead before pushing himself out of bed.

FIVE AND A half hours later, we're taxiing into Chicago, New York a recent memory. Holt worked the entire trip back, and I snuggled into one of the large reclining chairs and read. Now, Mr. Jones is waiting for us with his car and loading our luggage while Holt gets me settled in the back. Less than an hour later, I wake from a little nap as we're pulling into Holt's driveway.

"We're home." He wakes me with a kiss.

Home. As much as I've resisted the thought of losing myself in Holt so quickly, this does feel like home. Not the house, but Holt. Holt is home to me.

FIFTEEN

Holt

I LIE IN bed, replaying my mother's angry words repeatedly in my head, her eyes glistening with tears as she held onto my arms.

"Tell her, Holt," she begged. "You have to tell her."

I inhaled deeply. "I can't now. It's too late."

She squeezed my arms tighter, her eyes pleading. "It's never too late. You're going to lose her if you're not honest."

"Do you think I don't already know that," I snapped at her. Sighing, I shrugged out of her grip. "That's why I can't tell her. I will lose her."

She shook her head, her shoulders heavy with sadness. "Holt, how in the world did you get yourself into this mess?"

"I was trying to right some wrongs. I had no idea what to expect when she walked through that door." I raked my hands over my face and through my hair, resting them on top of my head.

"That is where it should have stopped. Do you realize what this could do to her?"

My hands fell from my head as my mom buried her face in her hands and cried. "I thought this was behind us."

The sound of Saige's whimpering pulls me from my thoughts. Her breathing quickens and her shoulders begin to shake. I pull her closer. "Saige. Baby, you're okay. I'm here." She awakens and shifts in my arms. "You okay?"

She nods her head quickly and rubs her neck. "Yeah." Drops of sweat line her forehead and she swipes at them.

"Same dream?"

"Same nightmare," she corrects me, her voice dripping with sadness.

"Want to talk about it?"

"Not really . . ." She hesitates, and settles into the crook of my arm. Her head rests on my chest and her arm is draped over my stomach.

I sigh. "Someday, I hope you'll trust me enough to tell me."

"Someday, I hope I won't have these, and we won't need to talk about it," she says quietly. "One can hope."

She sounds so hopeless, my heart aches for her. "I love all of you, Saige. The good parts, the bad parts, the parts you don't like, and the parts that scare you. I love all of them because they are what makes you who you are." Her arm tightens around me, and she presses a soft kiss to my chest. "Think about that . . . dream about me," I whisper to her.

It doesn't take long for her to fall back asleep while I struggle to bury the guilt I have for lying to her about who I really am. Every word my mother cried rings through my ears, keeping sleep at bay.

MONDAY MORNING, WE'RE sitting in typical bumper-to-bumper Chicago traffic, even though we're only a few miles from the office. Saige is nervously fiddling with her hair and mumbles to herself as she settles into her seat.

Gripping the steering wheel, I weave around a car, trying to make an illegal left turn, and I curse under my breath. "What has you all worked up?"

"Nothing."

"Saige," I admonish her.

She sighs. "I love our weekends together, but the shit they give me at the office . . ." Her voice trails off, and she looks at me out of the corner of her eye.

I reach over and pull her hand into mine giving it a light squeeze. "You know why they do it, right? Because you let it get to you. Walk in; tell them you had a great time in New York. Tell them you found a dress and had a non-eventful dinner with my mother."

"It wasn't non-eventful." She nailed that on the head, but I don't respond.

"Saige, you know what I mean. If you offer it, they'll feel like they're getting what they need from you and they'll leave you alone."

"They'll instant message me for more details," she argues. "You don't know these people. They are ruthless," she says with an exasperated tone. She's being overreactive and she knows it.

I can't help but laugh. "I know these people, babe. I hired them."

"They're all, 'Tell me about Holt,'" she says in a high-pitched voice, scrunching her nose.

I cut her off. "Speaking of . . ." I glance at her, and she turns her head to look at me. "Hashtag, how hot is Holt? Really?" I grin widely.

Her cheeks instantly flush. "How do you know about that?"

"Saige. Everything is monitored. The IT guys get off on finding instant messages or emails, and they just thought it would amazing to bust my balls with that hashtag." I roll my eyes as I remember the shit our lead IT guy gave me when he tossed the papers on my desk that outlined their conversation about me.

"I want to die right now!" She throws her head back against the headrest and I laugh.

"I have to say, I'm honored."

She grumbles, "This is so embarrassing, but you know I didn't make up that hashtag. I'm positive it was Kinsley. I'm going to kill her," she mumbles under her breath and I laugh again.

"Nothing surprises me anymore, Saige. It's funny. But I wanted to warn you that everything is monitored."

"Noted," she sighs. "This Monday sucks so badly, and I'm not even in the office yet."

I turn into the secured parking garage and wait while the gate lifts. "Go get your coffee with Rowan. He always makes everything better."

"He thinks you're hot too," she admits grudgingly, looking out her window.

I can't contain my laughter anymore. "I already know this too."

She just shakes her head at me, stifling a laugh.

OUR ROUTINE IS the same all week. Saige stays with me; I drive her to work. We have dinner, make love, and fall asleep together. It's exactly how I want my life to be with her. Simple . . . perfect.

Saturday morning, I jog along the lake. It's unusually quiet, but I welcome the peace. Today is the day of the Jackson-Hamilton annual cocktail party, and Saige is at the spa with Kinsley and Emery getting pampered while I blow off steam hitting the pavement. My lungs are burning and my legs ache as I hit the final stretch of my run with about a mile left, but I push myself harder until I collapse on the lush grass in my front yard.

Lying on my back, I stare into the ominous sky, dark

clouds swirling overhead. The cool breeze off the lake casts a chill in the air, and within a week or so, we'll know the seasons have changed. Fall is not far off. Large trees are just beginning to shed some of their leaves, but the colors haven't changed as of yet.

I glance at the time on my phone and decide to head inside and shower before Saige returns from the spa. As I shower and dress in my tuxedo, I hear fits of giggles coming from downstairs. The girls.

I jog down the stairs and stand just outside the kitchen where Kinsley, Emery, and Saige all stand around the kitchen island, passing around a bottle of champagne. Their perfectly styled hair and Hollywood-esque makeup stand out against their yoga pants and t-shirts.

They all sip from crystal champagne flutes, and I chuckle to myself as Kinsley whispers loudly, "I can't believe I'm in Holt Hamilton's house!"

Saige rolls her eyes and Emery chimes in. "I can't believe Saige gets to sleep with Holt Hamilton whenever she wants."

"Enough!" Saige laughs and sets her glass down. "It's Holt. It's not a big deal."

Emery scoffs, "Not a big deal. You're dating the most eligible bachelor in Illinois, and he's head over heels in love with you."

"Alright, alright," Saige relents, and I decide now is a good time to make my presence known.

"Ladies," I say, entering the kitchen. All three women turn to look at me, and no one says a thing. "Everything all right in here?" I ask, wondering why they're all so quiet.

"Jesus H," Kinsley mumbles under her breath.

"Kinsley?" I raise an eyebrow.

"Nope. Yep. All is good." She lifts her glass of champagne and tips her head back, emptying the glass.

"You look amazing," Saige whispers, walking over to press a kiss to my cheek. "I've never seen you in a tuxedo before. It suits you well." She grins and hooks her arm through mine.

"Well, you ladies look beautiful." Saige is stunning, but I don't want to single her out.

Saige smiles at me. "We decided to just get ready here. No sense in sending Kinsley and Emery home to get changed, just to turn around and come back downtown."

My heart flutters a little when I think about her treating my home as hers. I nod once. "Absolutely. There is a guest room with an attached bathroom here on the main level. Please make yourself at home. I'll see if I can get Mr. Jones to get us a bigger car."

"No!" Emery interrupts. "We don't want to interrupt your evening. I can drive. Thank you for letting us get changed here."

"Very well." I won't argue with her, as I want Saige all to myself in the back of my car. "Saige, Mr. Jones will be here in thirty minutes. Ladies, will that give you enough time to change and touch up?"

"That'll be more than enough time," Emery answers.

Kinsley tops off their champagne glasses, and they disappear down the hall toward the guest room.

Saige leans against the kitchen island and taps the top of her champagne flute with her forefinger. "Sorry, I should've asked you if it was all right that they came over."

I frown at her. "Your friends are always welcome here."

Her face twists guiltily. "I know, but I should've at least given you a heads up."

"It's not a concern." I move over to Saige and wrap my arms around her waist, pulling her into me. She inhales sharply when I press my lips to her neck. "I love your hair pulled back," I mumble against the soft skin under her ear.

"It gives me better access to this beautiful neck of yours." I pull my head away and run my fingers over her skin.

"As much as I want to continue this, I have to get ready." She giggles and kisses me. "But I'd like to see where this was going after the party tonight." Her green eyes dancing in the light.

"You can bet your ass I'm going to show you where this was going," I snicker.

She pats my arm as she pushes away from the island. "Meet me upstairs. I'm going to need help with my zipper."

I raise my eyebrows, my lips twisting into a mischievous smile.

She smirks at me. "Just the zipper."

Following Saige upstairs, I find myself staring at her perfect body as she pulls off her casual clothes and stands before me naked—willing me to touch her. My pulse quickens as I watch her perfect body slip into nude-colored lingerie, covering all the parts of her I'm dying to touch . . . taste.

She steps carefully into her long, slim dress. She's stunning. The olive green color matches her eyes perfectly and the silk hugs her body, displaying every luscious curve. The cut leaves one arm and shoulder bare and covers the other, and a slit travels the length of her lean leg, stopping mid-thigh.

Everything about her takes my breath away. She walks toward me, everything moving in slow motion. She's like a cat stalking her prey—only I'd willingly let her destroy me. She stands before me and turns around, the span of her bare back on display. I zip the dress, but not before running my fingers gently over the curve of her spine, taking in her silky smooth skin.

"Everything about you is beautiful." I run my hands up and down her arms.

She turns to face me, locking her eyes on mine

affectionately. "And everything about you is perfectly handsome."

"I can't wait to get you back here tonight, Ms. Phillips." I run my thumb over her cheekbone, and she settles her head in the palm of my hand.

"We need to go," she says quietly.

I lean in and press a quick kiss to her forehead, sliding my hand into hers. She grabs her clutch off the bed, and I help her down the stairs in her long dress. Kinsley and Emery are in the kitchen waiting for us.

"You two should not be allowed to show up like that," Kinsley scoffs. "It's not fair that the two most beautiful people in the world found each other. Come on, Holt. You want to like a chubby, short girl with a foul mouth like me, right?"

"You're just as beautiful as Saige," I tell her politely. "And Emery, you look equally as stunning." Actually all three women are gorgeous, each in their different ways. We all leave the house together, Emery and Kinsley following behind us while Mr. Jones drives Saige and me.

Twenty-five minutes later, we're all in the elevator, ascending to the penthouse. When the doors open, the sound of laughter and classical music fill the usually quiet space. Hundreds of people are standing around, talking and drinking. Servers carrying trays of champagne, wine, beer, and hors d'oeuvres flitter through the sea of people.

"Holy shit," Saige says under her breath.

"It's always like this," I tell her. "Just enjoy yourself. There are clients here." I nod at Mr. Caruso, the CEO of Caruso industries and the owner of four of our planes. "There are even competitors here. We're a friendly industry, Saige. As cut throat as we make it seem, we're actually on very good terms with all of our competition."

She nods and grips my hand. Kinsley and Emery sidle up to a table, each grabbing a flute of champagne.

"Ladies, be sure to find our clients," I remind them before I guide Saige through the crowd. It's nice to have Saige with me. I'm used to doing these events alone. Speaking discreetly, I tell Saige, "Don't worry about Sergio Perez. He'll be here tonight, but he knows you're off limits. Be pleasant, but you're not expected to kiss his ass." I raise my eyebrows at her, knowing that she'll do whatever it takes to keep his business, but I'm not willing to negotiate Saige for any aviation deal.

"But—" she starts and I cut her off.

"We're not discussing this again. Understand?" I hate sounding like a dick, but this conversation is done.

"Mr. Hamilton," a male voice cuts in. I turn to see who's approached, and it's Robert Wellingford, the owner of Compass Aeronautical. His bright gray hair stands out against his tan skin and dark suit.

"Robert," I say, reaching out to shake his hand. "Nice to see you again."

"Likewise." He takes a sip of his glass of whiskey, smiling at Saige. "And who is this beauty?"

I squeeze her hand once before letting it go and introducing her. "This is Saige Phillips. Saige works for—"

He interrupts me, reaching for her hand. "I've heard wonderful things about you, young lady. So much so that I'd love to snatch you away from Jackson-Hamilton and bring you over to Compass." He laughs boisterously, and Saige laughs kindly in return.

She graciously reaches out to shake his hand. "It's a pleasure to meet you, sir."

"The pleasure is all mine." Instead of shaking her hand, he pulls it to his lips and kisses just over her knuckles. "However, from the looks of this, it appears that Holt here has secured you for more than a job." He turns back to me. "Nice work, son. She's smart, talented, and beautiful. She's a keeper." He pats me on the shoulder and I nod, not willing to discuss my relationship with him.

"Great party." He changes the subject, and I see Saige visibly relax. "You always know how to entertain."

"Thank you. I hope you're enjoying yourself."

"Always," he says, looking over my shoulder. "Hey, there's Monty Freeman. I've been looking for that asshole all night." He steps away, but not before quickly turning around to say goodbye. "It was a pleasure meeting you, Ms. Phillips. My offer stands," he says seriously. "Anytime you're ready to leave this handsome schmuck, I'll have a job for you." He laughs as he walks away, and I shake my head at the crazy old man.

"Is everyone in this industry old?" She asks me.

"Mostly. Jackson-Hamilton is the youngest aviation broker in terms of how long we've been in business, but also our employees. I'd like to think we have a leg up on our competition because we're more technologically savvy and have a different business acumen than our competitors." I explain confidently.

I spy Sergio Perez across the room, tucked into a corner. He's watching us, and he nods at me when he notices I've seen him. "Perez at nine o'clock," I warn Saige. "Just stay close to me."

She squeezes my hand and I turn to her, offering her an encouraging smile. Her lips are pursed, but she fakes a smile in return and takes a deep breath.

"Jerry!" I greet the man standing in front of us. "Nice to see you again."

"Nice to see you, Holt." His voice has a slight Southern drawl to it. Jerry flew in from Georgia to join us. He juggles a glass of red wine in one hand and a woman's beaded purse in the other. "Vivian is in the restroom." He grimaces, holding up the purse. A slight blush covering his cheeks.

"And I'm sure she appreciates you holding her purse," Saige says with a giant smile, trying to make him feel comfortable, no doubt. That's just what she does. She draws people in and makes them feel good. I shift and let her take over conversing with Jerry.

Jerry chuckles. "I don't know what you women carry around, but this weighs more than a newborn."

"Our life," she says sweetly. "Trust me, everything and anything that could be needed is in there. Do not lose it!" She raises her eyebrows and smirks. Then they both break out laughing.

"I'm Saige Phillips," she says, extending her hand to him.

"I've heard a lot of great things about you, Ms. Phillips," he drawls. "Jerry Billings," he says, shaking her hand in return. "I'm CEO of Gulfstream Aerospace."

Saige's eyes widen in awe and she inhales quickly before speaking. "Amazing planes you build. I love working with all the different aircraft."

He smiles fondly. "Do you have a favorite?" He leans in and grins.

She smiles back at him. The personable and outgoing Saige is in full effect. "I wish I did. There seems to be something different about all the aircraft that I find simply unique."

"You're good," he says, pointing a finger at her while his wife's purse hangs from his wrist.

"Good?" Saige questions.

"You're a good bullshitter. I like that, Saige!" He tips his head back and lets out a hearty laugh.

Saige shakes her head slowly and glances at me out of the corner of her eye.

"Mr. Billings, enjoy yourself tonight. It's always a pleasure doing business with Gulfstream." I reach out and shake his hand.

He nods politely. "And vice versa, Holt. We'll catch up soon. You need to come golf Augusta National with me." Jerry Billings is the world's biggest golf fan. That man does more business during an eighteen-hole round of golf than most companies do in a month.

"That sounds like a plan." I pat him on the shoulder as we walk away.

"Everyone is so nice," Saige whispers.

"They better be. We're negotiating multi-million-dollar deals with these companies." I stop and grab two glasses of champagne from a waiter walking by, handing one to Saige.

"So do you know everyone here?" She asks, taking a sip of champagne.

I glance around the room and survey the faces, the men all dressed in tuxedos or suits and the women in evening dresses. "Most everyone. Every once in a while, someone catches me off-guard, but not often."

"You're that good." She smirks.

"I'm that good." I laugh and sip my champagne.

"So everyone invited is somehow associated with Jackson-Hamilton, I assume?"

I nod. "Mostly they're business associates or clients, but we also make a point to include our outside legal team, a marketing firm that works with our internal department, and other various vendors. We want to be sure everyone that helps make Jackson-Hamilton successful is here and appreciated."

Saige hands me her glass of champagne and reaches over and adjusts my bow tie. "Crooked." She winks at me. "Now it's not." She looks at me tenderly and places her hand on my chest.

"Everything about you is breathtaking," I tell her quietly. In a room full of people, I feel like she's the only person alive. She looks like a model in her long dress, statuesque and beautiful.

She leans in and rests her head on my shoulder as we take in the chaos around us. People standing around, sounds of laughter, and clanking glasses.

"You two are adorable," Rowan says, sneaking up behind us.

"Ro!" Saige whips around to face him.

"Whoa!" he says in response as Saige's lean figure turns toward him. "I swear, if I wasn't a gay man, I'd be doing everything in my power to steal you out of the arms of Holt." He grabs Saige's hands and steps back to take in all of her. I smirk at Rowan and say a silent prayer that he's gay and not competition.

Whistling, he shakes his head. "You shouldn't be cooped up in a stuffy Chicago office building. You need to be walking the runways of Paris, my dear."

I jokingly step toward Rowan with my hand up. "Hey, hey. First you insinuate you'd like to steal my woman, and now you're trying to ship her off to Paris?"

We all share a laugh, and Rowan gives Saige a side hug. He looks every part the dapper gay man that he is in a fitted navy blue tuxedo and plaid bowtie.

"You look handsome," Saige tells him as Kinsley and Emery join our little group, followed not long after by Isaiah. Everyone catches up while sipping champagne and I smile as Saige glows with happiness. She wraps her arm in Rowan's, and they stand off to the side, talking and giggling.

A firm hand grips my shoulder and a thick accent fills the air. "Mr. Hamilton." Sergio Perez's unmistakable voice pulls me away from watching Rowan and Saige. I turn to him and politely offer my hand to him, even though I'd like to rip his head off.

Ever the politician that he is, he fakes a tight smile and

accepts my handshake. "Thank you for the invitation." He reeks of whiskey and cigar as he squeezes my hand tightly in a show of dominance. I'll never submit.

I offer him the most polite smile I can muster. "I'm glad you could join us, Mr. Perez."

Suddenly, I can feel the air around us chill. Voices become hushed, and Sergio looks over my shoulder, obviously staring at Saige.

"Ms. Phillips," he says, dropping my hand and stepping aside. He tries to move past me, but I step to the side and place myself in front of him, stopping him from getting near Saige.

"Mr. Hamilton, is there a problem?" His eyes narrow slightly and his lips twist into a smirk before he licks his lower lip like a dog drooling over a bone.

Rage courses through me. "No problem. However, I was wondering if I may have a word with you . . . in private. Preferably downstairs in my office." I cock my head to the side in a display of cockiness.

"Of course." He takes a step back, but he never removes his eyes from Saige. "After you, Mr. Hamilton." He nods.

He holds his arm out in a gesture for me to lead the way and we head toward the elevators. As we walk, I can feel my jaw muscles working, the tension in my shoulders building. Every part of me is instinctively telling me this is not going to go well.

SIXTEEN

Saige

MY HEART BEATS so wildly in my chest, I swear I can feel it pound against my rib cage. Holt's eyes narrowed and his hands were balled in fists as he walked away.

"We're going to lose the Perez sale," I whisper to Rowan, my voice panicked. He stands shoulder to shoulder next to me with his arm wrapped behind my back.

"We don't want that fucking crooked asshole's business anyway," Zay chimes in.

I blink at him. "It's fifty million dollars, Zay. Jackson-Hamilton can't lose his account."

Kinsley pipes in, "From the look on your boyfriend's face, Holt doesn't give a fuck about fifty million dollars."

"Just stop!" I bark, rubbing my temples. "Fifty million dollars is a lot of money to lose for a one-evening commitment to a party." Even though every fiber of my being doesn't want to go, is scared to go, I'd do it for Jackson-Hamilton . . . I'd do it for Holt.

"It's never just one night, Saige," Emery says quietly. "With Sergio Perez, you never know what you're getting yourself into. He's shady as fuck. I don't trust him, and I agree with Zay. Jackson-Hamilton is better off without him.

This is one sale. We have plenty of others that we're close to securing."

I sigh loudly. "I understand that, but you guys . . . I don't ever want to be the reason that Holt's company loses a client. It's just so silly—"

"It's not, though," Rowan jumps in, placing his hand on my shaking arm. "I've known Holt for a long time. He'd do that for any one of his employees. He wouldn't put their safety in the hands of a corrupt Colombian politician who toys with guns and drugs on the side. He just wouldn't. He doesn't run his business that way."

I nod, feeling a bit better.

Rowan gives my arm a gentle squeeze. "Saige, don't even stress about this. Let Holt handle it the way he needs to. This isn't about you; this is about Sergio."

"I know, but . . ." I rub my stomach as it twists and turns as I wonder how the *meeting* is going between the two men downstairs.

Emery grabs my hand. "No buts." She smiles at me, but I know she understands my concerns. "Now let's enjoy this party. I mean, it's free booze." She winks at me, then everyone begins talking again and the mood around us shifts. I plaster on a smile and say hello as guests wander past, pretending all is fine. If I've learned one thing in my life, it's fake it till you make it.

"Em," I say, turning around. "I'm going to the restroom for a minute to just take a breather. I'll be back." It's a flat out lie, but I don't want my friends looking for me.

I weave through the tables and politely smile at people as I pass them, making my way toward the elevators. I press the down button, tapping my foot impatiently as I wait. When the doors slide open, the elevator is full of people arriving for the cocktail party. As they filter out, I step inside, and seconds later, I'm on the dark floor of

Jackson-Hamilton's main offices.

I walk quickly down the main hall that leads to Holt's office, noticing the office lights peeking through the fogged privacy glass. The office door is cracked open and I go still as I contemplate whether to knock or just listen to the two raised voices exchanging words behind the door.

"She's not negotiable," Holt barks.

"Everything is negotiable, Mr. Hamilton. Everyone can be bought for a price," Sergio snarls. My heart begins racing again.

"I beg to differ, Mr. Perez." Holt's voice is calm but deadly. "Ms. Phillips told me she spoke with you and that she's not interested. Please respect her wishes—and mine."

"This is about you, Mr. Hamilton," Sergio says, laughing bitterly. "You've taken an interest in her. I saw you walk in together, and I saw the way you kept her glued to your side." There's a moment of silence before Mr. Perez begins speaking again. "Well, I'm interested as well. And fifty-two million dollars says that Ms. Phillips will be accompanying me to my dinner party."

"You're wrong. Ms. Phillips won't be going anywhere with you." Holt's voice is laced with anger.

I hold my breath and stand up straight as Holt puts Sergio in his place.

"You're willing to risk losing my business for a stupid woman?" Sergio snaps at Holt, his accent growing thicker the faster he speaks.

"I'm willing to risk everything for her," Holt says, and my throat goes dry. "She's worth more than your fifty-two-million-dollar airplane, and any other business you'd send my way." His voice is firm and commanding and I almost faint when I hear him say I'm worth more than this sale.

Sergio chuckles. "You are a foolish man, Mr. Hamilton."

"We'll see about that," Holt growls.

Hearing the shuffling of footsteps, I quickly step to the side and around the corner so they don't see me. My heart is racing and my stomach is still in knots knowing that Holt just threw away a huge deal and lost a longtime client. I watch Sergio Perez disappear down the main hall, then I step around the corner. Holt is sitting at his desk, leaning back in his chair, his face turned to the ceiling.

"You okay?" I ask softly, standing in the doorway.

Holt spins his desk chair around to face me. "How long have you been standing there?" he asks, letting out a deep sigh.

My knees shake unsteadily. "Long enough to know that I think you made a mistake. Long enough to know that I'm shocked you'd do that for me." Tears sting the back of my eyes when I think about what Holt has just done for me.

He nods, his eyes dropping to his desk. "It wasn't a mistake. You're worth that. You're worth a million times that." My heart swells with emotion hearing him say this.

"Holt—" I begin walking toward him.

"Saige. Can we not talk about this? I made my decision. I'm at peace with it." He grins at me and takes my hand, his thumb caressing the top of it. "We have a party upstairs that we need to get back to."

He stands up and pulls my other hand into his. We're face-to-face, staring into each other's eyes. I feel like I can see his soul through his blue eyes, and I've just witnessed his heart. There is nothing about this man that I'm not head over heels in love with, if I could just find the words to tell him. I step forward and into his arms. He wraps them tightly around me, and I press my nose to his neck, inhaling the light scent of his cologne.

"I'd risk everything for you, Saige," he whispers, running his fingers over the back of my neck.

Suddenly, a loud knock startles me, and I jump back as Holt turns to see who's standing in the doorway.

An older gentleman dressed in a suit is watching us, adjusting the sleeves and cufflinks on his tuxedo. "Holt," he says with a slight grin. "Been a long time."

Holt pulls my hand into his, squeezing it tightly, and I notice his face turning red. "What are you doing here?" he bites out through clenched teeth.

The man runs his fingers through his white hair and adjusts the watch on his wrist before responding. "I would have thought after all this time you'd at least invite me into your office. You grew up with me demonstrating the proper way to treat clients. I'd expect you to have better manners," he says smugly, his voice dripping with arrogance.

It's Holt's father. It must be. My breath hitches, and I scramble to replay the details of Holt and his father's relationship, but all I can remember is that it's strained and there has been no contact for years.

Holt's grip nearly crushes mine, and I wriggle my hand out of his. With a deep breath, I take a step forward on shaky knees, thinking that maybe I can diffuse this situation. "Hello." I smile at the man, but he remains planted just inside the doorway.

"Hi," he says in response, no emotion in his voice. His face is devoid of any semblance of happiness as he stares over my shoulder at Holt.

I look back at Holt, who is also cemented in place, his hands fisted at his sides.

"I'm going to go back upstairs," I whisper, planning a quick escape. I need to let Holt and his father deal with whatever they need to deal with.

He simply nods in response. My shaky legs carry me across the quiet office until I'm directly in front of Holt's father, but he doesn't make an attempt to move and let me exit, so I stop.

Finally, he turns his attention to me, and my stomach flips nervously when I see the void in his blue eyes. The same blue eyes that Holt has. Ones that can stop you in your tracks, only his are hollow. The deep wrinkles in his face are accentuated by his frown, but his upper lip curls into a sickening smile.

"Pardon me," he says, taking one step to the side, still not enough space for me to get past him. I smile and take another step forward, praying he'll just let me through. "I hope I wasn't interrupting anything," he says, turning his attention back to Holt.

"No, no," I stutter. "We were just headed back upstairs. I'll give you two some privacy." Taking another step forward, I silently urge him to move out of my way, but he remains still.

"You really are a pretty little thing, aren't you?" There's a hint of laughter in his statement. "I didn't catch your name." He tilts his head to the side as he studies my face.

I force a smile. *I'm getting really good at this*, I think to myself. "Saige." I extend my hand. "Saige Phillips."

At that, his entire body stills, his eyes flashing to Holt. Then he erupts in laugher, tossing his head back. "You have really outdone yourself, son!" he roars, looking back at me. "My, my, my you have grown into a beautiful little thing." His quiet laughter continues. He holds his fist in front of his mouth, trying to stifle it back.

I glance back at Holt. "What is he talking about?"

Holt's face twists with agony and anger. "Saige. Go upstairs."

I take a deep breath and stand up straight, raising my chin as Holt's father continues to chuckle behind his fist.

"I didn't catch your name either," I say, my voice unwavering.

"Now!" Holt commands, but I hold my gaze on Holt's father. His eyebrows shoot up, but he finally stops laughing.

"Don't," Holt orders, but I'm not sure if he's talking to his father or me.

His father's baby blue eyes remain fixed on mine, and he holds out his hand. I slide mine inside his firm grip. He squeezes gently, holding it for a moment before he shakes it. "Jonathan Berkshire."

My entire world stops.

My heart ceases to beat. The blood from my head and chest rushes to my feet at the sound of that name. My mouth goes dry, and my lips separate as if I'm trying to speak, only my tongue is paralyzed.

I'm barely able to turn my head to the left in time to see Holt come bounding across the room and pulling me into his arms before I feel my knees give out.

I BARELY HEAR their raised voices, accusations, and verbal attacks on each other between the pounding of my heart and swooshing of blood overcoming my hearing.

A thunderous crash pulls me from my haze, and I see Holt land a punch directly to his father's jaw. Jonathan Berkshire falls backward against an office chair and catches himself on the conference table.

"Get the fuck out of here!" Holt barks. "You've done more damage in this lifetime than others could do in a hundred. I meant what I said when I told you I never wanted to see you again."

His father simply rubs his jaw and smirks at me.

Holt's chest rises and falls while tears sting my eyes and rage begins to overtake me. I look at Jonathan dressed in a designer suit, wearing a watch that probably costs more than all of the land my family owns—probably bought with the money he stole from my father. I close my eyes, quickly shaking off the sight of my father's lifeless body on the barn floor before I open them as the sound of flesh hits flesh.

Holt lands another punch square to the middle of Jonathan's face, knocking him completely to the ground. Blood spills from his nose and into his mouth, but he never loses the sick smirk on his face.

Holt draws back for a third punch when I finally find my voice. "Holt, stop." It's not powerful, it's not loud, but it stops Holt in his tracks. It's weak, but it's all I have left in me at the moment.

He turns to me as I stand up from the couch he placed me on minutes ago, and I walk over to Holt's desk, lifting the receiver on his phone. "We have a security issue in Mr. Hamilton's office and need immediate assistance," I say though a shaky voice into the phone. I calmly place the receiver down and, with a deep breath, find the courage to say everything I ever dreamed of saying to the man that destroyed my family. I close my eyes, allowing the tears to finally spill over. I hear the shotgun firing in the distance and smell the odor of gunpowder and blood.

I open my eyes and speak through the blurry tears. "Mr. Berkshire . . ." My legs tremble obnoxiously as I make my way to where he sits on the office floor, holding his nose. He's pulled a silk handkerchief from his pocket, and I watch as blood soaks the clean white cloth. I think about the blood that spilled from my father and how much more blood Mr. Berkshire deserves to lose.

As I approach, something inside me twists. This man, this waste of human breath, was my father's friend, his mentor, his partner. Of all the times I imagined this moment, I never imagined crumbling, falling to my knees in front of him as heaving sobs escape me.

"I hate you," I mumble between exasperating breaths.

"I hate you." My tight long dress rips at the seam as I kneel awkwardly. I ball my hands into fists and pound against this man's chest. He tries to push away from me, but I fall into him, hitting him continuously. "I hate you," I scream through my tears.

Holt takes a step toward me, but I hold out my arm to keep him at bay. "And you," I turn to look up at him. "You lied to me." My tears turn from anger to hurt as Holt moves in.

"Saige, let me explain." He squats, bringing himself down to me. I can tell he's in agony. I don't care.

I shake my head vigorously. There's nothing he could ever do to fix this. Nothing. I trusted him.

Holt's office door bursts open, bouncing off the wall behind it, and three security guards enter the office. I bury my hands in my face as two of them help Jonathan Berkshire up and Holt explains what happened. The third asks me if I'm all right. I ignore his questions.

I'm not sure I'll ever be all right. I'm not sure I'll ever forgive Jonathan Berkshire, or Holt, for that matter. I reach for the edge of the conference room table and pull myself up, straightening my ripped dress once I'm back on my feet. I swipe at the bitter tears on my cheeks and turn to Holt.

"Why?" I ask him, needing an explanation as to why he kept this from me for so long. I inhale a shaky breath.

He stands, his shoulders slumped in defeat, and he runs a hand through his dark hair.

"Answer me, Holt."

He sits down on the edge of the couch in his office and buries his face in his hands. "Saige, there's so much to tell you—"

"Liar," I shout, the rage in my voice building. "You are nothing but a liar. Were you ever going to tell me?" He doesn't answer. "So in New York when we were at dinner at your mom's house. Was that a distraction too?"

His pained face is genuinely confused at that. "What're you talking about, Saige? What do you mean 'a distraction'?"

"That night when you stopped talking to me. You told me you loved me." My voice cracks around the word. "Was that a distraction so you didn't have to tell me your mom figured out who I was? She knew who I was. She put the pieces of the puzzle together when I told her my last name." God, she figured it out that night. I press my hands against my stomach, trying to stop the ache. He inhales deeply and swallows hard, his lips pressing into a hard line. "Oh my God, Holt! How many more lies are there?"

"That wasn't a lie," he snaps angrily. "Saige, I would never lie about loving you."

"Bullshit!" I scream at him, the champagne in my stomach threatening to come up. The tears now fall in streams, and I can barely catch my breath long enough to speak. "Who else knew about me?"

He stares at me and I can see his hand shaking.

"Who the fuck else knows about me?" I'm on the verge of a full-fledged nervous breakdown, and I know I'm losing control. I feel myself unraveling.

"Jack," he says quietly.

"I fucking knew it," I say through heaving sobs, fisting my hands at my sides.

"Saige," he says pleadingly, jumping up and walking over to me. His eyes are a mixture of anger and hurt and his face is twisted in agony. He reaches out to hold my arm, but I slap his hand away. "Don't touch me," I hiss at him. "Don't you ever fucking touch me again."

He startles, his hurt compounding.

A moment later, Holt's office door flies open and Rowan and Emery burst inside. Rowan is gripping a glass of champagne, his eyes fixed on Holt, but Emery rushes over to me, pulling me into her arms. She looks to Holt for answers, but he drops his head and shifts from foot to foot.

"This is not what I was expecting to walk in on," Emery says, surprised. "Saige, sweetie. Come on. Let's go clean you up." Her fingers swipe at my wet cheeks, and she brushes back the loose strands of hair that have fallen out of my bun. She gently tries to guide me toward Holt's private restroom.

"No!" I shout, yanking my arm from her grasp. "I don't need to clean up. I'm ready to leave." I turn to Holt, who has moved next to his desk, one hand in his hair, the other gripping the edge of his desk. His eyes are fixed on me, and he chews on his bottom lip while breathing heavily. I try to gain my composure and I stand up tall, pushing my shoulders back. "Mr. Hamilton, or should I say, Mr. Berkshire? Please accept my verbal resignation. I'm sure, under the circumstances, you'll understand why I won't be giving you the proper two-week courtesy."

"Whoa." A voice comes from behind me. I turn to see a confused look on Rowan's face as he steps forward. "Saige, let's not be irrational." He pulls my right arm into his hands and begins rubbing it in an attempt to calm me down. "Sleep on this. You two can talk on Monday. We all have arguments—"

"There's nothing to sleep on, Rowan," I snap at him. "Mr. Hamilton has been lying to me about who he really is. Holt isn't actually a Hamilton, he's Mr. Holt Berkshire, son of Jonathan Berkshire—the man who stole my father's money, and the man who ultimately destroyed my family when my father killed himself," I say weakly, my voice finally breaking. I feel everything inside me breaking.

Rowan stills and drops my arm, stepping away from me. He opens his mouth to say something, but closes it quickly and pulls his lips in between his teeth.

"Saige—" Holt says desperately, but I hold up my finger

to stop him, narrowing my eyes at him in disgust.

"No! You've known who I was and lied about knowing me this entire time." I turn to see Emery behind me with a hand pressed to her mouth and tears in her eyes. "So, no. There will be no sleeping on it." I breathe heavily, wrapping an arm around my waist. "Interesting turn of events tonight, huh?" I say, my tone snarky. I turn one last time to see Holt, his head fallen forward and his chest rising and falling quickly. "I'm ready to leave . . . now. Rowan, will you please drive me home?"

"Of course," he says, barely audible.

I walk toward Rowan, who reaches out his hand for me and I take it graciously. I need him to support me as I walk on legs I can no longer feel. My entire body is numb. He squeezes my hand tightly and nods at me, his eyes bouncing between Holt and me. He shoots a look at Emery before he finally speaks. "Let's go," he says, wrapping his arm around my shoulder, pulling me toward him.

We step through Holt's office door and out into the empty office. All the lights are off except for the small wall sconces that lead down the main hallway toward the elevators.

"I need to stop by my desk," I tell Rowan and turn to walk through the dimly lit office toward our cubicles. My voice is gravelly from crying and yelling.

"Not tonight, baby girl," he says tenderly. "Anything you need I'll get to you later. Now is not the time for this."

He's right. I can't even deal with my desk right now. It's stuff, meaningless stuff.

He adds, "But I'm really hoping you'll change your mind about resigning. Give it some time."

I shake my head, a sob escaping from the back of my throat. There will be no second chances, as no apology will ever fix this. My life as I knew it, as I was finally beginning to move on, will never be the same.

He pulls me tighter to him. "I'm so sorry, Saige," he says as we near the elevators.

I can't stop the sudden flow of tears that feel like a river running down my face, and I wrap myself in Rowan's arms and succumb to the sobs.

SEVENTEEN

Saige

THE PLANE LANDS with a hard thump and brakes quickly. Flying commercial on a small regional plane is quite different from the private plane I was last on when I flew to New York with Holt. As we taxi to the small terminal, I pull my purse out from under the seat in front of me and stash away the magazine I bought but never read.

The flight attendant opens the small plane door, and I take the narrow steps down onto the concourse. The ground staff guides us to the small door, taking us inside the terminal. I walk through the gate of the airport and wait in the small baggage claim area. There is one baggage carousel, as this airport handles maybe six incoming flights a day.

I turn on my phone before sitting on the edge of the metal carousel and prop my elbow on my knees. My phone pings with incoming text messages, all from Emery, Zay, Rowan, and Kinsley. They've tag-teamed checking up on me, and I've been neglectful in returning their messages.

The latest from Emery advises that she visited the apartment and spoke with Evelyn, who informed her I flew home to North Dakota. Sighing, I power down my phone again before finishing the message. For a moment, I understand my father's defeat. Finding a career you love, in a city you love, only to have it ripped away from you deceitfully is devastating.

"Piglet," Brent's voice calls to me as the sliding glass doors pull open.

He bounces toward me in jeans and a long-sleeved t-shirt; his trademark baseball hat turned backwards. My face crumples with emotion. I jump up and rush toward him, wrapping myself around him. God, I missed him. Brent, my mom, and North Dakota have always been my safe place and this is exactly what I need right now.

"Hey, hey," he says as I cry against his chest. "You're fine. You're home now. Let's get your bags and we'll talk in the car." He pulls me away from his chest and plants a quick kiss on my forehead before heading over to the carousel for my two large suitcases.

"Jesus, Saige. How long are you staying?" He cracks a smile as he lugs the two bags.

I wipe my cheeks with the sleeve of my sweatshirt and pull my purse onto my shoulder. "Indefinitely," I answer him.

He stops. "Oh, this is going to be good, isn't it?"

I shrug.

"You can say that again."

WE LIVE IN Deer Creek, which is almost ninety miles west of Grand Forks, the city into which I flew. While Brent drives carefully down the narrow country roads, I update him on what brought me home. He says very little as I outline every detail of my relationship with Holt, both professional and personal, from my first day at Jackson-Hamilton to yesterday at the cocktail party.

As we pull on to Main Street in Deer Creek, he veers the pick-up truck into a parking spot in front of the local diner. Downtown Deer Creek is a city-block long with small brick buildings that hold the local grocery store, hardware store, and the one diner we have. He kills the engine and turns to look at me, cracking another signature smile. "This calls for Martha's pie."

For the first time in twenty-four hours, I smile back. "I think that is an excellent idea."

Brent and I eat a piece of Martha's chocolate pie covered in extra whipped cream and sip hot coffee while we catch up on all things Deer Creek related. He fills me in on the crops from this summer, planned renovations for different structures on the farm, and Murphy. I cannot wait to get home and see my Murphy. I've missed that yellow lab more than I've missed anything.

Dusk has set in and, as we pull off the main road and down the winding gravel road that leads to our farm, I take in how different everything looks since I've been gone. The house I used to think was average is beautiful with its wraparound porch and new paint. The trees that line both sides of the gravel drive are turning colors. As we take the final turn that brings us up to the house, I see Murphy resting in the grass just outside the side door.

As Brent stops the truck, I hop out and run around the back. "Murph!" I holler.

The old dog jumps up, his tail wagging and his hind end shaking. He leaps and jumps into my lap, licking my face wildly. Small yelps replace the deep bark I'm used to.

"Looks like someone is as excited to see you as you are him." Brent laughs. He reaches out his hand to pull me up, and Murphy follows us inside.

"I'm going to shower and go to bed," I tell Brent. "It's been a long two days."

"I think that's a good idea. I'll set your bags in your room." He smiles at me warmly.

As I hold on to the old wooden banister, I turn around. "Brent?"

"Yeah, Piglet?"

"Thanks for coming to get me."

His eyes are tender. "I'd do anything for you, Saige. You know that."

"Thank you," I say against the growing lump in my throat.

"Go clean up and sleep, kiddo." Sleep sounds like heaven right now.

"Night, B."

"Night, Piglet."

I FEEL THE bed dip and a soft hand brush the hair off my forehead as I try to force my eyes open. I can hear her giggle before I'm able to see her. "Mom," I mumble, my voice hoarse.

"I got tired of waiting for you to get up," she says in a hushed voice. "It's almost noon, Saige."

"I was tired." I prop myself up on my elbows. Murphy is curled into a ball at the bottom of my bed. Oh, how I missed him.

"I don't know how he got up here," Mom says, gesturing toward Murphy. "He hasn't been able to climb the steps in months." Mom rubs my hair, tucking the messy waves behind my ear. "Brent filled me in on why you came home."

Of course he did. Suddenly, my eyes sting with tears, and I can feel the lump in my throat. I nod, my chin beginning to quiver. Mom runs her finger over my lips, and I lie back on the pillow.

"I'd like to talk to you about it when you're ready," she says.

"What if I'm never ready?" I whisper.

She sighs softly. "Saige, you have to start living. My greatest joy came when you accepted that job and moved to Chicago. That was the first time I felt like you were going to be okay. I've moved on, Brent has moved on, and you need to move on. We'll always love your dad, Saige, but it's time for you to let go of the past."

I exhale a long breath as I take in her words.

"Come downstairs and eat. I took the day off to spend it with you."

I smile at her. Her hair is showing a few streaks of gray now, but her face is still as beautiful as I remember.

After a late breakfast, Brent puts me to work on the farm, just like he did when I lived here. Since I still won't go in the horse barn, he brings the horses to me. I brush and saddle them in the small, secure pasture. Murphy sits in the grass along the fence line and watches as I talk to Lola and Mikey. Both are American quarter horses, and we've had them since they were foals.

Brent meets me as I finish, and we spend the afternoon riding the horses along the perimeter of the property and talking. We stop at the creek that runs through the south end of our land, allowing the horses to wade in the shallow water while I take in the setting sun. Brent has been quiet, and I can tell something is bothering him.

"Just say it," I finally say, breaking the awkward silence.

He sighs and shoves his hands in the pockets of his jeans. "You know I love having you home, Piglet. I've missed you, but . . ."

"But what?"

He lifts his baseball hat off his head, running his hands through his short hair before placing it back on his head. His tan face softens as he begins to speak. "There's nothing for you here. You're so smart and talented, and coming back here is just . . . it's just not where you belong."

I sigh. "I didn't say I was staying forever." But I just might.

"I know. It's just that I don't want you getting too comfortable here. You have a life in Chicago."

I shake my head, feeling that same emotion churning my stomach. "I don't. I quit my job, Brent. Even if I went back, I'd need to find something else." The thought of working with Holt, seeing him every day, makes me ill.

He calls for the horses, and they step out of the creek and trot toward us. "I think you should talk to him, Saige."

No way. "I think you've lost your damn mind," I respond as I step back up onto Lola. He rolls his eyes at me before I take off, and we race the horses back to the barn.

I SPEND THE next couple of days falling into a routine. I sleep late, help Brent on the farm, cook dinner, and spend my nights reading. Anything to keep my mind off Holt. Both Brent and my mom have been respectful and not spoken about him again, but I see the way they look at me. There's more they want to say, but they're holding back.

I sit on the old wooden porch swing, a giant blanket tossed over my legs, the moon casting a bright light on the field. Murphy hobbles out of the back door and lies down on the porch beneath the swing.

"Hey, old man," I call to him. I reach down and run my fingers through his soft fur and rub behind his ear. He lets out a low groan before finally dropping his head to his paws, and we sit in the silence. For the first time in three days, my thoughts wander to Holt.

I close my eyes and fight the memories of his smile, his eyes, his touch. I swallow back my emotion and remind myself that everything I miss, everything I thought was true, honest love was nothing but a lie.

EIGHTEEN

Holt

MY HEART HURTS at the void Saige has left in her absence. Every rational part of me is screaming at me to give her time, but love isn't rational and I can't lose her. So I pick up my office phone and call the hangar.

She's been gone four days. Four days that I haven't eaten and barely slept. After a moment, the phone rings, finally connecting. "I need you to prepare my plane and file a flight plan for Grand Forks, North Dakota," I instruct and rub my temple. "Approximate departure in three hours." I disconnect the call and power down my laptop. Pressing the intercom on my phone, I ask Joyce to join me in my office.

She enters and takes a seat across from my desk as she's accustomed to. The lack of coffee, smiles, and greetings have not gone unnoticed since she returned to work after the cocktail party. Apparently, everyone is *Team Saige,* and I don't blame them.

"I need you to clear my calendar for the next three days. Actually, just clear it for the week and reschedule any conference calls for next week."

She purses her lips at me but jots notes into her small notebook.

"Please be sure to send the thank you cards to our guests and have them out this week."

She nods and continues to scribble in her notebook.

I turn and look out my office window, the Chicago skyline hidden in low-lying clouds. The skies are gray and cool, fall weather beginning to settle in.

"Will that be all?" Joyce asks, clearing her throat.

"Hold all my calls too, unless . . ." I pause.

"Unless," she prods.

"Unless it's important." I turn around and look at her. She knows the meaning of important. Important is Saige. Important is only Saige.

"Yes, sir." She stands and walks out of my office. I follow behind her, and she offers me a sympathetic yet stiff smile, and I nod at her in return as I leave.

At the elevator, I pull my phone from my suit pocket, hoping, praying for any word from Saige. I don't know why I'm disappointed when I see nothing. She's gone. I confirmed her flight back to North Dakota on Sunday, but I hoped she'd break and reach out to me. She's stronger than that, though. I know her. She won't break.

"Mr. Hamilton." Rowan's voice surprises me. He's standing next to me, waiting for the elevator. Everyone has reverted to extreme formalities with me since Saige left. Just one more sharply painful reminder of how she brought life to this office—to me.

"Rowan," I acknowledge him less formally, and we wait together, quietly, until I finally turn to him. "Would you mind closing Mr. Perez's account tomorrow? Wire him a refund and add five percent."

He looks at me out of the corner of his eye and nods. "I will." He clears his throat. "Taking the rest of the week off?"

"Something like that," I mumble.

Rowan and I ride silently down until we reach the ground floor. When the doors slide open, Rowan steps forward but pauses. "Go bring our girl home," he says softly before stepping out of the elevator and walking away.

"I plan to," I mumble to myself. I plan to do whatever it takes to get her back.

NINETEEN

Saige

AFTER FIVE DAYS at home, I finally walk down to the creek like I did every day when we first moved back to the farm. It seemed so much further away than it does now. Murphy, slow and arthritic, hobbles along carefully behind me. The beautiful creek runs along the edge of our property. The water is crystal-clear and you can make out every rock that lines the bottom of the water. Cattails shoot up along the banks, except in the area Brent and I cleared out years ago. We lined that area with large river rocks to keep the area clear of grass and cattails, making for easy entrance into my favorite swimming spot.

I used to spend hours down here during the summer, wading in the creek to cool off from the warm, humid North Dakota summers. I'd ride the horses down and let them drink the cool water while I'd swim and lie out on the grassy banks for hours. I could get lost in the blue sky, tall grass, and clear waters.

There is a giant boulder that sits just up from the creek bank, and I climb up on top of it like I used to so many years ago. Murphy's legs give out just at the edge of the water. He falls and pants heavily before stretching out into the grass, my poor old boy. But he makes the effort to army crawl to the water's edge and lap at some of the cool water before finally resting his head on his paws. I stare at the giant oak tree across the creek, admiring how much it's grown. Its branches are more dense and full of brightly colored autumn leaves. It amazes me how some things become so much stronger over time, yet others become more frail, weak like me.

This is my place. I bared my soul on this very rock, in these very waters in the days, months, and years after my dad took his life. I cursed God. I cursed Jonathan Berkshire. I swore revenge, and I thought I'd finally made peace with my father's death. *Thought.*

But I've never felt rage hit me like it did when Jonathan introduced himself and I realized Holt had lied to me. In that flash of a moment, I realized I'd never truly be at peace with my father's death. I'll always be broken.

I pull my knees tightly to my chest and let the crisp autumn air sting my tender face. There is absolutely nothing better than fall in the Midwest. You can smell the change of the seasons in the air. The trees are colorful, full of vibrant reds, oranges, and yellows, and yet the grass is still green. It will be until the first freeze.

I sit in the silence for a while when Murphy lets out a quick bark and lifts his head, looking behind me. His ears perk up as I hear the footsteps approach from behind me. As I've always been able to, I can smell him. I can feel him. I've always been able to sense his presence. My heart races and I will myself not to turn around to look at him. I'm not ready. He betrayed me.

"Hey, old guy," he says as he walks right past me and over to where Murphy lies in the grass.

I catch a glimpse of him from the corner of my eye as he kneels down next to Murphy and runs his fingers through his thick fur. Murphy lets out an audible moan as he rubs that sweet spot behind his ears, his favorite spot to be rubbed.

"Traitor," I whisper under my breath while my dog rests his head on Holt's thigh, soaking up the attention.

"It's beautiful here," Holt says, his back to me.

Whether he's talking to himself, Murphy, or me, I have no idea, but I don't respond. I won't deny his words because he's right, but I'm not going to answer him. This farm, this land is the most beautiful place on earth. This is my home; it always will be.

After a long moment, he stands up and brushes off his jeans. Even dressed casually, Holt is the epitome of a runway model. Worn jeans and a cream sweater, he looks like a J Crew model, but I keep my eyes fixed on the creek. His feet shuffle through the long grass over to the boulder I'm sitting on.

I can't be near him. I'm not ready for this. I slide down the opposite side. "Let's go, Murph." Murphy struggles to get up, his old legs shaking, and it takes a few seconds for him to get moving. "Come on, boy," I encourage him, and he begins a slow, stiff walk over to me.

"Saige," Holt calls to me from behind.

I don't answer him, but I turn around to look at him.

His eyes are sad and dark circles have settled under them. "I'm not here to try and change your mind. I'm not here to grovel for your forgiveness because I know I'm not worthy of that. I just came to tell you I'm sorry. I'm so sorry. I know my words are meaningless because I lied to you. But I mean it when I say I never wanted to hurt you, Saige." He takes a deep breath and tips his head back, pointing his face to the sky while shoving his hands in his pockets.

My emotions fluctuate between anger and hurt. "Is that all?" I back away further from him. It's hard to be close to him because, even though I want to hate him, I still love him. I'll always love him. But I don't let any of that show. I keep my face devoid of any emotion. "Because I have to get back to the house."

He blows a puff of air from his mouth and looks at me sadly. "You know, I hired you because I wanted to do something good. My father destroyed many families, Saige. Not just yours. He robbed countless families, most of them close friends of his, and he got away with it. He walked away scot-free, leaving a trail of destruction behind him, and I've spent the last thirteen years trying to make up for his sins."

He clears his throat. "He destroyed our family too, Saige. My mom walked away with nothing. She wanted nothing from that marriage. She believed nothing he provided for us was earned, and assumed everything we had was stolen from others." He raises his voice.

Rage fills me, and I don't know why, but I become emotional, feeling my throat clench. "Do you want me to feel sorry for you, Holt? Because I'm really struggling to find a sympathetic bone in my body right now for your luxurious upbringing—"

"I want you to hear me out," he yells back at me. "I was in college when all of this happened. I was humiliated. My father was all over the news, my family was dragged through the mud, and people called *me* a thief. I was just nineteen. I didn't have a clue what he was doing."

I swallow hard, shaking my head as he speaks. "Again, I'm really finding it hard to feel sorry for you. Because you see that?" I point to the oak tree across the creek. "That's where my father rests. His ashes are under that tree. So I'm sorry your ego was hurt, I'm sorry your name was run through the mud, but my father's life is under that tree. His best friend and mentor took everything he ever earned—betrayed his friendship in the most vile of ways. My father trusted Jonathan." My voice breaks. "And he lost everything—every single dime we had. We moved back to North Dakota with literally the clothes on our backs. It destroyed him, Holt. All he ever wanted was to provide for his family. Secure his future—and your father robbed him of everything." My voice breaks, and I feel the tears pool in my eyes.

I hate this. It's like I'm reliving it all over again. Why did he have to come back here?

My face goes hard again. "So I'm sorry, Holt. I don't feel sorry for you."

He looks desperate, his palms upturned. "I just wanted to make it right. I wanted to right his wrongs."

A few seconds of silence go by when I ask, "How did you find me? Why couldn't you just leave my family alone? We've been through enough hell to last a lifetime."

He looks away from me, fixing his eyes on the tree next to us. "I thought I was hiring a little farm girl from North Dakota. I was hoping to help her achieve a dream . . . offer her the life her father wanted. Call it repentance for what my father put your family through. But then you walked into Jackson-Hamilton and rocked my world, Saige. You were sexy and smart and witty; everything I wasn't expecting. You turned my world upside down. I fell in love with you, and that wasn't a part of my plan." He looks back to me, his blue eyes full of hurt.

He pulls his hands from his pockets and runs them through his hair. "I know I should have told you who I really was. But I fell in love with you, and I knew if you found out you'd run."

"And yet you continued to keep your secret," I snap at him.

"I did," he admits, his voice full of regret. "I haven't spoken to my father in thirteen years. When he walked into my office, it was the first time I'd even seen him since I legally changed my last name to my mother's maiden name. I'd written him off a long time ago. I honestly didn't think I'd ever see him again. It was easier to keep my lie, because the thought of living without you made me crazy."

"How many more lies are there?" I snarl at him.

"Saige, don't . . ." He takes a few steps closer, and I hold out my hand, gesturing for him to stop. He reaches into his back pocket and pulls out an envelope. Looking at it, he sighs and holds it out to me.

"What is it?" I cross my arms over my chest, not trusting him. Clouds have covered the sun, and the afternoon air has moved from chilly to almost cold.

"It's your last paycheck and a letter of recommendation." His jaw clenches, his hand visibly shaking as he holds the envelope out toward me.

"A letter of recommendation?" I ask, confused.

He swallows hard, looking sad and defeated. "I made a call to Compass Aeronautical. You have a job waiting for you there. You're talented, Saige. Don't throw away your career because you're angry at me."

My entire body shakes as the reality of the situation settles on me. He's letting me go. My breathing quickens, and my heart stammers in my chest. "I don't need your letter of recommendation—"

He nods. "You're right, you don't. Your work speaks for itself."

I scowl at him. "And I don't want your money."

"I understand. I figured you'd say that." He almost smirks. "For the record, Saige, I built this company from the ground up with my partner. The capital raised was legitimate. Not a penny of it came from my father or any Ponzi scheme."

I nod at him in understanding as my knees shake and my heart aches in my chest. This will be the last time I see

Holt Hamilton. "I think you should leave now," I say quietly, our eyes locked on each other.

I look into his crystal blue eyes for the last time as he walks toward me, stopping right in front of me. I keep my arms crossed against my chest as a protective barrier, not letting him close. Murphy wags his tail next to me and looks up at Holt.

Holt once again tries to hand me the envelope, and I shake my head at him. Finally, he drops it at my feet and swallows hard. His lips are slightly parted like he wants to say something, but he doesn't. My eyes drop to his chest because I can't stand to look into his eyes any longer. His firm hands reach out and grip my shoulders. I try to back away, but he won't let me. As if he is admitting defeat, his grip lessens as he leans in, pressing a gentle kiss to my forehead.

"Goodbye, Saige," he says softly before his feet begin rustling through the grass and he starts walking away. "Oh," he says, turning around. "There *was* one more lie, Saige. Since I'm laying it all out to you, you may as well know the truth about everything." He pauses and purses his lips. "You asked me when I fell in love with you . . ."

I shiver as he speaks, waiting to hear his answer.

"I told you in New York."

"I remember."

"I lied to you. I fell in love with you the minute you walked across Bar 51 toward me on those shaky legs. The way you looked at me like no one else on earth existed. And then I fell more in love with you when I felt your lips, but it was when you showed me your heart I knew I'd never be able to not love you. I was just too afraid to admit it to you, because somewhere deep inside, I knew the bottom would fall out and I'd lose you." His voice breaks and he chokes back his emotion.

It's like the air has been knocked out of me. He loved

me first. My heart shatters and my stomach lurches, and I swallow down the lump in my throat. He loved me first. I close my eyes at his confession, unable to look into his eyes anymore.

"Goodbye, Holt," I mumble under my breath, turning away from him just as the tears spill from my eyes and down my face.

I hear him walk away then and know I'll never be able to put the pieces of my shattered heart together again.

THE SHUFFLING OF forks and knives against dinner plates is the only sound at the dinner table tonight. No one speaks as I push roast and potatoes around my plate. Mom and Uncle Brent glance back and forth between each other and me before I finally just excuse myself from the table.

"Saige," Brent calls me back. "Sit down."

I feel like I'm being scolded, but the look in his eyes tells me something else. I've seen that look before. He's struggling with something. I slide back into the dining room chair and rest my hands on the edge of the wood table.

"Tomorrow," he says, pushing his plate away from him and clearing his throat. "I have an appointment."

"Okay?" I look between Brent and my mom. My mom's eyes are downcast as she fidgets with the napkin in her lap.

"For Murphy," he says quietly, his eyes full of pain.

"No!" I jump up from the table. "I'm not ready yet. It's not time."

"It is, Saige," he reasons with me. "It's not fair to him anymore. He can barely walk. Since you got back from the creek today, he hasn't been able to move."

I glance over at the fluffy dog bed in the corner, and Murphy lies there watching us. His yellow fur has turned almost white.

"He's old," Brent says. "Labs don't typically live this long. He's had a great life with us." His voice is affectionate and sad. "In the last week alone, he's started to decline. He can barely keep his food down. He struggles to stand up and remain standing."

No. No, not yet.

I burst into tears, falling off the chair to my knees. Letting Murphy go means letting the last thing my father ever gave me go. I can't do it.

"Saige." Brent jumps up from the dining room table. "It's going to be hard for all of us," he says. "But he's—"

"I know," I reply through my tears as he sits on the ground next to me.

"We can't let him suffer anymore, though, Saige."

I look over at Murphy, whose big brown eyes show me how tired they are, and I know Brent is right. "What time?" I ask.

"The vet will be here at nine o'clock."

I nod but can't seem to stop crying. "Can you lift him up the stairs so he can sleep in my room tonight?"

Brent rests his hand on my shoulder and gives it a squeeze. "You bet, Piglet."

Murphy spends the night in my bed, and he whimpers while I cry all night long. He tries to comfort me as he licks the salty tears from my face, and I just wrap myself around him as I weep. Hearing me cry is not new for him. Murphy spent many nights in my bed, licking my tears, listening to me talk, and just comforting me when I'd wake up from my nightmares. I've never had a better best friend.

On our last morning together, we watch the sunrise and he lets out a long sigh. It's like he knows his time with me is nearing an end. Resting his muzzle under my chin, he finally closes his eyes, falling into a comforting sleep. His little snores tell me he's at peace with the situation, and I'm going to have to try to be as well.

The vet normally likes to see animals in the barn, where they're contained, but I haven't stepped foot in that barn in ten years. It's not about to happen today either. So the vet quietly examines Murphy on the floor in our living room, listening to his heart, and checking his eyes and gums. Murphy doesn't flinch or even try to move. The vet agrees it's time and prepares an IV.

I'm not comfortable with death. Some people are so at ease with death and the whole fucking "circle of life" bullshit, but not me. Death robs us of those we love. Death leaves behind a trail of pain and suffering.

I kiss Murphy and tell him how much I love him as the vet inserts a syringe into the line that was placed in his right paw. My entire body shakes, but I hold him tightly as he takes his last breath. With a long and final sigh, he's gone.

I hold him for another half hour after that—clinging to the two things I'm not ready to let go of: Murphy and my dad. The vet is long gone, and my mom and Brent are sitting on the couch, watching me. I don't cry. I don't do anything other than hold Murphy in my lap and run my fingers through his coarse hair. I rub him behind his ears just like he used to beg me to do.

Suddenly, I feel the walls collapsing around me. I need air. Brent sees the change in me and quickly pulls Murphy from my arms. With a gasp, I jump up and run outside, trying to pull the brisk autumn air into my lungs, only I can't breathe. I struggle for air and find myself on all fours, heaving outside the back door. My fingers press into the leaves that have fallen to the ground, and I close my eyes.

My stomach lurches; I feel the bile rising. I try to swallow it down, but it's stronger than me and I expel the contents of my stomach into the grass. My stomach continues to twist and turn as it tries to purge what's left inside me, except there's nothing there. My stomach is hollow, much like my heart.

"Hey." I hear his voice this time before I sense him. I don't answer him, as I just don't have the energy. "Saige," he says, attempting to help me sit up. I pull my arm out of his hand.

"Goddamn, can you just go away?" I yell at him, tears falling. "I thought you left." I angrily narrow my eyes at him.

"Brent stopped me yesterday and mentioned that he thought you could use a friend today, so he asked me if I could stick around for another day."

Wiping my cheeks with the sleeve of my shirt, I snarl at him, "You're not my friend, Holt. I hate you." But I feel sick the moment those words leave my mouth. Hate is such a disgusting word, and I used it carelessly.

He winces, but he doesn't respond.

I pull myself up from the ground and begin to wander down the large yard and head toward the creek—my place. "And don't follow me," I yell over my shoulder.

I take my place on top of my boulder, where I used to feel like I was on top of the world. Now I feel like my entire world is collapsing around me. I feel so small atop this rock as everything I loved, everyone I believed in is now a part of my past.

I SIT ON the boulder for hours and watch Brent across the creek, digging a hole for Murphy under the large oak tree where my dad rests. As I suspected, Holt didn't listen to me. I heard him wander up behind me about ten minutes after I perched myself on the rock. He's been patiently sitting in the grass behind the boulder, just watching me.

I've spent these hours pondering what my life will be like now that I'm home in North Dakota. Will I stay here? If not, where will I go? What will I do? I make plans to call and check in with Evelyn, and I make a promise to myself to finally start answering the endless text messages from Rowan, Emery, Zay, and Kinsley. But mostly, I think about Holt.

I think about the first time he kissed me. The first time he made love to me, and all the times after that. I remember every time he touched me. There's no forgetting Holt Hamilton.

"I don't hate you," I say quietly, finally breaking the hours of silence. He doesn't respond, probably giving me a dose of my own medicine. I glance over my shoulder at him as he sits with his arms propped on top of his knees and his head down. "I shouldn't have said that, and I'm sorry."

Minutes pass and I've turned my attention back across the creek as Brent places a rock atop the freshly covered grave.

"You have every right to," he finally says.

"Well, I don't." I twist my body around to look at him, and he finally raises his head, our eyes meeting. I sigh loudly in aggravation.

"I will fight for you, Saige. I'm not just going to let you walk away." His voice is weak, maybe even timid. Not the confident Holt that I know.

"There's nothing to fight for," I say faintly.

"There's everything to fight for, Saige," he disagrees, sounding stronger. "Except you're so stuck in the past that you won't open yourself up to the present. Let go, and let me love you." His eyes are stained pink, and I wonder to myself if he's been crying.

My words are weak, but I get them out with a whisper, "I can't."

"That's not true. You are the strongest person I know. It's not that you can't, Saige. You won't." He speaks passionately.

I digest his words and do my best to contain my anger when he suddenly stands up and walks toward me.

"Do you love me, Saige?" My heart sinks as he searches for answers. My entire being begins to shake when he asks me this. Because I do. I always will.

His face is hard, begging. "Answer my question. I dare you. Do you love me, Saige?"

I swallow hard against my dry throat and nod. "I do. But I'm not sure I can forgive you, and if I can't forgive you—"

"I get it," he interrupts me. "I get it, Saige." His voice breaks. He reaches out and grabs my hand, placing it between both of his. "I love you. I always will, and if I could do things differently, I would. But I can't. I was wrong, and I lied to you, and I will pay the consequences of that lie. I just hope that someday you'll be able to forgive me."

"Let me go," I whisper to him. My eyes are cast down at my feet. I can't bring myself to look into his.

"I wish I could," he answers gently, tenderly. "I'll give you time, but I'll never let you go." He backs away from me, taking small steps backwards. "I love you, Saige Phillips." Those are the last words he speaks before he turns and walks away. His long legs carry him through the tall grass until he disappears over the hill.

I choke and a loud cry escapes from me. My stomach twists in pain, and I fall to my knees for the second time today, crying. I cry until I have no tears left, until I feel nauseous and tired. For a moment, I briefly understand why my dad gave up. The sense of hopelessness, despair, and pain having become all too consuming that it becomes easier to want to disappear rather than cope.

When my eyes finally dry out, I lay in the tall grass and stare at the gray sky while the clouds come and go and the air becomes colder, chilling me to the bone. I like the feel of the pain the cold provides, numbing my extremities. The physical pain provides an escape to the mental pain and the ache of my heart in my chest.

The sky grows dark, but I remain rooted in place, my back pressed against the hard, cold ground. My eyes are stinging from the dry air and from crying for hours, so finally, in my own way of giving up, I press my eyelids closed and succumb to the cold.

"JESUS CHRIST, SAIGE!" I can hear the voices and yelling, but it's easy to ignore because I'm so tired. It's only when I'm being lifted and jostled that I begin to understand what's happening and feel the cold.

"How long has she been out here?" I hear the male voice, familiar but not recognizable.

"Hours," Brent says, and I know he's carrying me. "She's freezing," he yells. "Open the door."

I find myself in the cab of Brent's pick-up truck. It's then that my body begins to shake uncontrollably, painfully.

"Hang on, Piglet," he says, sliding into the driver's seat. He presses the cell phone to his ear. "Found her. She's frozen solid. I'm worried." There's a pause. "House or hospital?" I assume he's speaking with my mom. The truck bounces over the uneven grass as the headlights shine on the dying grass. After a minute or two, we come to a screeching stop and my mom rushes out the back door, practically ripping the truck door open.

"Saige, what happened?" She asks, pressing her hands to my face. "Are you able to walk?"

I shake my head as my limbs ache and I try to move my fingers.

"Hypothermia," my mom says, looking worriedly at Brent. "We should go to the hospital."

"No," I'm able to manage to say. "Just inside."

"Help me get her inside," my mom says, rubbing my hand between hers.

Brent lifts me from the car and I feel bad. I know I'm dead weight right now. He sets me carefully on the couch in the living room, and my mom plugs in a heating blanket, laying it over me. She pulls off my shoes and checks my feet and my fingers.

"Brent, grab the thermometer from the medicine chest in the bathroom and my stethoscope from my dresser." She barks orders as if she's at the hospital. "Saige, what were you doing?"

I shake my head and take a deep breath. "Holt left."

She presses her lips together tightly. "He didn't want to leave."

"I know," I say groggily.

"You pushed him away, didn't you?" Her face is stern.

I nod and my body shivers excessively as the heating blanket finally begins warming me up.

"Here." Brent shoves the thermometer at my mom and she turns it on, placing it under my tongue.

"I need to listen to your heart and take your pulse." She presses the cold stethoscope just under the collar of my shirt and against my bare chest. Her fingers are pressed to my wrist as she looks at her watch.

When the thermometer beeps, Brent reaches over her and plucks it from my mouth. Ninety-five point two.

My mom shakes her head, displeased. "Take it again in five minutes. If it doesn't go up, she's going to the hospital." Standing up, she paces the living room floor. Brent starts a fire in the fireplace, and my mom takes my temperature again, then she sits on the edge of the couch and gently massages my arm.

"Ninety-five point eight," she says quietly with a

concerned smile on her face.

"I'm fine," I reassure her. "Just need to warm up." My teeth chatter, but I force a small smile. We all sit silently in the living room, Brent and my mom taking turns checking on me until sometime in the middle of the night, I give in to my exhaustion.

"MORNING, PIGLET," BRENT mumbles between sips of coffee. He rocks slowly in his recliner and rubs his eyes. I can hear pans clanking against each other in the kitchen, and I can smell the aroma of biscuits and gravy wafting through the air.

"Did you stay up all night?" I ask, stretching my arms over my head, finally able to move them without extreme pain.

"I dozed off for a bit," he admits.

"I'm sorry," I tell him.

He shakes his head slowly and swallows hard. I push myself up to a sitting position and rest my back against the arm of the couch.

He sets his coffee down before he speaks. "You scared us."

"I know." I instantly feel guilty thinking about how he and my mom must have felt. The same way we all felt ten years ago. "I didn't try to—"

"I know," he cuts me off. "But it's always in the back of our heads, Saige." He uses his feet to shove the footrest of the recliner back into place, and he leans forward in his chair. "Look. I know it's been a rough couple of days for you."

"Days?" I mutter.

"Days, years . . . whatever, Saige." He raises his arms and drops them again in agitation. "We get it. We do. And there is no easy way to say this, but we're all still hurting. Michael was more like a brother to me than a brother-in-law. Losing him was hard on all of us, but Saige, we can't change what *he* did. That was *his* choice. *We* have to live and move forward." He rakes his hand over his cheek.

I absorb what he's saying, exactly what Holt told me. I close my eyes against the sting of tears forming, and I nod my head. I'm barely able to choke out. "I know." Both of them are right. I do need to move on, but letting go of the grief feels like letting go of my father and I'm not sure I'm ready to let him go yet.

"Then give him a chance, Saige." He leans back into the recliner. "That man flew to North Dakota to apologize to you."

"Would you forgive him?" I ask, feeling that anger and bitterness rise up in me again.

He looks at me long and hard. His mouth opens to speak, but then he closes it. He rakes his hand over his face before he finally finds his words. "No one is perfect, Saige. I'm far from it. I know you're not going to like my answer, but yes. Yes, I'd forgive him. I'd give him another chance, and the opportunity to make it right."

I sigh. "What if I don't want to?" Because I'm hurt, because I'm angry . . . because I'm scared.

Brent's normally hard face softens. "Then you're letting the best thing that's ever happened to you get away."

I swallow hard and take in the depth of his words. "You like him that much, huh? Enough to believe him?"

He nods his head slowly. "Enough to know that he's crazy about you and he's tried to make it right. It's on you now, Saige."

It's on me, I think to myself, inhaling deeply.

TWENTY

Saige

I DROP MY last suitcase by the back door and throw myself into a chair at the kitchen table. Brent looks over the top of his coffee mug at me as I let out a deep sigh.

"What time is your flight?" he grumbles, setting down his mug.

Mom shuffles back and forth between the kitchen island and the table, setting down plates of bacon and bowls of scrambled eggs and fruit. One last home-cooked meal before I head back to Chicago.

"Noon." I take a sip of orange juice as Brent reaches over the table to pour me a mug of coffee.

"Have you talked to him since he left?" Mom asks casually while she stacks pancakes from the griddle onto a platter.

"No. I haven't checked any of my messages."

"Saige, you've been here for almost three weeks," Mom scolds me.

"I needed to disconnect, and I really needed this time to think; not be distracted by text messages and social media."

Brent grabs a piece of bacon and takes a bite, commenting with a full mouth, "Well, I think that's a good thing. Social media is a fucking waste of time anyway."

"You sound like such an old man." I toss my napkin across the table at him and roll my eyes. We laugh together, and Mom finally sits down at the table to join us. As we eat breakfast, we talk and laugh, and for the first time that I can remember, I feel content. I feel at peace. I look around the kitchen and my heart feels like it's slowly rebuilding itself, broken piece by broken little piece.

Whatever awaits me back in Chicago is yet to be seen. I'm anxious to move back to the city that I love so much and move forward with my life.

"Well, this old man is going to miss you," he says with a soft smile.

"I'm going to miss you too," I admit, swallowing down the small lump forming in my throat. I push the food around my plate and glance around the kitchen I grew up in. Everything I love so much is on this farm in Deer Creek. My throat tightens slightly as I fight the sudden rush of emotions.

I clear my throat and swallow. "As much as I hated why I came home, I'm really happy I did. I'm glad I got to be here with Murphy. I think I needed to be with both of you," I tell Brent and my mom.

"I'm so glad we got to spend these weeks with you too," Mom says, pushing her plate away. "But I'm not going to lie to you. Your life isn't here anymore. We'll always be here for you, but Saige, you aren't meant to be here."

I swallow hard and see Mom's giant smile through my blurry tear-filled eyes.

Smiling at me, she speaks quietly. "Use your wings— soar. Regardless of what happens when you go back, Saige. Embrace your life. You're living a dream that many would die for . . . literally." Her voice cracks and her face softens.

I nod and swipe at the tears that leak out of the corner of my eyes.

Brent heaves heavily and looks between both of us. "Why do you women always have to get so damn emotional? I'm trying to enjoy my eggs, and I feel like I'm watching an episode of *Dr. Phil*."

Mom and I burst out in laughter. "It's our job to make you uncomfortable," she says, swatting Brent's arm.

"Come on, Piglet. Let's get you packed up and on the road." He stands up and clears his plate from the table, leaving Mom and me.

My mom reaches her hand across the table and grabs mine, her eyes imploring me. "I mean it, Saige. Go. Live."

"I'll try," I whisper. And I will try.

Her lips press together into a tight smile. "Try hard."

"I will." I nod once in a promise to her.

Brent and I spend the next ninety minutes joking with each other and trying to keep the mood light as we inch closer to the airport. I hate goodbyes and he knows this.

When he finally lets me out at the curb, we trade insults and I slam the passenger door to his pick-up truck. He meets me at the back gate to help me get my suitcases out.

"Want me to help you get these inside?" he asks as he sets the two huge suitcases on the curb next to me.

"Nah, I can get them from here." I twist each of my hands through the pull-up handles on the bags, gripping them tightly.

We look at each other awkwardly before Brent finally speaks. "I don't know if I've ever told you, Saige, but I'm so proud of you." Tears prick the back of my eyes, and I exhale loudly. "Go get him," he says before stepping forward and pulling me into his arms.

"I'm going to try," I say into his shoulder as I hug him in return.

"Text me later. Let me know you got home okay. I worry about you, Piglet." There's a hint of sadness behind those dark brown eyes.

"I will. Take care of Mom for me."

"Always." He slips around the back of the truck and pulls away as I watch the taillights disappear around the curve.

I inhale sharply, breathing in the crisp fall air. The chill almost burns my lungs, but I savor the moment. As usual, the airport is a damn near ghost town. After checking my bags, I slide through security, and then wait at the gate for the call to board. One quick stop in Minneapolis for a plane change and I should be back in Chicago in about two hours. My hands begin to sweat as I think about my future and what it might look like.

THE BREATHTAKING CHICAGO skyline comes into view just as the late fall sun begins to set. The backdrop of Lake Michigan fills my soul and reminds me of the contentment I've always found here. We land and that's when the nervousness begins to settle in.

My stomach is in knots as every scenario imaginable runs through my mind. Where will I find him? What if he's not in town? What if he won't talk to me?

I shake off the negative thoughts and gather my bags, calling an Uber to pick me up. I haven't even let Evelyn know I'm back in town yet.

The black Mercedes picks me up, and the driver manages to get my two huge bags into the trunk of his small car. When we arrive at my condo, my sympathetic driver helps me get my bags inside. Evelyn isn't home and I don't even take time to freshen up. It's five o'clock and, while most employees of Jackson-Hamilton are well on their way out the door, I know Holt isn't.

I damn near jog the three blocks to the train station

with how fast I walk, and I find myself growing more impatient with each passing minute that I wait for the train. By the time I make it to the office tower, the sun has set and the sky is dark. The large lobby that is usually is bustling with people is now stark and dimly lit. Larry is behind the large security desk and offers me a quick wave.

"Ms. Phillips!" the old man says excitedly. "Haven't seen you lately."

"Had to take care of some family business, Larry," I say, rushing past him.

He waves me on, shaking his head and mumbling something about young kids always being in a hurry.

I step into the empty elevator and the doors slide closed. My heart is beating wildly the closer I get to Holt. When the doors open, I hesitate, pushing myself forward and out into the offices. The doors close behind me, and I let my feet carry me down the hallway I've become so familiar with.

Brent helped me realize that sometimes in loving us, people hurt us, but it doesn't mean they don't love us. It's rarely intentional but hurts like hell nonetheless. As I replayed what Holt told me, I believe him. I believe that he just wanted to right his father's wrongs. It's the only way he could control what happened.

I don't believe that Holt wanted to fall in love with me, but as I've learned, you have no choice with whom you fall in love with. Love finds us at the most unexpected times in our lives. One dare and I fell hopelessly in love with the one man who has the potential to help me move forward from my past—if I can just let it go.

The entire office is quiet; only the perimeter lights are on. Through the glass office, I see Holt's desk—empty—and his office is dark. I pause as my lungs constrict and my stomach drops. He's not here. I sigh, disappointed. Through the glass office, I can see the lights from the downtown skyline beginning to sparkle. I open his door and step inside, drawn to city. Then my heart literally stops. Standing in the dark, looking out of his window, is Holt. His hands are shoved deep in his pockets, his posture slack.

As I release the door handle, it clicks and Holt jumps slightly. However, he doesn't turn around. "Joyce, go home. We'll take care of everything tomorrow." His voice is low and lackluster. He sounds tired, defeated.

My hands shake as I scramble to find the words I want to say . . . *need* to say. I close the door quietly and clear my throat. My breath hitches as I wet my lips and I struggle to speak. "Holt?"

Even in the dark, I can see his entire body visibly stiffen. He remains facing the windows, looking outside, some eighty stories above Chicago. I take a few steps toward him but stop when he still doesn't answer or acknowledge me. Is this how he felt when I wouldn't acknowledge him at the farm? My heart sinks at how much I must've hurt him.

"I . . . I . . ." I stutter, trying to form my words. "I forgive you." My voice breaks, but I will myself to get through this. Taking a deep breath, I force myself to continue. "I love you, Holt. I know that means nothing right now, but I needed to tell you that. I'm sorry for the way I treated you at the farm; there's no excuse for some of the things I said to you. I was angry at you, but mostly, I was hurt—" I pause, giving him time to say something, anything.

He turns around slowly and looks at me, his eyes indecipherable in the dark office. Pulling his hands from his pockets, he rests his arms at his side, his broad shoulders slouching. As the moonlight casts a low glow in the office, and the city lights twinkle behind him, he is nothing more than a silhouette; however, he's still the most beautiful person I've ever laid eyes on.

"I trusted you," I say, my voice wavering slightly. "You

lied to me."

I hear him sigh quietly. He doesn't respond or move. He stands still and watches me intently. In the dark, you'd think it would be hard to see his reaction to me being here, but I don't need to see it. I can feel him. From six feet away, I can feel his angst, his hurt, and his anxiousness. I can feel the sparks that have always flown between us, but I can also feel his trepidation—his fear, just as I feel my own.

"But I understand why you did it, Holt, and I forgive you."

The silence in his office is chilling. I wait for him to respond, yet again, he says nothing. His silence answers every lingering question in my mind. He's done with me, and rightfully so.

"I just needed to say that." My stomach twists, nausea rolling through me.

I turn and slowly walk out of his office. He makes no attempt to stop me, and while tears sting my eyes, a sense of calm begins to settle in. Holt may have hurt me, but in doing so, he also set me free. He taught me to love again. This man with his lies brought me back to life. This man opened up my heart and dared me to love again.

As I reach my desk, tucked away in a dark corner of the office, I begin to gather my few personal items. A picture of Zay, Rowan, Kinsley, Emery, and me at happy hour, a small bamboo plant that is now turning brown, and some personal belongings from the drawer.

"What're you doing?" His voice startles me and I jump back.

"Cleaning out my desk," I say with my hand pressed to my chest.

"Leave it. You'll need it for work on Monday."

I blink. "Excuse me?"

"Leave it," he orders, his voice firm and his eyes dark.

Commanding Holt is back and stands before me.

I sigh heavily and pull my lips between my teeth before releasing my breath and speaking. "Holt, I can't work here. I appreciate you offering to let me stay, but it would be too hard to—"

"Too hard to what, Saige? Work with your boyfriend?" His eyes plead for an answer.

My eyebrows shoot up, and I'm at a loss for words.

"You're here," he says softly. "I'm not letting you go again that easily. I let you walk away that night at the cocktail party, and I should've stopped you, but I knew how devastated you were. I won't make the same mistake twice. You're not walking away from me again." His voice is strong and full of determination.

I swallow hard, taking in his words, but still wondering. "You didn't say anything back there, so I assumed . . ."

He shakes his head and rubs his tired eyes. "I was stunned. I haven't slept for more than two hours a night since you left. I honestly didn't know if it was really you standing there in my office or my hallucinations." He swallows hard, and I take a step toward him but stop short of touching him.

"It's me," I whisper, wanting him to know he's not hallucinating. I'm here. And I'm not leaving him again. Ever.

He swallows hard and clears his throat. "I know. Don't you ever leave me again." He reaches out his hand for me to take it, but I step forward and fall into his arms instead. I hug him and let him hug me back. It's there in his arms that I feel myself truly coming back to life.

I close my eyes and whisper against his neck, "It's so good to be home."

I can hear him smile. "I knew you'd miss Chicago." His arms tighten around me, and I feel at peace in his embrace.

"Not Chicago, Holt," I explain. "You. You are home."

EPILOGUE

Holt

"WHAT DO YOU think?" I ask as I turn onto the newly paved driveway. It's almost a half-mile long and is lined with trees that are probably a hundred years old. I can see why Saige loves this farm so much. October is the best month of the year in North Dakota, she says, and I can understand why from how beautiful it is.

"I can't believe they paved the driveway," she says, her hands pressed to her mouth in disbelief. "Brent says that the work has been moving along fast since they wanted to get it all done before winter." She sits back in the seat and peers out the passenger window.

The large SUV slowly rolls up the drive until we round the final bend, approaching the house.

"Oh my God!" she gasps. "It doesn't even look the same!"

The large farmhouse has been completely redone. New roof, siding, and the old front porch demolished and rebuilt.

"It's looks really good," I comment, worried that she's not happy with her childhood home's renovations.

She nods her head quickly and leans forward, looking out the windshield at the beautiful two-story house. "Hurry up," she says, urging me to park faster.

I barely have the gear in park before she's hopped down and sprinting across the front yard. She bounds up the four steps and stands on the giant wraparound porch. I know exactly what she was running for, and I smile when I see her tense body relax.

I meet her on the porch and she grins up at me. "They saved the swing."

I wrap my arm around her waist and pull her into me. "I knew they wouldn't get rid of it." I press a kiss to her temple.

She leans down and runs her fingers across all the initials carved into the old wooden swing. Saige's, her mom's, Brent's, her father's, and even her grandparents' initials are all there. The history carved into that swing was of utmost importance to her, and I'm happy to see it's still there.

"Come on. Let's get the bags inside and say hello." I pull her hand into mine, and we walk across the dead grass. With fall and the cooler temps, the lawn has long died out, but the beautiful colored leaves still hang from the trees.

As I pull the bags from the back of the SUV, Brent walks up from the barn, two small puppies following behind him.

"What are these!" Saige squeals, falling to her knees. The two puppies jump on her and lick her face. She tips her head back in laughter as they vie for her attention.

"The mutts," Brent says with a laugh. "Nice to see you again, man." He holds out his hand to shake mine and I accept.

"Good to see you too."

"I missed you, Piglet," Brent says, and I try not to laugh as Saige shoots him a look of death at his nickname for her.

She stands up and the puppies jump at her feet. "I missed you too." She leans in and gives him a quick hug.

"Your mom has been antsy all day waiting on you two.

Let me help you get these bags and get inside." Brent helps me gather the luggage and deliver them to Saige's old room. A minute later, we find Saige and her mom laughing together in the kitchen and catching up.

Brent grabs two bottles of beer, and we head out to the back patio to catch up. We take a seat at the patio table. Out here, it's even easier to take in the beauty of this land. Rolling hills and trees that are turning color highlight the landscape.

Swallowing a sip of the full-flavored microbrew, I ask, "So what do you have left for renovations?"

Brent looks over my shoulder and behind me, nodding. "Just the barn and a new chicken coop." He pauses and takes a sip of his beer. "I'm really glad you were able to bring her back here. That damn barn has been the source of so much pain over the years. I'm really hoping that demolishing it and building a new one will help her begin to heal."

He and I have the same goals. I swallow hard. "She's done so well this last year, but I hope this gives her some resolution."

Brent nods in agreement, inhaling deeply before changing the subject. "So, you nervous?" he asks with a chuckle.

"That would be putting it mildly," I admit.

"When are you going to do it?"

I turn and look over my shoulder at the beautiful land, then back to Brent just as the back door opens and Saige steps outside.

"What're you two doing out here?" She rubs her arms with her hands to warm them from the cool fall air.

"Just guy talk," Brent answers her, but she looks at me.

"Just guy talk," I confirm with a smile.

"Well, come inside." She waves us in. "Mom has food ready."

We enjoy a nice dinner, laughing and catching up. It is

so nice to see Saige laughing and happy. I know this place has mixed emotions for her and I always worry how she's going to handle being back here. After she helps her mom clear the table, she slides back into her chair next to me. "It's going to get dark soon," she whispers to me. "Let's go for a quick walk." She presses a quick kiss to my lips and smiles.

"Let's do it." I kiss her back.

Brent eyes me quickly, then turns to Saige's mom. "Should we start a bonfire?"

"Yes!" Brenda answers him quickly. "I've been waiting to use the new fire pit." She turns to Saige. "He finally installed a gas fire pit outside. No more smelly hair." She laughs.

"We'll meet you back there," Saige says as she stands up. Grabbing her puffy vest, she throws it on and wraps a scarf around her neck.

I throw on my wool blazer and follow Saige out the back door and across the newly paved patio. She laces her fingers through mine, and we walk the trail she blazed over the years trekking to and from the creek.

The late afternoon sky is beginning to darken as the sun lowers. The trail is stunning, lined by giant trees just beginning to spill their colorful leaves. Saige's cheeks and nose are tinged pink from the cool autumn breeze.

She pulls me down the trail until we hit the clearing, when she drops my hand. The large boulder sits off to the left and the creek flutters along. This place truly is majestic. Saige bounds down the remainder of the trail, stopping at the creek's edge. She bends down and picks up a rock, tossing it into the water, causing small ripples.

The sky is bright orange, the color of fire. Nowhere in my life have I ever been somewhere so perfect. I walk toward Saige, my hands stuffed in my front pockets. I pull out the oval diamond ring and hide it in my enclosed palm. As

I approach Saige, she slides her arm into mine, hooking it around my elbow, and rests her head on my shoulder.

"I'm so in love with this place," she says peacefully as we stare into the amazing sky. "Have you ever seen anything this beautiful?"

I swallow hard and pull away from her, positioning myself in front of her. "I have," I say gently, my voice hitching.

She looks at me, confused, sensing my nervousness. "What's wrong?"

I close my eyes and take a deep breath. Then I open them to look at her. She's breathtaking anywhere, even on her worst day. But there's something about being back here that lights her up, makes her simply stunning surrounded by the simplicity of this farm. Her long, dark hair is blowing in the breeze. Her lips are pressed together, and her green eyes shine in the remaining rays of the glowing sun.

Stunning.

Without another thought, I drop to my knee. Her eyebrows shoot up, her hands covering her mouth. Her entire body trembles as she takes in the realization of what is about to happen.

"Saige . . ." I start, having to pause and clear my throat.

Tears fill her eyes, and I find myself getting emotional. "For the rest of my life, I want you by my side. I want to be your husband, and I want you to be my wife. I want my children to have your eyes and your outgoing personality. Everything in my life that I've ever wanted, I want with you. Will you marry me?"

She drops to her knees in front of me and wraps her arms around me. Burying her face in my neck, she cries softly. Not exactly the reaction I was hoping for.

"Saige?"

"Yes." She pulls back, her eyes sparkling. "I'll marry you."

I feel the relief like a flood, and I can't stop smiling. She wipes her tears and we stand up. Her chin is trembling as she stares at me, not saying anything.

I frown. "Is everything okay?"

"I just keep reassuring myself that this is real life. I'm afraid I'm going to wake up from a dream and not be your fiancée."

Well, if that's her only worry, that's easily remedied. "Oh, you're my fiancée," I chuckle, "and then you're going to be my wife—"

"I knew you'd use those words against me someday." She laughs as more tears spill from her eyes. I'll never forget her spitting out those words on my patio . . . that she'd never be my girlfriend turned fiancée turned wife. I made it my mission to prove her wrong and, proudly, she's mine. *My fiancée.*

I wipe the tears from her cheeks and pull her into a hug. "I couldn't wait to."

I savor this moment with Saige in my arms while I envision our future. Nothing is certain, but with Saige by my side, everything will be perfect.

After a long moment, she wiggles out of my embrace. "Come on; let's get back to the house before we get stuck out here in the dark."

We walk briskly back toward the house, the wind picking up slightly as we go. Brent and Brenda are waiting for us, Brenda bouncing on edge of her toes. Saige drops my hand as we clear the trail, and she takes off running like a little girl. I laugh as she jumps into Brent's open arms, and he swings her around. Her mom wraps herself around both of them. I laugh at their yelps and laughter, and join them on the patio when I finally catch up.

"I'm getting married!" Saige squeals over and over again.

"Welcome to the family, brother." Brent shakes my hand.

"I'm not in quite *yet*," I tease.

"You were in a long time ago," he says meaningfully, squeezing my shoulder.

Brent has told me time and again how thankful he is that Saige has me. I know that I'm truly the lucky one, but nothing pleases me more than knowing that our relationship has her family's blessing.

"Can't wait to make it official," I say, feeling anxious just at the thought.

He gives me a quick nod as Saige shows her ring to her mom, tilting her hand back and forth under the patio lights.

Brenda walks over to me, her eyes misty, and pulls me into a tight hug. "Thank you for making her so happy," she whispers.

I don't reply. Because the truth is, she's made me happy; she's healed me. In finding Saige, I've learned to let go of my past just as she's learning to let go of hers. We can't hold ourselves responsible for the sins of our fathers and that has been the largest hurdle I've had to overcome.

As the sun goes down, we all enjoy the last few minutes of this gorgeous fall day outside, and for the first time ever, I'm at peace, and happy with everything in my life.

"HOW ARE YOU feeling?" I ask Saige as she finally begins to wake up.

She shrugs and moans but doesn't say anything.

"I think it's important you're there," I tell her, sitting up and leaning back against the headboard.

"It's just a barn," she grunts, pulling her pillow over her head.

I rub her back. "It's more than just a barn, Saige. Some

of your best childhood memories and some of your worst happened in that barn. You've been struggling for years to let go of your grief. When that wood comes down, I hope your pain is replaced with all the good things you remember about that barn." She stills as I talk. "Brent told me about your first pony, Cupcake. How you'd sit in that little stall and talk to her until they'd drag you into the house." I see her shoulders relax.

"And about all the hours you spent brushing the horses and the bonding with them in that barn?"

She still doesn't reply.

"I'll be there with you, Saige. I'll be right there holding your hand." I'll always be there. I need her to know that.

"Promise?" She mumbles from under the pillow.

"Promise."

She pulls the pillow from her head and rolls over. She presses her hand to my chest and looks at me. "You have the best heart, Holt Hamilton."

I grin. "We're a team, future Mrs. Hamilton."

"I can't wait," she whispers with a smile.

"Come on." I smack her ass. "Let's do this."

She grumbles but pulls herself out of bed and drags herself into the bathroom to get ready.

SAIGE PACES BACK and forth over the same ten-foot patch of grass, chewing on her thumbnail as the large tractors move into place. I can see her chest rising and falling with each heaving breath.

"Saige, come here." I'm sitting on one of the plush patio chairs, and I pat the chair next to me. She sighs loudly and tosses herself down into the chair. "You okay?"

Her eyebrows are pinched together, and her focus is trained on Brent, who is standing down next to the barn, talking to the general contractor who will rebuild the structure.

"I don't know," she finally answers me.

"I think this is going to be a good thing. New beginnings. Sometimes we have to leave the past there . . . in the past, so that we're able to move forward." I reach over and squeeze her hand.

As the group of men disperse, moving back to their tractors, Saige jumps up from her chair and jogs down the small hill toward Brent. She hollers something, and Brent turns around. I sit up straight, pausing as I wait to see what's happening. Brent places his hands on her shoulders and, with a nod, he steps back.

Saige shakes both of her hands next to her sides and begins to walk toward the large barn door. She pulls one of the large doors open and stands frozen in place. Brent jogs up behind her and opens the other door, turning around to look at me just as I stand up and trek down to meet them.

Saige turns around, our eyes locking for a moment before she spins on her heel and steps into the barn. A flood of emotions takes over me as I watch her disappear into the darkness. My heart thrums with worry.

I approach Brent, who keeps his eyes trained on her inside the barn but holds out his hand to stop me from coming any closer.

"Give her a minute," he says quietly.

I'm able to see over his shoulder. Saige is standing next to one of the empty horse stalls. She stares down at the ground, and her shoulders begin to shake. I try to step around Brent, but he holds out his arm, stopping me.

"Just hold on," he says. "She needs to do this."

"I know, but—" I stop when I see her turn around and begin walking back toward us. It's killing me to see her in pain.

She steps out, her pink cheeks wet with tears. Then she walks past us, her hands shoved into her coat pockets. As she finally passes us, she mumbles over her shoulder, "Tear it down."

Brent looks at me before signaling the guys to proceed with demolition. I glance anxiously after Saige, wondering if she'll ever be okay.

"Give her a bit," Brent tells me. "She needs a little time."

AN HOUR LATER, I stroll down to the creek where I know Saige has disappeared to. But the boulder sits empty where I expected her long body to be perched. Instead, I find her across the creek, sitting at her father's headstone. I contemplate leaving her, but I've left her long enough. I need to know that she's okay.

The creek is shallow and large river rocks poke up from the bottom so I'm able to step across, jumping into the tall grass on the other side. "Hey," I say quietly from behind her.

Her elbows rest on her knees and her head is propped in her hands. "Hey," she responds, barely audible.

"Mind if I sit down?" She shakes her head from side to side, and I sit down next to her. "You okay?" I ask her, resting my hand on her thigh.

"I am," she says unconvincingly, turning her head to me. Her face is splotched with red patches, and the remnants of her tears, but her eyes are dry. "I just needed to come here and talk to him."

"I'm glad you did," I admit to her.

"Did you watch them knock it down?"

"I did." I nod once, watching her carefully. "It's done."

She sniffs and nods, wiping her sad eyes. "Amazing how quickly something that holds decades of memories, decades of anger, and decades of history can be resorted to a pile of trash in just minutes."

I swallow hard, still worried for her. "The good thing about memories and history is that you remember them here." I tap her forehead. "And the good thing about anger is that you can leave it at the bottom of that pile where it belongs."

She huffs out a small laugh and leans into me. "Thank you for bringing me here." She rests her head on my shoulder. "I was just telling my dad how much he'd love you."

I smile, finally feeling hopeful. "You think so?" I ask, glancing at the headstone with "Michael Phillips" etched into the gray granite.

"I know so," she says, pressing a kiss to my cheek.

And that's where she leaves her anger, her fear, and her hurt—buried at the bottom of that barn, in a heaping pile.

CONNECT WITH REBECCA SHEA

www.rebeccasheaauthor.com

Sign up for Rebecca Shea's newsletter
for updates on new releases
http://tinyurl.com/jg89h2e

Follow Rebecca Shea on Facebook:
www.facebook.com/rebeccasheaauthor

Follow Rebecca Shea on Twitter:
@beccasheaauthor

Follow Rebecca Shea on Instagram:
https://www.instagram.com/rebeccasheaauthor

Email: rebeccasheaauthor@gmail.com

ALSO BY REBECCA SHEA

UNBREAKABLE SERIES:
Unbreakable
Undone
Unforgiven

BOUND & BROKEN SERIES:
Broken by Lies
Bound by Lies